HORRID

HORRID

KATRINA LENO

LITTLE, BROWN AND COMPANY

New York Boston

Little, Brown and Company
Hachette Book Group
1290 Avenue of the Americas, New York, NY 10104
Visit us at LBYR.com

First Edition: September 2020

Little, Brown and Company is a division of Hachette Book Group, Inc. The Little, Brown name and logo are trademarks of Hachette Book Group, Inc.

The publisher is not responsible for websites (or their content) that are not owned by the publisher.

Library of Congress Cataloging-in-Publication Data

Names: Leno, Katrina, author.
Title: Horrid / Katrina Leno.
Description: First edition. | New York : Little, Brown and Company, 2020. | Audience: Ages 14+. | Summary: Following her father's sudden death, Jane North-Robinson and her mother are forced to move to the old North house in Maine, where Jane uncovers her family's disturbing secrets.
Identifiers: LCCN 2019055174 | ISBN 9780316537247 (hardcover) | ISBN 9780316537186 (ebook) | ISBN 9780316537254 (ebook other)
Subjects: CYAC: Eating disorders—Fiction. | Sisters—Fiction. | Secrets—Fiction. | Ghosts—Fiction. | Parapsychology—Fiction.
Classification: LCC PZ7.L5399 Ho 2020 | DDC [Fic]—dc23
LC record available at https://lccn.loc.gov/2019055174

ISBNs: 978-0-316-53724-7 (hardcover), 978-0-316-59224-6 (OwlCrate signed edition), 978-0-316-53718-6 (ebook)

Printed in the United States of America

LSC-C

Printing 3, 2021

to my mom,
who often recited this poem to me.
in hindsight—a little creepy, mom.

There was a little girl
Who had a little curl
Right in the middle of her forehead.

And when she was good,
She was very, very good,
But when she was bad, she was horrid.

—A nursery rhyme adapted from
the poem "There Was a Little Girl"
by Henry Wadsworth Longfellow

There was a little girl

She couldn't remember the first book she had eaten.

What it had tasted like, how it had felt—the scratch of it as it slid down her throat.

She couldn't remember why she'd done it. She must have been a baby, a toddler, ripping pages out of a picture book about a talking stuffed animal.

Had the smell of books calmed her down then, as it did now?

Outside, the rain pelted down angrily, it sounded like muffled gunshots on the roof of the bookstore, but inside, inside, surrounded by books, surrounded by the smell of them, she felt calm and tranquil, momentarily at ease, like the past five weeks had never happened.

They'd made it to Maine about thirty minutes ago but the rain had driven them off the highway and into this town with the strange name—Kennebunkport—and Ruth had pulled over and idled on the side of the road until Jane searched *bookstore* on her phone and found this one.

"We might as well," Ruth had said. "I don't want to go any farther until this lets up a little."

She wasn't used to driving in the rain—neither of them was. It didn't rain like this in Los Angeles. If it rained at all, it was a delicate sprinkle that lasted ten or fifteen minutes and ended with a rainbow. Nothing as dramatic as this, sheets of water falling so thickly from the sky that Jane couldn't see a foot outside the window.

The woman behind the counter was unpacking a box of paperbacks.

"Let me know if you need anything," she'd said when they walked in. "Although we'll run into each other soon enough in here."

It was a tiny store, built in a one-car garage behind a big Victorian house. Jane walked down the center aisle, letting her fingers brush across the spines of books until she found one by Raymond Chandler, a collection of short stories called *Killer in the Rain*. She pulled it out and held it. The cover featured a woman in a sea of blue water, floating on her back, her hands outstretched over her head, one high heel on, one off.

Ruth squeezed by in the aisle and Jane showed it to her. Her mother wrinkled her nose.

"Because of the rain," Jane said.

"I'll be in true crime," Ruth replied.

She slipped past Jane. Jane brought the book up to her nose and inhaled. It had a sweet, musty smell.

No, she couldn't remember the first book she'd eaten, but she *could* remember the first book she'd eaten purposefully. And that was maybe more important.

Her tenth birthday. May 4. The book was *Alice's Adventures in Wonderland*. Jane had the same birthday as Alice Liddell. A happy coincidence she had locked away inside her heart when she'd first discovered it.

She liked to pretend, back then, that she and Alice shared more in common than just a birthday. That they might have been friends, if they'd grown up at the same time. That they might have been as close as sisters.

Jane had always wanted a sister.

She'd asked for a new bike for her tenth birthday, but her parents had gotten her a bright-blue scooter instead.

"You don't need a new bike, monkey," her father had said. "Your old one is just fine for now."

And the scooter *was* fun; she'd ridden it up and down their street after dinner. But that night, back in her bedroom, getting ready for bed, she felt a dull throb of anger. She hadn't *asked* for a scooter. She'd wanted a new bike with a basket and a bell. Her old bike didn't have either of those things.

Her breath came quicker and quicker. She felt her face go hot. She felt this warm ball of energy forming in the pit of her stomach, this growing anger that was threatening to spill out of her.

She blinked back tears and stared at the book on her lap, and it was like a little light switch had gone off in her head, and she'd thought, *Oh, I know.*

And she tore off a corner from the first page and put it into her mouth and chewed it.

When she swallowed, she could feel it very distinctly traveling down her throat. She'd imagined she could even feel the tiniest *thump* as it hit her stomach.

The feeling it brought was like some sort of liquid calm. Like she was Alice, for real, but instead of growing bigger or smaller she grew less angry.

She tore off another little piece.

And another.

And bit by bit—

She ate it.

Just one page.

And the next night, one more.

And the next night, one more.

After one, she felt full. But not a *belly* full. A *happy* full. A warm and tingly full. Like the words had dissolved on her tongue and melted into her blood and fixed something inside her. Smoothed out the edges of her ten-year-old brain, all the silly things she got so mad about.

It took her a year to finish the entire book. A page every few nights. Sometimes none, if she was too tired or if she'd had a good day at school, if she was feeling happy.

After a year, she had been left with just the cover, nothing in between it but air.

For her eleventh birthday, she asked her parents to pay for a bookmaking course at the local community college.

She made a journal. Two hundred creamy white pages. She wrote in it as soon as it was finished, the night of her birthday.

> *I just turned eleven. I like eleven more than ten. Ten felt very IMPORTANT.* (She underlined the word *important* three times.) *Eleven feels more manageable. Here are some things about me. My best friend is Salinger Lane. I'm in the fifth grade, and we have our own lockers for the first time. My favorite class is English. I don't want to get my period. Julie got her period in class and EVERYBODY laughed at her. I wore jeans to school last week and I cuffed them because my mom said they looked good like that and then Brenna and Andrea made fun of me. I don't know if I'll keep this journal forever. But for now it's nice to have somewhere to say things I don't want to say to Sal or to my mom. Anyway, I'm Jane North-Robinson. I'll write more later, maybe.*

She *did* write more later, most nights before she went to bed, and for a while that had been enough.

But then it wasn't enough.

And the second book she had eaten was *Peter Pan*.

She finished it just as she was filling up the last pages in her first journal.

So she made a new journal.

And on and on and on.

"Have you read *The Big Sleep*?" asked the owner of the bookstore. Jane blinked herself back to the present and forced a smile.

"Of course," she said. "Chandler's first book. It's genius."

"Ahh, a mystery fan," the woman said. "You've come to the right place. We only sell mystery books here. A little true crime in the corner and some thrillers thrown in to round everything out. I'll let in a couple horror books, but they have to be *very* good."

"I don't have a copy of this," Jane said, holding up *Killer in the Rain*.

"Appropriate pick for a day like today."

"Have you read everything in here?" Ruth asked, stepping behind Jane.

"Of course. I won't sell anything I haven't read myself. Wouldn't feel ethical. I'm Paula. Are you visiting from somewhere?"

"Ruth and Jane," Ruth replied. "We've just moved to Maine, actually. From Los Angeles."

"Some great mystery books set in Los Angeles. *The Big Sleep* being one of them, of course. Lots of true crime, too. Are you settling in Kennebunkport?"

"We have a bit farther to go," Ruth replied. "Bells Hollow."

Paula smiled. "Bells Hollow. Sure."

"You've heard of it?" Ruth asked.

"My two areas of expertise: mystery books and Maine. All these little towns have mysteries, you know. I could tell you a thing or two about Bells Hollow."

"No. Thank you," Ruth said quickly. Then her face softened. "We should probably get going. It sounds like the rain is letting up a bit."

"I'll get this, thanks," Jane said, handing Paula *Killer in the Rain*.

Paula slid behind the counter and Jane spotted an end shelf of books she hadn't noticed before—Agatha Christie.

"Oh, here we go," Ruth said, smiling as Jane started pulling out paperbacks. "Agatha Christie's number-one fan right here."

"Poirot or Marple?" Paula asked, referring to Agatha Christie's two most famous characters.

"Poirot, of course," Jane said.

"My kind of girl," Paula replied.

"I'll get this, too." Jane put a copy of *Destination Unknown* on the counter. "Can't pass up this cover." It featured a robed figure standing in the middle of a confusing background, all swirls of color and shapes. It looked like something Dalí would paint.

"Do you judge a book by its cover?" Paula asked as she picked up the Agatha Christie book and recorded its price.

"Guilty," Jane said.

"Sometimes you can't help it," Paula said, winking. "Especially when they're as good as this one." Paula slid the two books across the counter and said, "Nine fifty-seven."

Jane pulled her credit card out of her wallet and handed it to her. Ruth opened the front door and stepped outside.

"It's definitely slowed down," she called back.

Paula took the credit card and ran it through her machine, then paused to look at the name.

"North," she said softly. "That's an interesting surname."

Jane shrugged. "My mom's side."

Paula handed the credit card back to Jane. Something had come over her face, a sort of shadow. "You be careful up there," she said, just quiet enough so Ruth wouldn't hear. "In Bells Hollow. These old towns all have histories. Some of them are darker than others."

"Oh. Okay. Thanks." Jane took the card and the books. She opened her mouth to say something else, but Ruth stuck her head back in the store.

"Come on, honey, let's make a run for it," she said.

With a last glance back at Paula—who was still looking at her strangely—Jane shoved the books inside her jacket and followed her mom to the car.

Her stomach gave a weird little flop when she passed the U-Haul trailer they'd pulled all the way from California. Her entire life was in there. Well—what was left of it. Six years of journals. Her sizable collection of mystery books, largely made up of Agatha Christies, diligently collected over the years, old and fragile pulp paperbacks she adored for their often-silly covers and turquoise- and red-edged pages. Whatever clothes she could squeeze into her allotted three boxes. They'd been driving for a week, but it hadn't gotten less strange seeing the entirety of what they owned shoved into this tiny trailer.

Ruth had cried when they'd reached the large blue sign that said, in three-foot-high letters: WELCOME TO MAINE.

She'd pulled over in front of it and Jane had said, "I guess we're here?"

"Maine is a big state. It will take another few hours."

"*Hours*," Jane repeated.

WELCOME TO MAINE.

And then it had started pouring.

Jane let herself into the passenger seat and tossed her new books in the back.

"She was kind of weird, huh?" Jane said.

"She runs a mystery bookshop out of her garage," Ruth said. "I think 'weird' is exactly what she's going for."

"You're probably right."

Jane looked at her mother, then back at herself.

They were both a little worn and rumpled around the edges from a weeklong drive across the country. A week's worth of diner meals and takeout and fast food that had left Jane's body feeling heavy and slow. Too many carbs, not enough vegetables. Too much coffee and not enough water. Too much time sitting, feeling shaky and off whenever she had to walk somewhere. Rotating the same two T-shirts and the same two pairs of jeans. She was ready to be out of the car for good. She was ready to *burn* the car. And the clothes.

"Fuck," Ruth whispered next to her. Then, "I'm sorry. It just hits me sometimes."

Jane understood exactly, because it just hit *her* sometimes, too, even though it had been five weeks since her father's heart attack and four weeks since the funeral and three weeks since Ruth had revealed they were broke and two weeks since she had announced they were moving across the country and one week since they had set off, all their worldly possessions sold except the precious little they had managed to cram into the trailer.

"Fuck is right," Jane said, and for a moment she felt washed in anger, a sticky, red-hot anger that threatened to explode out of her like a scream. But she couldn't lose it now. She had to keep it together, for her mother's sake. She took a slow, quiet breath and said, in a voice that fell just short of any real emotion, "We'll feel better when we get there. Just a few more hours."

"A few more hours," Ruth repeated.

They hadn't been using GPS on their cell phones; instead Ruth had stopped at a gas station in every new state they drove through and bought a map, and sat in the car for a moment studying it, planning the route that would bring them farther and farther away from California, the only home Jane had ever known (the only home she had ever *wanted* to know, and for that reason just the sight of a paper map would, for the rest of her life, create an aching, lonely feeling in the pit of her stomach; she had learned to hate maps, to hate street signs, to hate the mile markers that appeared and then disappeared in the passenger-side mirror).

And so they'd made the entire trip, sometimes listening to

podcasts, sometimes to the radio, sometimes to books on tape, sometimes to nothing at all, because something would end and neither Jane nor Ruth would realize it was over because neither Jane nor Ruth had really been listening to it anyway.

But silence in a car wasn't really silence at all. The *whoosh* of opposite traffic. The errant horn. The pavement disappearing underneath them. The engine roaring away. The soft huff of air coming out of the vents. It all blended together to create something almost like music.

WELCOME TO MAINE.

Jane didn't feel welcome at all.

Instead, she felt ambushed—like even the week's worth of driving hadn't been enough to prepare her for the inevitability of actually arriving.

And here is something she hadn't anticipated: Every mile they put between themselves and California felt like it was bringing them further and further from her father.

Jane had *loved* her father—she'd been devastated when her mother had shown up halfway through second period on the second day of her senior year, reeking of cigarettes (a habit she only returned to on the darkest of days), somehow holding in her tears until they had made it back to the car, putting both hands on the steering wheel but not starting the ignition, staring straight ahead as Jane shrunk smaller and smaller in her own seat. Because somehow she knew what had happened. The details were fuzzy, unknown to her, but the truth was evident, loud, painful: *Something had happened to her father.*

"Mom?" she'd said, and when Ruth looked up at her, it had felt like her mother was returning from a long journey—her face was clouded over; it took her eyes a full minute to focus.

"Jane, I'm so sorry," she said. "I'm so sorry, but something happened. Your father...Jane. Your father had a heart attack. Sweetheart. I'm so sorry. He's gone."

Ruth had said more, but Jane hadn't heard a word of it; her ears were overcome by the sound of her own blood sloshing angrily through her veins, the sound of crashing waves, persistent and loud.

"What do you mean?" she said finally, interrupting her mother, her voice almost a shout. "What do you *mean* he's gone?"

"I'm so sorry, Jane. I'm so sorry."

It seemed like that was the only thing Ruth was capable of saying—*I'm so sorry*—and each repetition only served to make Jane angrier and angrier. She was aware that her emotions were confused, that she should be feeling *sad*, not angry, not resentful, not hateful, but there wasn't anything she could do about it; she felt the way she felt, and she couldn't do anything to stop it, to correct it.

"But what do you *mean*?" she'd screamed at her mother, and Ruth had stopped apologizing, Ruth had rested her forehead on the steering wheel and begun to sob.

Jane couldn't help feeling a pang of that same resentment, now, that same anger, that same rushing in her ears, as she sat, listening to her mother trying not to cry. Because a few days after Greer had died, Ruth had come back from the lawyer's office quiet, smelling like smoke again, and it took almost a week for her to finally tell Jane the truth: They were broke.

It seemed that lately it was taking longer and longer for Ruth to tell Jane the truth. Full minutes in the car to choke out what had happened to Greer. Days to reveal they were broke. Another week to mention the house in Maine, a house Jane had never heard of before, a house they were now barreling toward at sixty-five miles per hour.

What else had Ruth not yet worked up the courage to tell her daughter?

Greer Robinson (Ruth had kept her maiden name of North; Jane was a North-Robinson) had been a loving, devoted husband and father—but he had shared that one quality with his wife, that propensity for dishonesty. It had always been his dream to start his own business; their life as a family of three had been marked with financial ups and downs as Greer left steady, stable jobs to work for various start-ups that inevitably failed after six months or a year. Eventually, he'd taken their entire savings—apart from a few thousand dollars Ruth had in a separate account—and invested it in a business that had failed very quickly. All the money was gone. He had stopped paying the mortgage on the house months ago. He hadn't told his wife about any of it.

So Ruth had come up with a plan: They would sell their house in California, barely break even, and move across the country to her mother's estate in Maine. Emilia North had been dead for two years, and she had left the New England house to Ruth in her will.

"We'll only have to pay property taxes and insurance," Ruth had told Jane, like Jane had any idea what those two things meant or what they might cost. "We can manage that. I'll get a job, and we'll manage."

"Why can't we just sell that house and stay here?" Jane had asked.

"It needs too much work. It would never pass inspection. And there aren't any mortgage payments. I know this sounds counterintuitive, but I just don't have the money to sell a house like that."

Jane glanced over at her mother now. Ruth had been acting stranger and stranger the closer they got to Maine, and now here they were, one hour in, and Jane wondered if she should offer to drive.

But then Ruth took a deep breath, a purposeful breath, and when she looked over at her daughter, her eyes were dry and wide.

"Ready for this?"

"No," Jane responded bluntly. But she smiled a little. A sad smile that fooled no one.

"Me neither," Ruth said.

She pulled out of the parking lot.

And when they got back on the highway, Jane almost wished she felt something—a jolt, a shock, a bolt of lightning— just as she wished she'd felt something when they passed the state line into Maine—but it was just the same as every single mile since California.

Just another mile marker disappearing into the distance behind her.

It took just over four hours from Kennebunkport, with a bathroom break and a stop for lunch and a gas top-off and two cups of cheap coffee so hot Jane couldn't even take a sip for fifteen minutes.

They passed a sign that said: WELCOME TO BELLS HOLLOW. EST. 1680. "LITTLE PLACE IN THE FOREST."

"*Little Place in the Forest,*" Jane read. "What's that supposed to mean?"

"A lot of these old towns have slogans like that," Ruth replied.

"Weird."

"There's a *Blueberry Capital of the World* not far from here."

"I don't like blueberries," Jane said, perhaps because she was determined not to like anything about Maine, including any of its seasonal fruits.

Ruth smiled. "Me neither."

Another five miles down a quiet, tree-lined road and Ruth slowed the car and made a right-hand turn onto a street with no street sign. Jane thought maybe Bells Hollow was so small that it didn't even need street signs. Maybe the postal workers knew everybody by name. Maybe they didn't even *have* mail here.

They drove for a half mile more. There were only a few houses on the street, set far back from the road and from one another, big houses with big yards and big, long driveways. Each lot was cut out of dense woods, the dark trees skirting the edges of the property lines.

"*Little Place in the Forest,*" Jane whispered.

They were slowing down; Ruth gripped the steering wheel tightly, and gently eased the car to the side of the road. They were at the very end of the street. Jane looked past her mother out the driver's-side window and there it was—North Manor, a house Jane hadn't even known existed until her mother had slid an old Polaroid across the kitchen counter that night two weeks ago.

Like the other houses on the street, North Manor was set back from the road, a large colonial-style mansion with three gables at the front and four white columns supporting a white-railed balcony. The nine windows at the front had black shutters. There were two brick chimneys at either end of the house, and a faded brick path leading up to the front door.

In the Polaroid, the house had been pristine in its beauty.

Now, though, it was barely recognizable as the same place. All but two of the windows were smashed. One was boarded up completely. Two shutters hung at haphazard angles, and the grass was overrun with dandelions and looked like it would come up to about Jane's shins. The brick path was littered with patches of weeds that had pushed aside the stone and made everything uneven.

"Jeez," Jane whispered.

They hadn't gotten out of the car. Jane didn't even think her mother had looked up at the house yet; she was staring very purposefully at the center of the steering wheel.

"Mom?"

Ruth blinked rapidly and looked over at her daughter, keeping her eyes down. "What does it look like?"

"You want an honest assessment?"

"Please."

"It sort of looks like one big tetanus trap."

"Okay," Ruth said, nodding.

"Are you going to look?"

"I'm going to look."

"Soon?"

"Soon."

A few seconds passed. Jane saw her mother's lips moving quickly, silently—some private countdown she didn't want to intrude on.

Then Ruth took a breath, lifted her eyes, and looked out the window at the place where she'd grown up.

Jane had only ever lived in their small house in the Valley. She couldn't imagine leaving it, like her mother had, and returning so many years later to find it in near ruins.

"You okay?" Jane asked.

"Oh, I don't know," Ruth said, sighing. "Look at this place. It's a mess. I should have come back here so much sooner."

"Did all this happen in two years? Since Grandma died?"

Ruth frowned. "I don't think your grandmother was in her right mind the last few years of her life. I think she just let it go."

"But it's okay? For us to live here?" Jane asked. "Without, you know, contracting a staph infection or something?"

Ruth laughed. "The windows are the main thing. I called ahead and had them measured. They'll start to replace them in the next few days, before winter sets in."

The phrase *winter sets in* was entirely alien to Jane. In Los Angeles, *winter* meant it was sixty-five degrees out for a few weeks and people leaped at the chance to wear too-heavy jackets and floppy beanies. She had seen snow on a family trip to Tahoe when she was twelve, and she remembered it being exciting at first—but that excitement had worn off when her boots soaked through and she'd lost feeling in her toes.

Jane opened the car door and slid out. It was colder than she'd expected; there was a bite to the air that even the chilliest nights in California hadn't managed to carry, and there was a breeze that blew Jane's waist-length, wavy blond hair around her face. She caught it in her hands and trapped it in a low ponytail.

Jane heard Ruth's door open and shut, and a few moments later, she was standing next to her, staring up at the house.

"It's *freezing*," Jane complained. "It's only the beginning of October! Isn't this supposed to be fall? I thought fall was, like, a gentle breeze and a pumpkin-spice latte."

"That's September," Ruth replied. "October is basically early winter. Although we can still get you a latte, if you want."

"Maybe later," Jane mumbled, just as a gust of wind blew across the front yard, raising goose bumps on her arms and the back of her neck.

Ruth put her arm around her daughter's shoulders. "I know none of this is what we wanted. If there was any way we could have stayed in California, honey . . ."

"I know."

"We just owed too much on that house. I never would have been able to catch up. And Los Angeles is so *expensive*. It's two lattes for the price of one, here."

"I know."

"And I love you very much, and I promise this won't be forever. You'll be applying to colleges this year. You'll get into one back home, and you'll go, and I'll eventually sell this place and follow you there with my tail between my legs. We'll make it work."

"I know."

"Can you say anything except *I know?*"

"He chose the worst time to die," Jane said, just a little morbid humor between mother and daughter that made Ruth smirk and nod in agreement.

"Tell me about it. He certainly did throw a wrench in things."

Jane had a flash of her father lying in his casket, looking waxy and strange in death, no outward signs of the heart attack that had killed him.

In the flash, his hands were clasped on his chest. He was holding a wrench.

Jane's mouth felt suddenly chalky and dry.

"Mom—how come you never came back here?" Jane asked, a little nervous all of a sudden, like the chill of the air had worked its way into her skin and settled itself in her belly, to twist and writhe like some alive thing.

Ruth hesitated. It felt to Jane like she was deciding what to say, like she was carefully arranging her words into the most appropriate order. Jane thought back to Paula at the bookstore, the strange look that had come over her face, the way she had told Jane to be careful. Finally, in a forced kind of way, Ruth said, "It isn't always easy. Returning to the past. Now, come on—let's get inside and have a look around."

She started walking to the house.

Returning to the past . . . Jane turned the phrase over in her head as she followed Ruth to the front door. She didn't understand what it meant, or what it might be like to *not* want to return to the past. That was all she wanted to do; all she wanted in the entire world was to rewind, start the tape over, go back a few weeks or months and try a do-over, get her dad back and drag him to the doctor's office before it was too late, fix whatever had gone wrong in his body that had made his heart turn against him.

Ruth fit the key into the lock, fumbling just a little to get it to move. When she finally pushed the door open, a wave of dusty, stale air hit them.

It was the smell of disuse, of empty rooms, of empty hallways, of two years without anyone walking around, without any air circulation. It was like mothballs stuck into the backs of closets, that sickly sort of smell that caused your throat to go dry, your saliva to evaporate.

It was a thick thing, a heavy thing. The feeling of neglect seemed to radiate from all around them. They stood in the doorway, peeking in, letting their eyes adjust to the dim light, and then Ruth stepped inside and Jane followed her and there it was, that phrase again, because walking through the front door felt *exactly* like returning to the past, in such a quick, immediate way it left her feeling a little dizzy.

Like walking through a familiar room in the dark and missing your step, knocking your hip into a chair you could have sworn was three feet away from you.

Like raising your hand to wave at someone in a crowd before realizing it isn't who you thought it was at all.

Like a hollow swoop in the pit of your stomach from standing up too fast.

"What *is* this place?" Jane whispered.

Ruth actually laughed—and her laugh helped break the spell a little, helped return Jane to reality.

"It won't be that bad once we fix it up," Ruth promised.

"It's like the creepy house in *And Then There Were None*," Jane said. It wasn't one of her favorite Agatha Christie novels, but the house on Indian Island gave her the chills just like North Manor did. She wouldn't be surprised if a spooky voice started playing out of a gramophone, announcing their crimes.

Whatever Jane's crime was, she was sure the punishment was too great to fit.

"I don't remember that one," Ruth murmured. She flicked the light switch next to the door—nothing. "Shit. That should have been on by now."

"We are absolutely going to be murdered," Jane said.

"This is not an Agatha Christie novel," Ruth replied sensibly. "Get your cell phone out."

Jane took her phone out of her pocket and checked it. "Great. No service. We are *definitely* going to be murdered."

"Stop being so dramatic and turn the flashlight on."

Jane did.

In the soft beam of the light's glow, the foyer looked even spookier than it had a few minutes ago.

There was a faded Oriental carpet running the length of the hall; a wide, open staircase spun upward and disappeared into shadow; and the banister and entranceway table were covered in a thick blanket of dust.

Jane couldn't imagine this house filled, as it once was, with people—let alone her mother as a child, her mother as a baby, her mother as a teenage girl, attending school and kissing boys and doing homework and playing games.

"It's cold in here," Jane said.

"The heat was supposed to come on with the lights," Ruth replied.

Their house in California hadn't even had heat. Jane looked over at her mother. She seemed to have shrunk two inches; her shoulders were hunched and sagging, her arms folded on her chest like she was trying to make herself as small as possible.

"How are you holding up?" Jane asked.

Ruth shrugged. "Not sure. You?"

"Not sure," Jane repeated.

Ruth took a step forward. She rubbed at a spot on her left wrist, then she reached her hand out and placed her palm flat on the banister. "I broke my wrist on this staircase," she whispered. "I slid down the whole thing on a trash-can lid."

"Sounds unsanitary."

"My mother almost killed me. I think she *would* have, if she hadn't first needed to drive me to the emergency room."

Jane had only met her grandmother three times. Emilia North had visited for Christmases when Jane was four, eight, and twelve. They had never gone east to see her.

She doesn't like visitors, Ruth had explained once.

"Where should we start?" Jane asked.

"This way," Ruth said, and walked through an open doorway into a big sitting room. Someone had taped cellophane over the broken windowpanes, and some bigger pieces of furniture were covered with dusty, yellowed sheets. Jane could make out the shape of a piano in one corner; a large bookcase or hutch against one wall; a long, low sofa in the middle of the room.

"Who played the piano?" Jane asked.

"My father."

Jane had never met Chester North; he had passed away when she was just five years old.

She wondered, now, whether it had hurt her mother to lose her father as much as it had hurt Jane to lose hers—

It must have.

"That's a 1925 Steinway," Ruth said. "We could sell it. It would probably pay for your first year of college."

They walked into the next room. And the next room. An endless stretch of rooms, each with its collection of sheet-covered furniture, each alike in its feeling of loneliness.

They kept walking until they reached a room at the far end of the house. An enormous fireplace took up much of one wall. "We'll sleep in here tonight," Ruth said. "We'll light a fire. We should be nice and toasty."

"Are there doors?"

"*Mais oui.* Observe." Ruth hooked a finger into the pull of a pocket door and slid it out of the wall.

"So fancy," Jane said.

"I know, that's why I said it in French."

"So we'll just sleep on the floor?"

"It'll be like we're camping."

"We hate camping."

Ruth sighed. "Yes. I know we hate camping."

"But a fire will be nice," Jane added quickly. "Can we get stuff for s'mores?"

"Now you're talking. Come."

She led Jane through a door to a dining room at the back of the house, a dining room bigger perhaps than their entire house in California, with a long table made of dark wood and tall, wide windows that overlooked the backyard.

"Fancy again," Jane said.

"I hated eating in here," Ruth replied. "We only used it for company. Boring dinner parties. When it was just the three of us, we ate in here—"

And she darted off to the left, through another set of open pocket doors that led into a large, roomy kitchen—high ceilings and a double oven and a fridge you could fit an entire person inside. There was a recessed nook at the back of the house with a little kitchen table and chairs. There was enough light back here that Jane turned her flashlight off and put her phone back in her pocket. She wandered around. She opened a cabinet and found a dusty set of antique china. Another drawer held various kitchen utensils. Another drawer held a set of delicate glass mixing bowls.

North Manor had become like a time capsule, she realized—unchanged and preserved in the absence of occupants.

There was something in the air here, some smell that came in through a broken windowpane, where the cellophane had come unstuck and was flapping in the breeze. It was a sweet smell, an out-of-place smell, the smell of...

"Is that roses?" Jane mused aloud, walking over to the window and peeking out.

"Hmm?"

"I think I smell roses."

"It's not the season for them," Ruth said distractedly, running a finger across the table to see how much dust had accumulated there.

"You don't smell them?"

Ruth came over to the window. She wiped her hand on her jeans, then ran her fingers through Jane's ponytail.

"I hate roses," she said.

She walked out of the kitchen, through a bare pantry to a hallway that ran from the front of the house to the back. Jane followed.

Ruth paused in front of a heavy wooden door with an enormous brass handle. She tapped it.

"This was my father's study."

She opened the door.

It was darker in here—the two windows at the back of the room were covered in thick green, velvet curtains. Ruth went and opened them, and Jane imagined the room hissing at being exposed to light after all those years.

The walls were covered with dark wood paneling and the air had a lingering smell of old tobacco. There was a massive desk that took up most of the space. The walls behind it contained floor-to-ceiling bookshelves, completely stuffed with old hardcovers.

Jane felt a twinge in her gut. Something deep stirring inside her. A longing for comfort she tried her best to ignore.

"I was never allowed in here," Ruth said, smirking a little.

There was a pen case on the desk. Jane opened it and pulled one of the pens out; it was an expensive-looking black, heavy thing that said *Montblanc* on the side. She pulled her phone out of her pocket to see if it might be worth something, but she still didn't have service.

She raised the phone above her head, moved to the window, did a little dance—

"I wouldn't hold your breath," Ruth said.

"Nobody would find our bodies for *weeks*," Jane muttered.

"Relax, Detective Poirot. Let's keep going."

Ruth left the room, and Jane took a moment to replace the pen in its case. When she stepped out of the office, her mother had already disappeared. Jane shrugged and went left, toward the back of the house. The smell of roses was overwhelming now; how did Ruth not notice it?

The hallway ended in a little mudroom. There were hooks on the wall for coats and a shoe rack by the door. A pair of galoshes; a pair of house slippers; a pair of old, dirty white sneakers.

Jane had the feeling, again, that the house was like a time capsule—like a glimpse into the last hours and days of her grandmother's life. Emilia Banks North had passed away in her sleep, found the next day by the nurse who visited every morning. Jane imagined nurses were trained for things like that. Maybe it was nothing more than a gentle shock: finding your employer dead.

Emilia had left everything to Ruth, her only heir.

And then Greer had lost it all.

Well—except for this house.

Jane looked at the mudroom door. It had a window in it that was cracked but not broken through. It was as if something had been thrown at it—there was a small point of impact with splinters spreading out around it like a spiderweb.

She opened the door and the cold hit her at once—a big blast of it that chilled her completely. The backyard was in the same state of disrepair as the front yard, but Jane could tell just by looking at it how beautiful it had been once, when it had been maintained. There was a great fountain in the middle of a large expanse of grass, with different stone paths branching out from it in a wagon-wheel pattern. There were little patches of garden—now overrun and dead with the cold—that at one time must have been lush and flourishing.

Jane walked out to the fountain. It was bone-dry now, the stone covered with a thin fuzz of old moss. She looked back to the house and saw a light turn on in a second-floor room. So the power must have finally kicked on. She gave a little wave to the shadow that passed in front of the window and checked her phone again. Still no service.

It must have been all the trees; the backyard was completely surrounded by them.

Jane had never been one to be easily spooked—she spent most of her free time reading mystery books and watching horror movies—but she couldn't help feeling just the tiniest bit creeped-out in this place. Maybe it was because everything was so brown and brittle. Maybe it was the rustle of fallen leaves blowing against stone walkways in the breeze. Maybe it was the smell of roses. The smell and... Wait a minute. There *were* roses. She could just make out the bright spots of red and pink and orange at the far end of the lawn. She knew it! It felt nice knowing *something* could survive out here. Jane started walking toward them.

Ruth had said it wasn't the season for roses, but she had never had much of a green thumb—they hadn't even had a grass lawn back in California; instead, their property was filled with succulents and mulch and little patches of small rocks. Greer had called the style *drought-tolerant*; Ruth had called it *low-maintenance*.

Maybe roses were low-maintenance, too, and that was why they were the only thing, besides the shin-high grass, that had survived the years without tending.

But they weren't just surviving, Jane noted as she got closer, they were *thriving*—lush, green plants that vined up white arbors to form a covered walkway. Up close, the smell was thick and heavy and made Jane a little dizzy. She sat on a white bench and took the closest blossom in her hand. It was a deep, vibrant red. So bright she felt like she could eat it.

The wind whistled outside the arbor and eventually she realized she could hear something else—Ruth, calling her name.

She stepped out of the protection of the rosebushes and waved at her mother. Ruth hurried over, hugging her arms across her chest for warmth.

"I *told* you I smelled roses," Jane said excitedly, pointing.

"These should be dead already," Ruth replied. "Jesus, it really *is* freezing. Let's go get a few things for dinner."

"And s'mores."

"And s'mores." Ruth took Jane's hand and pulled her back toward the house.

"You didn't even look at the roses," Jane whined.

"Honey, my toes are going to fall off. You were right about the roses. Would you like a medal?"

"Rude."

"*Freezing,*" Ruth retorted.

Jane looked up at the house. It was dark again. The light in the upstairs window was off.

"Well, at least the electricity's finally on," she said.

"Not yet. I just checked," Ruth replied. They reached the mudroom door and stepped into the house. Ruth flicked a light switch on and off. Nothing happened.

"But I saw a light upstairs," Jane said.

"Are you trying to scare me? I think the fear part of my brain is frozen solid."

"No, I'm not trying to scare you. I saw a light. And I saw you at the window."

"I didn't even go upstairs. There might have been an electric surge or something." Ruth shrugged. "I didn't notice anything."

"A surge?"

"These old houses have old wiring. Old everything. I'll call the electric company from the car."

"Old wiring sounds like a fire hazard," Jane said.

"Not everything is going to cause your imminent demise, my love."

Jane wasn't so sure of that.

There was only one grocery store in town, a tiny co-op with low ceilings and poor lighting but plenty of organic produce. They got tomato soup for dinner; bread, butter, and cheese to make grilled cheese sandwiches; and stuff for s'mores. Ruth made a fire and assembled the sandwiches on a cast-iron skillet, which she put over the embers. She heated up the soup in a saucepan next to it.

"You are a true mountain man," Jane observed.

"My father made me go to Girl Scouts," Ruth replied. "He was afraid if I didn't do something outdoorsy, I'd turn into one of my mother's society ladies. Or even worse—I'd turn into my mother herself."

"Emilia wasn't that bad, was she?"

"She was on her best behavior when you saw her. She could be a proper pain in the ass, though. I was sent to my room once for not remembering which of my many forks was for salad."

"And yet you slid down the staircase on a trash-can lid."

Ruth smiled proudly. "That was my dad's influence."

"I wish I had met him," Jane said

"Yeah, I wish you had met him, too. He was a good guy."

"Like Dad?"

"Couldn't be more different." Ruth laughed. "Chester was always a little...I don't know. Hesitant. Reserved. I think it maybe came from living with my mom all those years. But still, every now and then, when she wasn't looking, I think I got a glimpse of who he might have been."

"Honestly, Emilia sounds like a real piece of work."

"My dad once compared this house to a mousetrap," Ruth said conspiratorially. "You let your guard down and all of a sudden you're trapped for life."

"But you left."

"Yeah. I left. And look at me—right back where I started."

"Are you okay?" Jane asked, because Ruth's eyes had become unfocused; she seemed distant and strange.

She took a moment to answer. She looked up at the ceiling, then stared into the fire. "I don't know," she admitted finally. "It's weird. I never thought I'd be saying this, but...I miss her. Emilia. Being back here makes me miss her." She bit her lip, paused again, folded her hands in her lap and interlaced her fingers. "When she died, I felt so many things. This rush of pain, of sadness, of guilt, of regret. I should have come back to see her. I should have moved her out to California with us after my dad died. I should have done more to take care of her. But I don't know. I don't know that she really did that much to take care of me." Ruth closed her eyes, and when she opened them, they were red and wet, and Jane reached over and took her hand.

"I'm sorry, Mom."

"I'm sorry, too, because now you know what it's like. To lose a parent," Ruth whispered. "It's a terrible thing. And yours was so good. So much better than mine."

Jane was crying now, too, and they sat in silence for a few minutes, holding hands, crying, letting their soup get cold.

"I want you to know that I'm here for you, Janie," Ruth

said. "I never want you to feel how I felt with Emilia. I never want you to feel like you have to go through this alone. You can always come to me."

"I know," Jane said. "I know."

"Grief is different for everyone," Ruth continued. "There's no right or wrong answer. Just remember that, okay?"

"Okay, Mom."

"For example, sometimes grief is crying onto your grilled cheese sandwich," Ruth said, wiping at her cheeks.

"Does it make you feel any better that these look like the best grilled cheese sandwiches ever made? Tears or no tears."

Ruth smiled. "It does, a bit, yeah."

"Let's do this."

They ate cross-legged in front of the fireplace, dipping their sandwiches into the bowls of tomato soup. The food and the fire warmed Jane's body until her skin had a faint pink glow to it, and neither of them spoke until there were only a few crumbs left on their plates.

It was only after they'd eaten two s'mores each and cleaned up all the dishes, leaving them out to dry on the counter, that Jane felt the first wave of fatigue wash over her.

"Oy," she said.

"Same," Ruth agreed.

They'd brought in sleeping bags and pillows from the back seat of the car, and they spent a few minutes getting every-thing unrolled and set up.

"Is it okay to leave this burning?" Jane asked, already buried in the sleeping bag, just the tip of her nose showing, her voice muffled.

"It'll be fine. We need the warmth," Ruth replied.

A few moments of rustling as Ruth settled into her own sleeping bag. As soon as she was still, the only noise was from the fire, crackling and popping as it burned away. Behind that, if she strained her ears, Jane could hear nothing but an overwhelming silence. She almost said something, but she realized Ruth was already sleeping, snoring gently, passed out in ten seconds flat.

Jane rolled over onto her back, the fire warming the right side of her face, the left side feeling abruptly chilled.

So this was it. The first night of her new life. She pulled her phone out of the sleeping bag and checked it. Still no service. She hadn't even texted Salinger—her best friend back home— to let her know she'd made it.

She opened her messages now, even though the phone was useless, even though the battery was almost dead. She wrote a text to Sal. *I miss you so much. I hate it here. I want to come home.*

She didn't hit Send. She clicked back to her messages. She scrolled down until she found *Dad*.

The last message he'd sent her said: *Outside!*

He'd been picking her up from Sal's house. The night before his heart attack.

Jane ran her thumb over the text.

Outside!

She squeezed her eyes closed and imagined he'd just sent

that text, that he was outside now, waiting for her, the heat blasting in his old pickup as he drummed his fingers against the dashboard in time to whatever was playing on the radio.

She almost imagined she could hear his truck idling, the driver's-side door creaking as he opened it and stepped out onto the driveway, his faint footsteps as he walked up to the front door, to knock lightly, to come and fetch her since she didn't have any cell service to respond to his text. She almost imagined she could hear those knocks—*tap-tap-tap*—and then her eyes opened suddenly, because she *had* heard them, or no, of course she hadn't, she'd just been concentrating so hard, trying to hear them, that she'd tricked herself into believing they were there.

She sat up in her sleeping bag, wiping at her eyes (had she started crying again, or had she never really stopped?), peering into the darkness of the house, the flickering shadows that the fire cast on all the walls, the unfamiliar shapes of furniture jutting out of the floor like icebergs.

Tap-tap-tap.

She froze.

She'd heard it that time, she was sure she had, and she was up and on her feet, running to the window at the front of the house, pushing the cellophane aside to peer out of the dirty, cloudy glass.

The moon was bright in the sky. The driveway was empty. Of course the driveway was empty, because her father was dead and his pickup truck had been repossessed and he would never again come to pick her up, never again come to drive her back home.

Tap-tap-tap.

It was only an old tree, the wind knocking it against the side of the house, its branches clicking against the windows like long, dry fingers.

Tap-tap-tap.

Grief is different for everyone, Ruth had said, and maybe Jane's grief manifested itself in visions, in thinking she could almost see the outline of Greer's truck in the driveway. Almost. But when she blinked—it was gone.

She was still holding her phone. She looked down at the screen now, open to her father's text, and felt a heavy, cold ache in her stomach.

Outside!

She looked out the window once more.

She'd give anything—*anything*—if that were true.

Although Ruth had told her she could wait until Monday to start school, Jane woke up early the next morning and got dressed while her mother slept. It was Friday, and Jane figured it would be nice to ease into it, to have only one day of school and then a weekend, instead of five straight days of classes.

She made instant oatmeal they'd bought at the co-op and ate it standing over the kitchen sink. She kissed Ruth on the forehead before she left. Her mother mumbled and rolled over; she'd never been much of a morning person.

The bus stop was at the beginning of the street, a ten-minute walk. It was a gray, chilly morning. Jane wore a flannel and her jean jacket, and after three minutes her fingers were numb. Jane was sure she'd be the only senior riding the bus. In California, she had walked to the high school or else gotten a ride with Sal and her brother.

She reached the end of the street and looked down the road. She could just about see the bus now, about a quarter mile away, making the occasional stop, dutifully extending the bright-red stop sign.

Another minute and then it was pulling up in front of her, brakes screeching, and she climbed the steps before she could change her mind.

The smell hit her first; it was like she was eleven years old again on the first day of middle school. It was the smell of whatever plastic they used to make the drab brown seats, the smell of a dozen packed lunches, the smell of unwashed hair and sweaty skin and runny noses.

All school buses were the same.

She tried not to cry.

She took an empty seat in the middle of the bus and pulled out her phone, staring at it until it lit up with a couple of bars of service. She sent a message to Sal:

Got to Maine yesterday. Haven't had service. I'm omw to school now. I miss you so much and I don't feel good, slept on the floor and will never be warm again. Also will definitely be murdered in this house. Other than that everything is great.

It was a thirty-minute ride to the school. Bells Hollow High School was a small, unassuming building, nothing at all like her enormous high school back in California, which was brand-new and housed over fifteen hundred students. There were currently eighty-one seniors at Bells Hollow High.

Well—the fewer students, the easier it would be to avoid them all.

She pushed through the double doors and walked into the front office, which was right across from the entrance.

"Hi," she said to the woman at the front desk. "I'm Jane North-Robinson. It's my first day."

"Jane, of course! It is *so* nice to meet you. I'm Rosemary," she replied. "This is a lovely surprise; we weren't expecting you until Monday!"

Jane forced a smile and shrugged. "I thought—why wait?"

"I like that attitude! I have all your paperwork ready somewhere...." Rosemary opened a filing cabinet next to her desk and pulled out a manila folder. "Your locker assignment is in here, and your schedule of classes. Let me just call Alana—I think I saw her walk in a few minutes ago. She'll be your buddy. It's something we do here; we just find it's really helpful to have someone you can turn to with all your questions."

Rosemary lifted a telephone receiver from her desk and

Jane heard the announcement system crinkle to life in the hallway.

"Alana Cansler to the front office please," Rosemary said into the receiver. She hung it up and smiled at Jane. "So, how was your trip here?"

"Fine," Jane said. "Thanks."

"What do you think of Bells Hollow so far?"

"I haven't really seen that much of it. It seems nice."

Rosemary seemed to have exhausted her supply of small talk. She smiled a bit awkwardly until the door opened behind Jane, then she lit up and said, "Oh, here she is now! Alana, dear, this is Jane!"

Jane turned around. Alana was a white girl with shoulder-length brown hair, bangs, and tortoiseshell glasses. She was wearing overalls with a white long-sleeved shirt underneath. She stuck out her hand energetically, and Jane took it.

"Nice to meet you!" Alana said.

"It's nice to meet you, too."

"Why don't you two get going; Alana, will you show Jane to her locker? Jane, if you need anything, just let me know, all right?"

"Thanks," Jane said.

"I thought you weren't starting until Monday?" Alana said as soon as they were in the hallway.

"My internal clock is a mess. I woke up super early. It was either this or help my mom clean."

"You're from California, right? This way." She led Jane

down one of the hallways that branched off from the main entranceway.

"Los Angeles," Jane confirmed.

"I've always wanted to go to California. Is it nice?"

"I love it, yeah."

"Well, Bells Hollow isn't that bad. As your first-day buddy, I'm supposed to tell you it's amazing, but it's definitely not *amazing*. It's just not bad. It's fine." Alana laughed. "Sorry, I should be selling it more. This is you."

They'd reached locker 101. Jane consulted the paper that Rosemary had given her and found her combination. She opened it on the first try, put her jacket inside, then closed it.

"So have you seen much of the town yet?" Alana asked. "Where do you live?"

"I live in my grandmother's old house," Jane replied.

"Oh, who's your grandmother?"

"Emilia North."

Alana blinked. "Emilia North?" she repeated.

"Did you know her?"

"It's a small town; everybody kind of knows everybody." Alana paused, fidgeting a bit. "Do you mind if we stop at my locker first? We still have a minute."

"Sure, of course."

Alana's locker was in the next hallway; it just took a few seconds to reach it. She opened it and started pulling books out, then asked, "So... you live in North Manor?"

"Yup."

"It's been empty for a while."

"Two years. Since my grandmother died."

"I'm sorry."

"Thanks. I didn't really know her that well."

Alana zipped up her backpack, shut her locker, and turned to Jane. She looked a little embarrassed.

"What?" Jane asked.

"It's so stupid."

"Just tell me."

"I feel like a jerk. But if I don't tell you now, someone is definitely going to tell you eventually."

"Tell me what?"

"It just has a nickname. That house."

"A nickname?" Jane repeated.

"Like . . . a not-nice nickname."

"Okay. . . ."

"People call it the creep house. It's so juvenile, I know."

"Creep house?" Jane laughed. "I can think of at least a dozen more imaginative names for that house."

"I didn't say it was imaginative," Alana said, smiling. "But still, it's rude. People here are just bored. There's not a lot to do, you know? The closest movie theater has been closed for renovations for two years. What's California like? I'm sure there's just, like, too much to do, right? On Friday nights do you just go hang out with celebrities?"

"There are a lot of celebrity meetups, yeah," Jane said seriously. "They get kind of boring after a while."

"And was everyone . . . You know?"

"Was everyone what?"

Alana gestured at Jane's hair. "I mean . . . So *blond*?"

Jane laughed out loud. "Yes," she replied. "Only blonds allowed."

They had the first three classes together, and later, when the bell rang for lunch, Alana led Jane to the cafeteria. Jane purchased the least offensive-looking thing on the lunch menu: a semi-greasy piece of cheese pizza. Her old school's cafeteria had been huge, with options for every single kind of diet. There wasn't even a salad in this place; she made a mental note to start bringing her own lunch.

"Over here," Alana said, leading the way to a table near the middle of the room, where she introduced Jane to a handful of people whose names Jane forgot almost immediately. She sat between Alana and Susie, a black girl with box braids that fell long and straight down her back.

Jane thought Alana must have prepped her friends that Jane would be sitting with them for lunch, and although everyone was perfectly nice and welcoming, Jane couldn't help sensing a tiny bit of wariness from them. She swore two girls across the table whispered something about North Manor as she sat down, and one guy with glasses to her left seemed determined not to make eye contact with her. The only ones who acted normal were Alana and Susie.

"Alana told me you live on my side of town," Susie said as Jane took a bite of pizza. "I'm just a few streets over."

"Oh, really?" Jane said.

"Yeah. What do you think of Bells Hollow so far?" Susie asked.

"There are a lot of trees," Jane said. "I guess I didn't know there would be so many trees."

Susie laughed. "A lot of trees. A lot of deer. Alana claims she saw a moose once."

"I *did* see a moose. Do you know how big moose are? I mean—too big. Unnecessarily big," Alana said.

Jane took another bite of her pizza and felt a dribble of grease slide down her chin. She wiped it away quickly, and looked up just in time to notice a girl walk by their table and kick the leg of Alana's chair as she passed it. She was white with stringy, dyed-black hair that fell to her shoulders and a piercing on her lip, a little hoop that curled over her bottom lip.

"What was that about?" Jane asked Alana.

Alana sighed. "It's complicated."

"She's terrible; it's best not to dwell on it," Susie said. "So besides the trees, are you enjoying your first day at our famed Bells Hollow High School?"

"It's all been uphill since the bus," Jane replied.

"The bus?" Alana repeated. "Oh no. You took the bus?"

Jane shrugged in reply.

"You probably have lice now. My friend Marian took the bus once, and she had to shave her head," Alana said sadly.

"Don't listen to her; that is absolutely not true," Susie said. "I can give you a ride home. We're so close."

"I couldn't ask you to do that," Jane said.

"Don't be ridiculous," Alana replied. "Susie doesn't mind. She drives me home, too."

"Are you sure?"

"Totally," Susie insisted. "It's no problem at all."

Jane felt a little awkward about it, but she shrugged and thanked Susie for the offer. It definitely *would* be better than taking the bus.

The bell rang a few minutes later and they headed to their lockers for their afternoon classes.

Salinger texted back around two, a string of emojis meant to convey how much she missed Jane. Jane had last period with Alana and Susie. They sat together at the back of the room, and when the last bell rang, the three of them walked to the student parking lot. Susie had a small SUV; Alana got into the back, insisting that Jane take the passenger seat. Susie let the car heat up for a minute before pulling out of the spot.

Alana only lived a few minutes from the school, in a little ranch house that reminded Jane of California.

"See you tomorrow, Jane!" Alana said as she let herself out of the back seat.

"Thanks again for the ride," Jane said as they pulled away from the curb. "I really appreciate it."

"My parents pay for my gas," Susie said. "So it's no problem. I can pick you up in the mornings, too."

"Are you sure?"

"Yeah, of course."

"Well, thanks. It's really nice of you to offer."

The silence in the car was just slightly uncomfortable, like being in an elevator with a stranger. Finally, Susie cleared her throat and said, "So...North Manor?"

"Yup. We moved in yesterday. Alana told me about the nickname."

Susie groaned. "She did?"

"Somebody would have told me eventually."

"I guess you're right. It's been in your family for a while?"

"It's always been in my family, yeah. We were never supposed to live in it. But...things changed. So here we are."

"You didn't want to move?"

"No. It was really sudden. But hopefully I can go back to California when I graduate."

"I don't blame you," Susie said. "For not wanting to move, I mean. My parents were talking about moving to another town—literally, like, ten miles away—and I started having nightmares. I couldn't imagine moving across the country."

"We didn't really have an option," Jane said softly. She didn't elaborate, and Susie didn't ask her to.

Susie seemed to know where she was going, which was good, because Jane wouldn't have been able to give her directions. All these streets looked the same—tree-lined country roads that wound their way through the town.

"Give me your number; I'll text you Monday morning,"

Susie said when they reached North Manor. She handed Jane her phone and Jane inputted her number and saved it.

"Thanks again for the ride," Jane said.

"Of course. Have a good weekend. It was nice to meet you."

"Thanks. You too," Jane replied, sliding out of the car.

Inside the house, the electricity was on and it felt a lot warmer. The window people were there and had already replaced most of the windows on the first floor. With the lights on and the windows fixed and the curtains open and the heat going, North Manor actually felt marginally less creepy than it had the night before.

Jane found her mother in the kitchen, sipping a cup of coffee. She wore her standard cleaning outfit—ripped jeans, a holey T-shirt, and a bandanna to keep her hair out of her face.

"You snuck out so early!" Ruth exclaimed, hugging her.

"I gave you a kiss!"

"Really? I thought I dreamed that. Ugh, I've been going *nonstop* today. Let's order in for dinner. Do you have any homework?"

"Not really."

"And? How was it?"

Jane shrugged. "Not bad."

"'Not bad' coming from a teenager is basically a ringing endorsement," Ruth said, kissing Jane on the temple. "Let me finish up and take a shower, and we'll eat early. I'm starving."

A few hours later, they'd gone to pick up Thai food for dinner and were eating it in front of the fireplace. Ruth had poured herself a glass of wine and given Jane a half glass as a little celebration of surviving the first day of school. Ruth didn't want to sleep upstairs until all the windows were fixed, so they were camping in the living room again. They'd found a stack of old board games—Monopoly, Scrabble, Yahtzee—and Jane had picked Scrabble as their first choice.

"You know—this isn't so bad," Ruth said as she set up the board. She had a container of curry in front of her and kept spearing hunks of potato with her fork.

"You might not feel that way when I destroy you at Scrabble."

"I mean, it's not ideal. I know that. And I guess we could always drive to a motel. It's just . . . Why spend the money if we don't have to, you know?"

"At least it's not windy tonight," Jane said. "Last night there were moments I thought the house was going to collapse around us."

"This is a solid house, Jane," Ruth said, laughing "They built them right back then."

"We'll have to explore the upstairs tomorrow; I haven't even seen your old room yet."

Ruth smiled. "Up the stairs, take a left, second door on the left. Although my mother turned it back into a guest room when I left home. You won't find many childhood trinkets."

"How come she did that?"

Her smile faded. "I told her I wouldn't need it again."

"You never wanted to come back for a holiday or anything? To visit?"

"Oh, gosh. Life just sort of got in the way, Jane. I met your father, and then you came along, and it was so much easier for Emilia to come west to visit than for Greer and me to lug you all that way. And it was cheaper, too, one ticket versus three. It wasn't on purpose," she added—although her words felt too much like a careful afterthought to carry much water. "It's just the way it happened."

"I guess that makes sense," Jane said, although it didn't make sense to her, not at all.

In fact the longer they spent in this house, the less sense everything seemed to make. Why did it feel like her mother was hiding something? Why did it feel like she had another reason for never wanting to return to North Manor?

Ruth played the word *secret* for sixteen points.

Jane thought that felt fairly accurate.

Ruth fell asleep early, and Jane covered her up in her makeshift bed and put the leftovers away, then settled back in front of the fire and took a sip of her wine. She didn't usually drink, and as a result it was going right to her head, making her sleepy and warm. The fire was still going strong, and she stretched out her legs, letting the heat warm the soles of her feet.

She must have fallen asleep, because when she opened her eyes the room was darker and the fire had died down to just a few barely burning embers. She had a crick in her back from the way she'd been sitting, so she slowly stretched her arms over her head and then froze as she heard it—the sound that must have woken her up.

It was a muffled crack, a brief *pop* with a long silence after it.

Jane didn't immediately feel afraid; rather she felt a sort of prickling of her senses, like how in a darkened room you might move to avoid hitting something you couldn't even see, because you just *felt* it was there. She got to her feet quietly, trying to pinpoint where the sound was coming from, straining her ears in the darkness of the house. Her first thought was the tree that had tapped against the window last night—but this was different from that, louder and farther away.

She was used to living in perpetual noise. Their house in California had been adjacent to a main road, and there were always cars rushing by and parents pushing baby strollers and kids zipping around on bikes. Enough noise and it all eventually fades into the background, becoming something other than noise, a distant lull to sing you off to sleep.

She had never experienced quiet as profound as nighttime in New England, where even the sound of your own breathing became deafeningly loud.

And there was another noise.

A steady *thump-thump-thump*.

The sound of her own heart, she realized.

A sound that quickened when she heard the cracking noise again.

It came from the back of the house.

She pulled out her phone, turned on the flashlight, then

dimmed the beam with her hand, letting out just a splinter of light to see by.

The house was still a mostly unknown thing to her. Furniture crept up on her, the piano seemed to move by a few inches in any given direction, floor lamps erupted out of the dark like people dressed in bronze.

And now the sound—like a sharp scream. And another sound, following it. The shattering of glass.

And suddenly Jane wasn't scared anymore; suddenly she knew exactly what the sound was, and it didn't frighten her; instead it filled her with a sharp kind of anger.

She took off at a run, making her way to the mudroom at the back of the house, not bothering to shield her flashlight anymore.

She stopped just in time. One of the panes of glass in the mudroom door—one that had been replaced that day—was shattered. The floor was littered with glass, and there was a rock in the middle of all the pieces. She bent down and picked it up.

Someone had thrown a rock through the window.

That was why all the windows had been broken; someone was using them as target practice.

Angrier now, she knew she shouldn't risk it, but she picked her way carefully through the mess of glass, standing on barefoot tiptoes as she made her way to the door. She fumbled with the lock and pulled the door open hard, almost throwing herself back with the effort.

The cold hit her like a slap, and she pushed her body out into the night and strained to see anything in the immaculate darkness of the night.

Nothing, nothing—

Wait!

Movement, the sound of laughter, an exclamation of surprise—"Oh shit!"—more laughter and feet running away, two or three or four shadowy figures darting across the backyard.

"I'll call the police!" Jane screamed into the dark. "If you come back, I'll call the police!"

Silence.

Anger coursed through her body like a thing with weight, with substance, fiery hot and burning underneath her skin. She took a step out into the backyard, knowing she should go back inside, knowing she couldn't catch whoever it was, couldn't even see where they had gone—

Another step and the wind whipped her long hair around her face so violently that it tangled and knotted.

Another step, even though she couldn't see anything, even though the darkness was so complete out here she could barely register her own hand held in front of her face.

She couldn't think, she couldn't concentrate on anything other than her anger, the sharp cut of it, the way adrenaline made her fingertips tingle.

But then—a light?

She turned back to the house, expecting to see Ruth in the mudroom, about to yell at her to come inside, but no.

The mudroom light was still off.

But upstairs—

Upstairs there was a light on.

And as she watched, a hand pressed itself against the glass of the window.

And then the light went off.

And everything was dark again.

Someone was in the house.

Who had a little curl

S omeone was in the house.

Jane's entire body was on fire; her heart was beating so rapidly in her chest that she thought it might burst. It seemed to pulse in time to one panicked thought that kept running through her mind:

They're inside they're inside they're inside.

Whoever had thrown the rock through the window was just distracting her so someone else could slip past her into the house.

Her body felt frozen in place, unable to move.

But not frozen in fear...

Frozen in anger.

Motionless in rage.

She was going to go upstairs. She was going to hurt them.

But then the mudroom light had turned on and there was Ruth, looking sleep-rumpled and confused, blinking to wake herself up.

"Honey? What happened to the window?"

Jane couldn't reply. She couldn't speak. She still couldn't *move*. How had she gotten back in the mudroom? Wasn't she still outside?

"Jane, what—oh my god. Honey, oh my god. Don't move! Your feet!"

Somehow, that broke the spell. Jane looked down at her feet and saw tiny rivulets of blood branching out from underneath them. The glass. She was standing in glass, and she hadn't even felt it.

"Mom," she croaked, finding her voice again. "Someone broke the window. And someone is inside. I think...someone came inside."

"What is the door doing open? Were you out there?" Ruth's face changed. "Jane—you weren't trying to go *after* them, were you?"

"No, I just... There was another light. And...and a hand. Upstairs."

But even as she said it, Jane doubted herself. She hadn't been standing far enough away from the door for someone to sneak past her. Had she even seen anything at all? Or had her brain played tricks on her, feeding off the intensity of the moment to create the next thing to panic about?

"Honey, it's just the wiring. I'll go unplug everything

tomorrow. We'll have an electrician come in. We need to get you out of there. Don't move. There should be a broom in here—" Ruth opened a tall cabinet and pulled out a broom and dustpan. "Jesus, it's *everywhere*. Don't move."

Ruth began sweeping the glass to the side, carefully brushing it away from Jane's feet. She cleared herself a path to the door and pulled it shut, locking it. She put her hand up and gently touched the broken pane of glass.

"Did you see who did it?" she asked.

"It was too dark."

"I heard yelling," Ruth said. "And then I rolled over and you weren't there. Fuck, it scared me. You should have woken me up or called 911."

"There's no service, remember?"

"I'll call the phone company. We'll get a landline. And we'll go to the cell phone store and ask about our options. And—oh shit. Are you crying? What am I doing? We need to look at your feet. Can you lift up your foot, honey?"

Jane placed a hand against the wall and lifted up her left foot. Ruth was wearing socks; she pulled one of them off and used it to gently brush the sole of Jane's foot, sweeping tiny shards of glass away.

"Okay," she said. "The other one."

Jane lifted her other foot and Ruth repeated the process.

"It doesn't look too bad," Ruth said. "Fuck, the blood scared me, but...It's just a couple scratches. Can you walk? Can you make it to the kitchen?"

"There's nobody upstairs, right? There's nobody in the house?" Jane asked. Her brain felt fuzzy, like she was coming out of a dream, waking up from a nap she'd only been half-asleep for.

"There's nobody in the house, honey," Ruth said quietly, putting her hand on Jane's cheek. "Come into the kitchen, okay?"

Jane followed Ruth down the hallway and into the kitchen, taking a seat at the table as Ruth disappeared and returned a minute later with rubbing alcohol and bandages.

Now that her body was calming down, Jane could feel her feet. They stung, like a dozen little fiery pricks.

And there was another pain—a stinging on her right knuckles that had nothing to do with what had just happened. A phantom sting from years ago. She squeezed her eyes closed as Ruth took a cotton ball of rubbing alcohol to the soles of her feet, and suddenly she was six years old again, and the boy next door had taken the white LEGO horse from her.

"That's mine," she'd said. "If you want to play, you can have the brown one."

She'd held it out to him helpfully, but he'd kicked it out of her hand. It went flying across the driveway. He had refused to give the white horse back.

The next thing she remembered, she'd been standing over him. He was writhing around on the driveway, holding his nose. He'd dropped the white horse. Jane had bent over and picked it up.

Her hand stung.

She'd looked down at it, surprised to find it bleeding in one spot, the rest of her knuckles red and raw.

Underneath her, the boy had finally managed to get to his feet. He'd stood up and run home.

The anger had left as quickly as it had come. It had gone with the punch, as if that physical act had been enough to dispel it from her body.

Of course the boy had told his mother, who'd called the house and gotten Greer on the phone.

Greer had sat Jane down on the couch and she'd begun to cry. Through her tears, she had protested that the boy had deserved it.

"I have no doubt about that," Greer had said. Jane's father had always been fair, willing to listen and reason. "I've always thought he was a little punk. But, Jane—you can't go around punching all the punks in the world. First of all, it's not right, and it's not the way to solve your problems. Okay?"

"Okay," Jane had said quietly.

"And second of all, you'll end up doing more damage to your hand than you'll do to them. Just look at it." And he'd taken her hand gently in his and turned it knuckle-side-up, so they could both see the tiny cut and the raw redness of her skin. He'd kissed her softly on the back of her wrist.

Jane could feel that kiss now, as plainly as if Greer were standing over them in the kitchen, watching as Ruth cleaned Jane's feet. She rubbed her knuckles as he faded away again, until the only thing remaining was the sharp absence of him—the place where he had been and wasn't anymore. The place where he would never be again.

She wrapped her arms around her stomach.

"Does it hurt?" Ruth asked.

"Not really. Just stings."

Ruth raised a hand and touched Jane's cheek. Jane hadn't even really registered it, but she realized now she was crying.

"I miss him," Jane whispered. "And I hate him for leaving us."

Ruth leaned the broom against a wall and wrapped her arms around her daughter.

"Oh, honey. I miss him and I hate him, too. And I think that's okay, for now."

Jane woke up late the next morning, to sunshine streaming in through the windows, to the smell of coffee. For once Ruth was up before her. Jane stretched and groaned a little—she was exhausted, and nights on the floor weren't doing her back any favors. She wiggled her toes and flexed her feet, looking for any pain, but felt nothing. The cuts had been small, and Ruth had been diligent in cleaning them.

It had taken her hours to fall back asleep.

Ruth had made them tea after covering up the broken window with cellophane. They'd built up the fire again and sat in front of it, sipping the tea and trying to relax.

"I'm sure it was just kids," Ruth had said. "Kids who probably thought this house was still empty. You must have scared the shit out of them, Jane, chasing them into the backyard like that. They won't be back."

Jane pulled herself out of her sleeping bag and grabbed a sweater from the couch—it was one of Ruth's, an old fisherman's sweater, oversize and soft. She pulled it on and ran her fingers through her hair, tangled and messy from the night.

She stood up carefully, testing her weight on her feet. They hurt a little, but nothing unbearable. She made her way into the kitchen slowly, stepping lightly, expecting to find Ruth with a cup of coffee, but she wasn't there. So she wandered around the first floor, peeking into different rooms, finally reaching the foyer, where she paused for a moment at the bottom of the stairs, looking up.

She couldn't quite bring herself to go up there.

If Ruth was right, and there *was* some sort of faulty wiring, it still didn't explain the shadow Jane had seen. It didn't explain the hand pressed against the windowpane last night. But in the morning light, she really wasn't sure she'd seen a shadow or a hand at all. Probably the light had just flickered. Probably her imagination had been on overdrive. Probably it was what Ruth had said before—*grief is different for everyone*—and for Jane, it was making her see things, making her imagination run wild. And, she reminded herself, there was *no way* someone could have snuck into the house behind her back. It was just the adrenaline. She knew from personal experience—adrenaline did strange things to your body, to your brain. It made your own mind a thing you couldn't trust anymore.

She shook her head and moved on.

She made her way to the mudroom. The galoshes that had been there were gone. She squinted out the shattered window but didn't see Ruth anywhere. But the dead bolt was unlocked, so Jane slipped a pair of tennis shoes on, opened the door, and stepped outside.

It was a mild day, with almost no breeze.

Jane took a deep breath. It smelled like pine trees, like a scented candle they used to burn during Christmastime in California, when it was eighty degrees outside and the Santa at the outdoor mall must have been sweating buckets underneath his suit.

Her feet protested a little more as she walked into the backyard, but the air felt good in her lungs. She took a deep breath through her nose. It smelled kind of amazing, actually, like pine and wood and dirt. Los Angeles never smelled like that.

She became aware of a strange sound—a metal-on-metal sound, like a giant pair of scissors opening and shutting.

She closed the mudroom door and walked toward the fountain.

The sound grew louder. She looked back toward the house, which was large and cold-looking in the morning light. The windows were all dark. Most of the curtains on the second floor were drawn closed. It wasn't a very welcoming house. Jane couldn't blame her mother for leaving; she didn't understand what kind of a person *chose* to live in a house like this. Too many rooms, too many chimneys, too many windows.

And that sound again. What was that sound?

She turned back around and finally saw Ruth, at the very edge of the lawn, near the rosebushes. She wore jeans and a flannel, and her hair was in a messy bun on top of her head. The galoshes came up almost to her knees. She was wielding a giant pair of garden shears, and she was attacking the rosebushes with a singular purpose, cutting down great chunks of perfectly healthy plant.

She was standing in a heap of oranges and pinks and reds; the colors stood out in stark contrast against the gray of the morning.

Jane started walking toward her. "Mom?" she said, when she was close enough.

Ruth looked up with a start. Her eyes were strange, like she was in a trance; she shook her head, and they slowly came into focus.

"Morning. I couldn't sleep."

"What the hell are you doing?"

"Just a little pruning."

"Pruning? You're murdering these things."

Ruth laughed. All the strangeness was gone from her eyes now. She just looked tired and weary. She brushed some hair back from her face. "They would have died in the first frost. It's a miracle they've made it this far. The plants will come back stronger in the spring if they're properly cut back now."

Jane had no idea if this was true or not, and if it *was*, she had no idea how Ruth knew that. Ruth hated gardening. She hadn't even owned a trowel back home. And she certainly didn't seem to be taking much care with the process. She was hacking away at random, leaving some bushes with no more than an inch or two of green pushing through the soil.

"How are you feeling? How are your feet?" Ruth asked.

"Not bad, surprisingly."

"You know what helps foot injuries?"

"What?"

"Pancakes. We need pancakes. I hope Sam's is still open. It was my favorite diner when I was your age. The best chocolate-chip pancakes I've ever had."

"Let me go get dressed."

"All right, go on. I'll be right behind you."

"Hurry up! You made me hungry."

Jane started back toward the house. As she passed the fountain again, she heard the *whoosh* of the shears' blades as Ruth resumed her frantic cutting.

For some reason, the sound made her skin crawl.

Sam's Diner—a little place on the main square of Bells Hollow—felt like walking straight into the 1950s, with an old-fashioned counter to the left, an actual jukebox in a far corner, and the daily specials written on a vintage green chalkboard. They waited a few minutes for a red vinyl booth, then ordered chocolate-chip pancakes, a side of fries, and an egg scramble loaded with cheese and veggies.

When the food arrived, Jane cut herself a bite of pancake and dipped it in the syrup.

"Holy. Shit."

"I know," Ruth said, popping a fry into her mouth. "I can honestly say, one thing I missed about this place was Sam's."

"Is there actually a Sam?"

"There was! He was a hundred years old when I lived here. I'm sure he's not around anymore. But his legacy lives on."

They ate in silence for a while. The diner was busy around them; every time a booth cleared, it was filled again immediately. The counter was taken up by old men reading newspapers, groups of kids eating breakfast sandwiches, and one mother reading a romance novel as her baby slept in a car seat by her feet. It was warm and smelled amazing, and Jane couldn't help thinking, *Greer would have loved this place.* He would have been one of the men at the counter, reading a newspaper, drinking eight cups of coffee one after another, eating sourdough toast spread with too much butter.

Jane flinched. Those memories—those visceral, sudden memories—appeared without any warning, like a slap to the face, and left her reeling in sadness, the smell of phantom sourdough toast almost suffocating her.

"What's up?" Ruth said softly, somehow sensing this, reaching across the table to take Jane's hand briefly.

"Oh, just nothing. Just . . . He would have loved this place. You know."

Ruth smiled sadly. "Yeah, I know."

And for a moment, he was almost at the table with them, stealing bites of pancake, ordering a third cup of coffee, spreading butter on toast. Jane let him sit with them for a moment before pushing him away again, because he *wasn't* here, because he'd never be here again.

"Okay," Ruth said. "I've been *very* patient. Tell me a little bit about your first day?"

"Oh, it was fine. I mean, it wasn't anything special."

"I know it's all been such a big change. I'm just proud of you for keeping it together."

"Thanks, Mom."

"I reached out to some old friends yesterday. One of them, Frank, owns a construction business. He said he could use some accounting help, so I'm going to lend a hand. Just three days a week to start, but maybe it will turn into something more."

"Really? That's amazing. And you were worried you wouldn't find a job."

"It'll be good. Keep me busy. And we need the cash."

Ruth ate another fry. Jane finished the last bite of the egg scramble, then let her gaze wander around the diner. It was still packed, and there were a few small groups of people waiting for tables. The counter seats were all filled, and Jane noticed an older man sitting at the very end, his stool swiveled so he was facing the direction of their table. Although most of his face was hidden by a newspaper he held, his eyes were visible over the top of it. And Jane swore he kept looking up at them, shifting his vision from her mother and back to her.

"Do you know that guy?" Jane said, leaning toward her

mother. "Don't turn around. At the end of the counter. He keeps looking over here."

"If I don't turn around, how can I tell you if I know him?" Ruth asked, smiling.

"I mean, look, but don't make it obvious."

Ruth turned her body to the side and acted like she was reading the specials board. She took a quick glance behind her, then turned back to Jane. Her face had changed. She looked almost sad.

"Dick Carrington. Dr. Carrington," she said.

"Was he your doctor?"

Ruth didn't answer for a moment. She flagged down a server and motioned for the check. "No. Not my doctor."

"Oh. Why do you think he keeps looking at us?"

"Because you're beautiful," Ruth said. It was clear she was trying to keep her tone light. She winked. The server came back with the check and Ruth pulled some money from her wallet and put it on the table. "Let's get out of here, okay?"

They had to pass the man to get out of the restaurant, and when they were close enough, he lowered his newspaper and said, "Ruthellen North. I thought that was you."

"Dr. Carrington. How are you?" Ruth said, taking his outstretched hand.

"Old," he said, laughing. His gaze switched to Jane. His laughter died and his expression turned serious. "What a lovely girl."

"My daughter," Ruth said. "Jane."

"Jane," he repeated. "It's a pleasure to meet you."

"Nice to meet you."

He turned to Ruth. "Are you back in that house?"

"Yes. Jane and I moved into North Manor," she said. "It was nice to see you, but we really have to—"

"It can't be easy," he said softly. "Being back there."

"*Really* nice to see you," Ruth said pointedly. She put a hand on his arm and squeezed, then reached back and took Jane's hand and led her out of the diner.

Once they were outside, Jane tugged at Ruth to get her to stop walking.

"What was that about?"

"What was what about?" Ruth asked.

"The creepy old man being creepy? 'It can't be easy being back there'?"

"Oh, honey. He's a hundred years old. Who knows what he meant."

"It seems like he meant he's surprised you're back in North Manor. Why would he be surprised you're back in North Manor?"

"Would you like to go ask him, sweetie? I'm not a mind reader. People are weird. Did you notice he was also holding his newspaper upside down?"

"He was?"

"Yes. Stop being such an alarmist." Ruth smiled. "Look—there's a bookstore across the square."

"Where?" Jane mumbled. She had the distinct impression Ruth was trying to change the subject, and she was annoyed that it was working.

She looked around the town square. She didn't think she had ever been in a town quite this tiny before, where you could turn in a circle and pick out the post office, the diner, the general store, the coffee shop, and the bookstore. Actually, these last two were connected, and the sign above their shared entrance said BEANS & BOOKS.

"Fine. I'll go in," Jane said.

"If I twist your arm?"

"Maybe I'll see if they're hiring. If you can get a job, I can get a job."

"Honey, take some time and settle into things a bit. You don't have to rush into anything like that."

"Nothing too bad. A few hours after school or something," Jane said.

"All right. Well, here, get me a coffee to go," Ruth said, digging in her purse.

"My treat," Jane said, and took off before her mom could argue.

The shop was deceptively roomy on the inside. The coffee counter was to the left, and there were a few scattered café tables in front of it. The bookshelves started to the right, five or six long stacks of them with places here and there to set your coffee while you browsed. The combined smell of coffee and used books felt like the intersection of all things good and necessary, as far as Jane was concerned. Any residual weirdness from the man in the diner melted away as she stepped between the first shelves of books.

She did what she did in every bookstore she visited—she went to the mystery section and scanned the shelves for Agatha Christie books. She was pleased to find a fairly large collection of little vintage paperbacks, some of them even in individual protective sleeves. She picked up a copy of *The ABC Murders*—it was one of her favorites, and she owned multiple editions. She had never seen this one before, though. It had a purple cover, which she loved, with illustrations of various bits of the novel on it: a yellow stocking, a woman with a red scarf around her neck, a stack of letters addressed to M. Hercule Poirot.

"Help you find anything?" said a voice behind her. She turned around to see a black guy a few years older than she was. He was cute, with jeans and a buffalo-plaid flannel rolled up to his elbows.

"Oh, just browsing for now, thanks."

He peeked behind her at the shelf she was looking at. "Agatha Christie?"

"Yeah. She's great."

"I could never get into her," he said, shrugging. "It's impossible to figure out who the murderer is."

"That's exactly why I like them. Once you get to the end, you realize that you should've known all along."

He smiled. "Well, let me know if you have any questions."

"Actually . . . you aren't hiring by any chance, are you?"

"You might just have perfect timing. We had a couple people leave at the beginning of the school year." He paused, then held his hand out. "I'm Will. My dad owns this place, but I'm the manager."

"Jane." She shook his hand. "I just moved here. I'm a senior, but I can work after school or on weekends. Or both. Anything you need, really."

"That sounds perfect. Where did you move from?"

"Los Angeles."

"Los Angeles, California, to Bells Hollow, Maine. An interesting trajectory."

"That's one way to put it," Jane said, laughing.

"What do you think of it so far?"

"So far it's . . . fine." She shrugged. "We just got here. I haven't formed any huge opinions yet. I mean, the bookstore is nice."

"The bookstore is the best," Will said, spreading his arms out. "Let's go to the counter and I'll get your number. Can I get you a coffee or something? On the house."

"Oh, thanks. That would be great. And I think I'll take this book, too."

Will took the book from her and looked it over. "*The ABC Murders*, huh? Is it a good one?"

"One of my favorites."

"All right. This is on me if you'll let me borrow it first."

"Sure," Jane said. "It's a deal."

They walked over to the coffee counter. Will put the book behind the desk and got her a piece of paper and a pen. She wrote down her number as he poured a cup of coffee.

"Do you have any barista experience?" he asked, fitting the lid on the cup.

"I make a mean latte."

"That's half the battle." He laughed. "Well, welcome to Bells Hollow, Jane." He slid the coffee across the counter.

"Thanks. And thanks for the coffee. It was nice meeting you."

"You too."

Jane slipped a dollar into a tip jar with a sign that said SCARED OF CHANGE? LEAVE IT HERE, then found Ruth waiting on a bench outside.

"Mmm, thanks," Ruth said, taking the coffee. "How did it go?"

"Cute barista."

"Not a bad little morning we're having—good pancakes, cute barista."

"Free coffee," Jane added.

"Free coffee? Does life get any better than this?"

But she said it with a sad half smile, and Jane knew exactly what she meant.

Yes, life got a lot better than this.

If Greer were still alive, he'd have ordered the silliest thing on the menu. He unironically loved weird drinks, like marshmallow and crème brûlée and gingerbread lattes.

Jane looped her arm through her mother's and leaned into her and didn't reply. She didn't have to.

After a quick trip to the mall to buy new winter coats and a little box that was supposed to make their phones work in the house, they returned home and spent the rest of the day cleaning. They focused on the downstairs while the window company worked upstairs, replacing the rest of the windows before doubling back to fix the one in the mudroom.

"Let me know if you have any more trouble," the foreman said as Ruth signed the invoice. Jane peeked over her shoulder and saw the price—what had been paid already and what was still left to pay. And on top of it all, an extra cost for the Saturday work. Who knew windows were so *expensive*?

They had never been rich in California—not like some of the students at Jane's school, who drove Porsches and Teslas to class—but Jane had also never really had to think about money before. Now, though, it was creeping up on her: the price of *things*.

"Thanks," Ruth said. "I will."

After the window people left, Jane installed the booster from the cell phone store. As soon as she plugged it in, her phone lit up with six messages from Salinger:

Hello I miss you more today than I have ever missed anyone in the history of the world

Janiieeeeeee

are you dead

WHERE ARE YOU

You know that store near my house that sells the really good smoothies, they're going out of business so not only is my best friend all the way across the country, now I don't even live near a good smoothie place

Are you actually dead I miss you

"Tell Sal I said hi," Ruth said. "I'm going to start dinner."

Jane collapsed onto a freshly vacuumed sofa and texted her back:

RIP to the good smoothie place. I miss you more than I can possibly express in words

my mom says hi

it's cold here

ILY

When Sal didn't text back right away, Jane wandered into the kitchen. Ruth was finishing up the salad she was making; she placed the bowl down while Jane stared out the window, remembering the morning slaughter of the poor roses.

"Set the table, will you?" Ruth asked.

"Sure." Jane got plates and silverware as Ruth took two potatoes out of the microwave. "Salad and baked potatoes. I think this is the most New England meal you've ever cooked."

Ruth shrugged. "When in Rome." She put the potatoes on two plates and brought them over to the table. Jane sat down across from her and started dishing out the salad. "We can start cleaning upstairs tomorrow so we can finally sleep up there."

"It'll be nice to get off the floor," Jane replied.

"Agreed. We'll go to the outlets next weekend, maybe. They're two hours away, but they have great stores. We can get new bedding, new pillows. A few things to make this place a bit homier."

"Sounds great."

Jane looked past her mother, out the windows again. The sky was already dark. She didn't like this house at night, when the shadows grew longer, the air grew chillier.

"Honey? Is something wrong?"

"What? No. I didn't know windows were so expensive." She didn't know what made her say it, but at least it was easier to explain than her sudden fear of the dark.

Ruth laughed softly. "Of all the things I thought you might say, that wasn't one of them."

"I saw the invoice."

"Oh, Jane. You do *not* have to worry about stuff like that."

"But you have to worry about money now. You have to, like, budget and stuff. Didn't Dad do all the budgeting?"

Ruth laughed—a short, bitter laugh that Jane didn't like. "Your father did all the budgeting, yes. And look where that got us." A long quiet. Ruth reached across the table and took Jane's hand. "I'm sorry. I shouldn't have said that."

"It's okay."

"But please, let *me* worry about money. You just worry about making friends and doing your homework. Okay?"

Jane shrugged. "Okay."

"How's the potato? You know Maine is famous for potatoes, right?"

Jane took a bite of the potato, chewed, and swallowed. "What a weird place," she said.

Ruth snorted softly. "You're right about that, sweetie."

That night, after dinner and a game of Scrabble, after brushing her teeth and washing her face, Jane slid into her sleeping bag for what she hoped would be the last time in a long time. Maybe it would be the last time ever. Maybe, tomorrow night, they would burn the sleeping bags in a ceremonial bonfire in the backyard, along with the maps that had gotten them here in the first place, along with the entire car and the greasy fast food they'd eaten and the clothes they'd worn that, Jane imagined, would never not smell faintly of gasoline.

In her own sleeping bag, Ruth was already breathing heavily, a faint rattle in the back of her throat as she left Jane alone in the quiet, too-big house.

Even closing the pocket doors didn't really help to lessen the feeling of being lost in a vast forest. They'd taken the sheets off all the furniture, but the antique high-backed chairs and tall lamps and bookcases and fancy hutches seemed to tower over Jane, casting strange shadows across the room. It didn't help that the only light source was the fire, which seemed to have a mind of its own, its flames dancing wildly every time a draft blew across the floor.

Jane stared into those flames and tried to turn off her brain. The day had seemed to pass in a blink of an eye, and Jane felt tired and achy from so much cleaning. Not just tired—exhausted, really—but it was the type of exhaustion that didn't lend itself to immediate sleep. It was the type of exhaustion that inexplicably kept you up, that kept poking and shaking you awake, just to remind you, again, of how tired you were.

Jane rolled over, away from the fire, trying to get comfortable. She hit her pillow with the palm of her hand and stretched her legs out, long...

Something grazed across her bare foot.

The tag of the sleeping bag?

No, this was too soft for that. This was something velvety and smooth and small.

Jane sat up and reached inside the sleeping bag, leaning forward to find it.

Her fingers closed around whatever it was, and she pulled it out of the bag and held it up so it caught the light of the fire.

For a long moment, she just stared at it, her brow gently furrowed in confusion, her mouth slightly open.

She didn't know what to make of it. It was so out of place, so confusing to find it here, and her brain struggled to make sense of it, struggled to understand the path it had taken to end up in her sleeping bag, of all places.

It was a single rose petal, a large one, about two inches in length. It was a deep red, and when Jane could finally move and brought it up to her nose, it smelled fresh and rich, like she had just plucked it off the flower.

Am I dreaming? she wondered, because she honestly couldn't tell; she might have fallen asleep without even realizing it. But what a strange dream this was. What did it mean?

Sleepily, she thought of the flowers from *Through the Looking-Glass*, the tiger lily and the rose that mistake Alice for a flower herself. Was Jane a flower? Was this petal from her own body? Was she turning into a rose?

She closed her eyes and opened them again when she swayed dangerously.

Lie down, she instructed herself, and she did, slowly lowering herself back into her sleeping bag, her brain half–shut off already, her thoughts confusing and slow.

She laid the rose petal on the floor next to her, eye-level, and it was the last thing she saw before she fell asleep, three seconds later, and dreamed her skin grew thorns.

When she woke in the morning, the petal was gone, and its existence at all was so muted in Jane's memory that she could hardly even recall it as a dream. Probably it *was* a dream, but Jane only knew that she'd slept like the dead, falling deeply asleep and not waking up again until morning.

After a breakfast of coffee and toast, Jane and Ruth headed upstairs. It was Jane's first time seeing the second floor, which was basically just one long hallway with doors on either side of it.

"Nothing up here but bedrooms and bathrooms," Ruth said.

There were eight bedrooms in all, four at the back of the house and four at the front. Two of these were locked—the master bedroom, where Jane's grandparents had slept, and the room right next to it, which Ruth said had been used for storage.

"Let's stay out of those for now," Ruth said. "I don't think I'm quite ready to tackle them."

"You mean I only have six bedrooms to choose from?" Jane complained.

"Ha-ha."

Jane stuck her head in one room after another and settled on one at the front of the house, with a private bathroom and a four-poster bed and two enormous windows. There were sheer white curtains to match the white bedspread. There was even an empty bookshelf—plenty of room for her mystery novels.

"Good choice," Ruth said. "I think I'll be just down the hall."

"Your old bedroom?"

"Nope. Starting fresh."

Jane went downstairs to get her boxes, which were stacked neatly in the foyer. She carefully carried each one upstairs and into her new bedroom. The last one was the heaviest; it contained all her journals and a few dozen Agatha Christie paperbacks. She hoisted it into her arms and started slowly upstairs, putting one foot in front of the other, groaning with the effort.

She'd just passed the first landing when the bottom of the box gave out. Books tumbled out in a heavy cascade; one particularly large journal landed on Jane's foot. She almost lost her balance, but she managed to drop the box and grab onto the railing before she fell backward.

Most of the books and journals slid only a few steps down,

coming to a rest on the landing, but a few of them tumbled farther down, toppling over and over until they reached the first floor.

"Shit," Jane said. *"Shit."*

"Janie, you okay? What was that?" Ruth appeared at the top of the staircase. "Oh shoot. Was that the heavy one? Let me help you, honey."

"Shit!" Jane repeated. Her foot throbbed where the journal had hit it, and even though she hadn't thought about them all day, she swore the cuts on the bottom of her feet started to sting again, too.

"Honey, not a big deal," Ruth said calmly, skipping down the few steps to meet Jane. "Deep breaths, okay? Did you hurt yourself?"

"Shit. Yes. No. I'm fine. You don't have to help, let me just do it myself."

"Baby, baby. *Breathe.*"

Jane squeezed her eyes closed. Her body felt hot and itchy. The familiar first pangs of anger. She put a hand on the banister and squeezed the wood as hard as she could, squeezed it until her hand throbbed.

If Greer were still alive, he'd be the one carrying the heavier boxes upstairs, but—Jane realized bitterly—if Greer were still alive, there would be no boxes to carry, because they never would have had to move to Maine. He would have figured out another solution. He would have come here alone, maybe, and fixed up the house enough to sell it. He would have made their money back. He would have made everything okay again.

Jane closed her eyes and suddenly she wasn't in North Manor anymore, suddenly she was back in their old house, sitting cross-legged on her bed, working on homework, and Greer was nudging the door open with his foot. He came into the room holding an enormous box, and as Jane watched, he dumped its contents out on the bed next to her.

Agatha Christie paperbacks! At least three dozen of them. She picked one up greedily, then looked up at him and asked, "Where did these come from!"

"Mother lode, right?" Greer said, clearly proud of himself. "Estate sale. End of day, no one had taken these yet. Guess how much for the lot of them."

To Jane, these books were nothing short of priceless, but she did some quick math and said, "I dunno...two hundred?"

"Free!"

Greer began doing a silly dance around the room, stomping all over the carpet, waving his arms around wildly. Jane looked at the book in her hand. *Poirot Loses a Client.* She couldn't wait to read it.

Jane could hear Ruth now, gathering books into her arms, picking up the ones that had fallen on the landing. She heard her jostle the box upside down, so the rip was at the top. There were still some books in it; they tumbled around as Ruth carried the box past Jane and up to her new bedroom.

Jane struggled to breathe evenly. She opened her eyes. *You're fine.*

She made herself go collect the books that had fallen down

there. Ruth reappeared and grabbed another stack from the landing. Jane met her back in her bedroom.

"See?" Ruth said, depositing her load of books on the floor. "No big deal. Are you okay?"

Jane put her own books on the floor and nodded stiffly. "I'm fine. Sorry. I just . . . It was just stupid."

"No big deal," Ruth repeated. "I think I'm going to take a quick shower. You're good?"

"I'm good, Mom."

Ruth touched Jane's hand, then left her alone, shutting the bedroom door behind her. The carpet was littered with journals and books. Jane took a seat in the middle of them and started stacking them into piles, organizing them into groups. Her hand paused as she picked up one of the books. *Poirot Loses a Client*. The cover had become one of her favorites, made even more special because Greer had given it to her. Poirot's infamous bowler hat and mustache. An enormous mansion surrounded by topiaries in the shape of giant birds, a revolver, and a skull bleeding red roses from its base.

The cover had ripped in the book's fall. It had twisted backward and torn down the middle. Right through the bowler hat.

Jane threw the book violently; it hit the side of the bed and fell to the floor.

She covered her face with her hands. Her heart was beating too quickly; she could feel it hammering against her rib cage. She tried to remember Ruth's easy tone: *No big deal*. But her fingers were shaking. Her hands were shaking. She was having trouble getting air into her lungs; her vision was starting to turn to white.

Then her hands landed on a book within arm's length—a battered hardcover of *The Lion, the Witch, and the Wardrobe*. She grabbed for it in a panic, letting it fall open on her lap to the first page in the book. Page 51. Pages 1–50 were gone.

Without ceremony, without pausing to think, she ripped page 51 from the book, then tore off a small corner and put it into her mouth.

Almost instantly, she felt like she could breathe. She let the paper sit on her tongue for a minute, turning pulpy and clumpy as her saliva coated it.

And then she swallowed.

Again and again until the entire page was gone.

Again and again until her anger—the dull throb that never seemed to completely leave her—receded a little.

Again and again until she felt safe.

A knock at the door.

She closed the book and slid it into the bookcase.

"Come in," she said.

Ruth opened the door and stuck her head inside. She had a towel wrapped around her hair. "Everything okay in here?"

"Yeah, Mom. Just trying to organize."

"Why don't you strip that bed and we'll get a load of laundry going?"

"All right. I'll meet you downstairs in a few."

Ruth closed the door again and Jane took a deep breath, then let it out slowly, just like Greer had taught her to do.

She reached across the floor and picked up *Poirot Loses a Client*. She traced her fingers over the ripped cover.

If her father were here, he would have found tape and taken the book from Jane to mend it. He would have said there was nothing sad about a book with a few dings in it. That was how you knew it had been enjoyed.

He was the one who had always known the exact thing to say to help her calm her anger. He would sit with her, breathe with her, listen to her. Who would do that for her now? She knew Ruth tried, but there was just something *different* about Greer. He seemed to understand her in a way she didn't even understand herself. He understood her anger, why it sometimes exploded out of her in waves of red.

That anger was faded now, replaced with sadness, replaced with a gnawing in her stomach that she identified as the place that had been ripped out of her when Greer had died. The absence of Greer.

She stood up and placed the book carefully on the bookcase, then walked over to the bed and pulled the heavy comforter to the side. She unbuttoned the duvet and made a pile of linens on the floor. The door creaked open as she was pulling a pillow from its pillowcase. She turned around, expecting to see Ruth again, but there was no one there.

She crossed to the door and shut it again, making sure

it latched. When she turned back to the room, she paused. What was that? A buzzing noise? She stood listening for a few moments before she realized it was her phone.

"Shit," she said, kneeling in front of the pile of linens. The buzzing was coming from underneath them; her phone must have slid out of her pocket and gotten buried. She pulled the sheets to the side and found it after a minute of searching. She'd missed the call, but as she held the phone in her hand, it lit up with a voicemail. She hit Play and held it to her ear.

"Hi, Jane! I'm realizing now it's a bit early—sorry for that; I've been here since six and you sort of lose track of time. Anyway, oh—I haven't even said who I am. It's Will, from Beans & Books. Just wanted to see if you were down with doing some training this week. How does Tuesday after school sound? It's all right if it's too late notice; you can text me back at this number and let me know. Thanks!"

Grinning, she texted Will that Tuesday sounded great, then she slid the phone into her pocket, rebuilt the pile of linens, gathered it all in her arms, and stood up. She turned around and paused—

That was weird.

The door was open again.

Something must be wrong with the latch.

She dropped the linens and crossed the room, then closed the door again. She gently pulled without turning the handle. It wouldn't open.

She left it closed and took a few steps back, waiting.

Nothing happened.

She shrugged, opened the door again, gathered up the linens, and headed downstairs. The laundry room was empty, but Ruth had already started a load. Jane dropped her pile in front of the machine and paused as she heard footsteps on the floor above her. Like someone was running down the hallway. What was Ruth doing?

"Mom?" she yelled to the ceiling.

"What?" Ruth answered from the doorway; Jane jumped a mile and turned around, her hands covering her heart.

"You scared the crap out of me!"

Ruth dropped more linens onto the pile and laughed. "Sorry. Thought you heard me coming."

"No, I thought you were upstairs. There were footsteps."

"Footsteps?"

"Yes, footsteps!"

The house creaked. As if on cue. Like a long exhalation of muffled pops. Ruth smiled knowingly.

"It's these old houses, Janie," she explained. "They're constantly making noises. It's called *settling*; you'll get used to it. Come help me get some curtains down."

They stayed busy the rest of the day, doing endless loads of laundry, stripping and making beds, dusting and vacuuming the rooms they were going to sleep in.

And it was fine, really. Nothing else weird happened. But still . . . Jane couldn't shake a strange feeling. Like a tingle down her spine that never quite went away. It was silly, of course, just nerves and overtiredness and the time change messing with her head.

That night, when she finally said good night to Ruth and went upstairs to her new bedroom, she pulled the bookshelf in front of her door.

For what exactly, she wasn't sure.

But she felt a little safer, anyway.

She didn't sleep well. She had the same dream, over and over, a fuzzy dream that became fuzzier if she tried to focus on it. Long corridors. Closed doors. The sound of footsteps and the feeling that there was someone in the shadows, watching her.

When her alarm went off she moaned and hit Snooze, but she couldn't fall back asleep. She stared up at her ceiling for a few minutes before getting out of bed and pulling on a sweatshirt. She dragged her bookshelf away from her door. She'd been silly to put it there—what was she afraid of?

Ruth was already in the kitchen, eating a piece of toast spread with peanut butter and jelly, drinking a cup of coffee.

"Morning, honey," she said. "How did you sleep?"

"Meh," Jane replied.

"Same." Ruth sighed, and Jane watched her struggle to put on an encouraging face. "We'll get used to it. It's only been four nights."

"At least no one threw any rocks at the windows."

"Small favors," Ruth agreed. "Get yourself some toast. Excited about your first full week?"

"Meh," Jane repeated. "Excited for your first day at work?"

"Meh."

"Word of the day."

"It appears so."

They ate in a silence that felt even more profound because of the silence of the house. Jane found herself missing the noises of California, the constant car horns, music blasting from a distant stereo, Greer mumbling aloud to himself about some new business idea as he roamed throughout the rooms with a cup of coffee gone tepid.

What would Greer think of North Manor?

He would probably love it; he had an affinity for old things, for things past their prime, for things that needed a little imagination to find their true beauty. He'd probably have replaced all the windows himself, and given everything a fresh coat of paint by now, and kept them up at night with the sound of hammers and table saws and sandpaper sliding roughly against wood.

He would have filled up all the silence of this house with noise. He would have made it feel like a home, as opposed to just another place to sleep.

Jane finished her toast and carried her dish to the sink just as her phone buzzed—Susie was in the driveway.

"Ride's here," Jane said.

"Hey," Ruth replied, taking Jane by the wrist. "I'm sorry I'm such a grump this morning."

"Ditto."

"It'll get better," Ruth continued, but she wasn't quite able to make herself sound convincing. She smiled weakly to make up for it, and Jane kissed her on the cheek.

"Love you."

"Love you, Janie."

Jane grabbed her backpack and pushed out into the brisk morning. She slid into the passenger's seat of Susie's car and tried to sound as cheerful as possible when she said good morning.

"Hey!" Susie said, backing out of the driveway and starting off down the street.

"Morning. Thanks for picking me up."

"Don't mention it."

"How was your weekend?"

"I feel like it was ninety percent homework. What about you? Anything exciting?"

Jane thought back to Friday night, to the smashed window. That definitely qualified as *exciting*, but for some reason, she didn't want to tell Susie about it.

"Well, I cleaned for approximately thirty-eight hours. But I actually slept in a bed last night. So that was nice. Oh, and I got a job."

"Already? Where?"

"Beans & Books. I start Tuesday."

"Are you serious?" Susie said, brightening. "That's my dad's place!"

"Wait, are you Will's sister?"

"Yes!"

"Small world."

"Small *town*," Susie corrected. "You'll like Will. Technically, my dad owns it, but he's totally hands-off. It's basically Will's thing now. He goes to state school a half an hour away, but he only has classes two days a week. So he's at the shop the rest of the time. He wants to franchise it eventually; he's trying to open one near his school."

"That's cool."

"Maybe he'll finally leave me alone now; he's been trying to get me to work there. I just prefer drinking the coffee rather than making it, you know?"

Jane laughed. "Well, I guess I'll be the one making it for you now."

"Have you worked in a café before?"

"Yeah, back home, just a couple days a week."

"I bet there's very fancy milk in California."

"Oh, the fanciest. Macadamia, pea, walnut."

"Macadamia milk sounds amazing, I mean, why did you ever move? You had to know Bells Hollow wouldn't have macadamia milk."

Susie was joking, of course, but Jane paused anyway. Did she tell Susie the truth? It was still hard, saying it out loud—*my father died.* The words always seemed to catch in the back of her throat. But not telling her seemed worse, like an insult to Greer's memory.

Finally, with a deep breath, she said, "Actually, we moved here because my dad died." She paused, trying to keep her tone light. "To be honest, he loved macadamia milk, too. He would have been super bummed you guys don't have it here."

"Jane, I'm so sorry," Susie said. "I had no idea."

"Thanks. It's been . . ."

"Terrible?" Susie supplied bluntly.

Jane looked at her and smiled sadly. "Yeah. It's been terrible."

And it *had* been terrible, but it was strange. . . . The more distance they put between themselves and North Manor, the better Jane felt. Like a weight was lifting from her shoulders. Like something huge and dark was dissolving from her heart.

She settled back in her seat and tried not to think about how good it felt to be away from that house.

Transferring to a new school was a lesson in makeup work. Jane had done a fair amount of homework over the weekend, but she still felt behind in her morning classes, struggling to figure out where the rest of the class was in the lesson. She was exhausted by the time the lunch bell rang; Alana found her by her locker, not putting anything away, just sort of staring into it blankly.

"You okay?"

Jane blinked. "I think I fell asleep with my eyes open."

"Long night?"

"Long night, long morning."

"Anything I can do to help? I *am* your buddy, you know."

"I haven't missed a coffee shop on campus, have I? Maybe tucked behind the science wing or something?"

"Are you telling me you had a *coffee shop* in your high school?"

Jane nodded sadly. "They actually made great cappuccinos."

"Of course they did."

Just then someone emerged from the crowd of lunch-bound students and bumped their shoulder against Alana, hard. It was the same girl who had kicked her chair at lunch Friday, the girl with the dyed-black hair and dark eyes. She was trailed by a guy in cut-up jeans and a stained Henley shirt.

"Did you bring it?" she asked, not looking at Jane.

Alana rolled her eyes. "Yes, Melanie."

"You were supposed to put it in my locker."

"I've been busy. With classes."

"Busy with classes? Or busy making new friends?"

Melanie looked at Jane for the first time. Her expression was hard to read, but she was looking at Jane like she was pathetic, not worth the time it took to glance in her direction. And there was something else there. . . . Something like anger or recognition. Jane couldn't quite pinpoint it.

"Melanie, this is Jane. Jane, Melanie," Alana said stiffly. She dug around in her backpack for something, pulled out a small, stapled stack of paper, and handed it to Melanie.

Melanie took it but didn't look away from Jane. A funny smirk spread across her face. "It really is you."

"What do you mean?" Jane asked.

"I *told* you it was her," the boyfriend said.

"Yeah, you were right," Melanie said.

Her boyfriend laughed. There was something familiar about that laugh, something that nagged at Jane's memory.

Oh, right.

Of course.

Jane could almost hear his exclamation in the middle of the night—*Oh shit!*—right after Melanie had thrown a rock through her window.

He had laughed then, too.

"Can you go away now, please?" Alana said.

"Shut up, Alana," Melanie snapped. "I'm just talking to our new friend."

"Jane is not your—"

"You do realize I could go to the cops, right?" Jane interrupted.

Melanie's smirk grew wider. "Are you threatening me?"

"What are you talking about?" Alana asked. "Mel, what is she talking about? Go to the cops for what?"

Melanie turned toward Alana. "How about you tell your new friend that if she threatens me again—"

"I'm not *threatening* you," Jane said, her voice rising, her blood starting to pump faster. "I'm *telling* you: If you come to my house again, if you throw another rock through one of my fucking windows, I *will* call the police."

"You did *what*?" Alana screeched.

"Stay out of it, Alana," Melanie snapped.

"Babe, let's go," the boyfriend said, tugging Melanie's arm. "Mr. Foster just came out of his classroom."

Melanie let him pull her a step away from Jane. Jane's eyes were burning; she could feel her cheeks getting hot.

"Look," Alana said, her voice quiet. "You don't have to worry about Jane telling the cops. Because if you do anything to Jane or that house again, you or Jeff, *I'll* tell your mom, okay?"

"You were always such a little tattletale," Melanie said.

"And *you* were always such a little bitch," Alana shot back.

They stared at each other for a moment and Jane realized they had the exact same color eyes. And the way Alana had said *your mom*.

The boyfriend—Jeff—kept pulling at Melanie's arm until she finally broke eye contact with Alana. Jeff practically dragged Melanie down the hallway. Jane watched Mr. Foster nod to himself and go back into his classroom.

Jane was losing it. Breathing heavily, she turned and faced her still-open locker, putting one hand on the door. The metal felt cool underneath her fingertips. *You can't lose it here. You can't lose it in front of Alana.*

"I'm so sorry. I can't believe she came to your house," Alana said.

Jane made herself reply, struggling to keep her voice even. "All the windows in the house were smashed when we moved in. She threw a rock through one on Friday night."

"What an asshole," Alana said.

Calm down calm down calm down.

Jane took a long, shaky breath. She could feel Alana lean a little closer to her.

"Are you okay, Jane?"

"Sorry, just . . . She just made me a little mad."

"I totally get it. She's been making me mad my whole life."

Jane turned to her, curious, letting the curiosity replace the anger, letting *anything* replace the anger.

"You guys are . . . ?"

"Cousins, unfortunately," Alana confirmed.

"Is everyone in this town related?"

"Pretty much."

"Has she always been like that?"

"Not this bad. She's always been a little . . . off, I guess. But it's gotten worse."

"Did something happen?" Jane asked, because Alana was whispering now, and something had changed in her face. She looked almost sad, almost wary.

Alana took a deep breath. "Melanie's older sister is very . . . ill. Because of something that happened when she was younger."

"What happened when she was younger?"

"We don't have to talk about it," Alana said quickly. "But recently, her sister has gotten worse. A few years ago, she took a bunch of pills and . . . She's been in the hospital ever since. Mel kind of . . . broke. After that. At first, I tried to be there for her. I really did. I mean, she's my cousin, too. But Melanie's made it clear that she doesn't want my help. She doesn't want anyone's help." She paused. "Now that you're here . . . I think you should just try to stay away from her."

"Now that I'm here? What do you mean?"

Alana's expression darkened. She opened her mouth, but it was a moment before she spoke. Like she was deciding what to say. "I just mean . . . you have nothing to do with her issues. So just . . . stay away from her. I'm sorry she did that to your house."

"Let's just hope she doesn't come back." Jane paused. "You weren't . . . doing her homework for her, were you?"

"Just every now and then. An essay or two," Alana said. "I don't know why. It's guilt, maybe. She spends a lot of time at the hospital. With her sister. I just . . . I want her to be able to do that. I want to be able to do *something*. So here we are."

"You're a good person," Jane said. Her breathing was returning to normal, her skin was cooling down.

Alana shrugged. "Part of me hates her. Part of me just feels really, really bad for her."

Jane closed her locker. "That sounds fair to me."

"I'm glad it sounds fair to someone." Alana smiled sadly. "Come on, let's go eat."

Ruth wasn't home when Susie dropped Jane off after school. North Manor was quiet and still, the emptiness a palpable, alive thing. Jane went up to her bedroom and changed into pajamas and sat on the floor in front of her bookcase.

She hadn't written in her journal in such a long time. She pulled it out of the bookshelf now and held it. The last entry was from just a few days before Greer had died. So maybe she didn't want to use it now, because in its pages, Greer was still alive. If she never wrote another word, Greer would always be alive. Whatever happened to this journal after Jane died, if anyone ever picked it up and read it, they would never know he had died.

She put it back on the shelf.

She dug around in her backpack for her homework and spent the next hour or so working on it, then she pulled out the copy of *Destination Unknown* she'd bought at the little mystery bookshop and held it on her lap.

You be careful up there, Paula had said. *In Bells Hollow. These old towns all have histories. Some of them are darker than others.*

Some of them are darker than others.

What the hell had that meant?

Jane thought back on earlier, on meeting Melanie, and Alana saying something had happened to her sister *when she was younger.*

Was that a dark history? Alana had seemed slightly evasive about details, and Jane hadn't pressed her—she knew firsthand how it was better to sometimes keep the past in the past. It was less painful that way.

Jane shook her head. Whatever had happened to Melanie's sister wasn't any of her business. She opened *Destination Unknown* and read it until she heard the front door open and close.

"Janie, I'm home!" Ruth called from downstairs.

"Be down in a sec!"

Jane finished up the chapter she'd been reading; when she went downstairs a few minutes later she found Ruth working on paperwork at the kitchen table.

"Mom, it smells amazing in here," Jane said, collapsing into a kitchen chair. "You already started dinner?"

"Oh, I just put a lasagna in the oven, honey. I had it ready to go in the fridge; I'm *starving*. Didn't get a chance to eat lunch."

"How was your first day?"

"Oh, it was fine. Busy. They're in terrible shape, accounting-wise. Hence this." She waved her hands over the small mountain of paperwork.

"They're lucky to have you."

"What about you, honey? How was school?"

"Not bad."

"Good." Ruth yawned.

"Can I pour you a glass of wine?"

Ruth laughed. "Do I look like I need it?"

"Kind of, yeah," Jane said, smiling. She got up and patted Ruth on the top of the head. She got a wineglass down from the counter and poured a generous amount of Cabernet into it. She set it on the table in front of Ruth.

"Thanks, honey," Ruth said. "I'm gonna go wash up. Be right back."

Ruth left the kitchen and Jane stole a sip of her wine. It smelled rich and oaky, like some kind of deep fruit and...

Roses?

Jane put the wineglass down on the table. She sniffed the air. She could definitely smell roses, overpowering even the smell of the lasagna.

She walked over to the window and cracked it open; the smell of roses wafted in so strongly it almost took her breath away.

She went to the mudroom and opened the door. It was just after seven, and although the sky was dark, it had an almost-purple quality to it. The color of a bruise. She stepped out into the backyard and closed the door behind her.

Outside, the smell of the roses was so strong it made the back of her throat itchy.

It wasn't a nice smell anymore.

There was something deeper about it, almost rotten. A thick, too-sweet odor that took up more space than it should have.

She started walking to the rose arbors.

Ruth had left big piles of the dead plants she had cut down. Jane could see them, rotting there—was that why the smell was so strong?

But no—

That wasn't possible.

She took a few steps closer, then paused.

How was that possible?

Because she was close enough now to see that the arbors were covered with roses again, even thicker than before, twice as many blooms that crowded one another and fought for space—

But they weren't the reds and pinks and oranges they had been before.

No, as Jane got closer she could see that every single rose was black—

A dark, thick black, a black like the night sky, a starless expanse of nothingness.

Jane stared at them.

She knew nothing about gardening. Was it normal for roses to grow back this quickly? Were they supposed to be black? Ruth had only just cut them, but they already covered the arbor again. Jane moved underneath the archway and it became instantly darker; all the light was blocked by the cluster of leaves and thorns above her.

The smell was even stronger than before.

Wrong and overwhelming.

It brought tears to her eyes.

As she stood underneath the rosebushes, a breeze blew through the arbor.

It gusted among the plants and sent a shower of black petals down around her.

She held a hand out and one petal landed in the center of her palm.

And as she held it, it curled dramatically in on itself, rotting before her eyes, drying up and dying in a matter of seconds.

She let it drop to the ground.

She suddenly found she didn't like the smell of roses anymore.

Right in the middle
of her forehead

Ruth refused to talk about the roses; in fact, she wouldn't even go out to the backyard to look at them. She ate dinner without saying so much as a word, then she refilled her glass of wine, told Jane she was tired, and went upstairs to bed.

Jane cleaned the dishes and put away the leftovers and felt a growing pit of strangeness in her belly.

Why was Ruth acting so weird? Was it really *just* because she was tired? Or was something else going on?

She got her laptop out of her backpack and set it up at the kitchen table to facetime Salinger. It rang three times before Sal picked up; she was lying on her bed with her long brown hair spread out around her, and Jane felt her eyes well up with tears immediately. She wanted to be in that bedroom so badly, working on homework or trying on Sal's clothes or making Sal braid her hair into a crown around her head.

"I'm sorry, who are you? I don't have this number saved in my phone," Sal said, not yet looking at the camera, rolling her eyes back in her head. When she did finally look, she sat up, her face instantly concerned. "Jane? Are you crying? What happened?"

"I don't know. Everything. I hate it here. Everything sucks. I just want to come back to California."

"Fuck, I picked the wrong time to guilt-trip you for not facetiming me sooner," Sal said, softening.

"You really did."

"Great, now I'm crying. Stop crying, you're making me cry. I miss you so much."

"I miss you, too."

"What is going on?"

"I don't know how to explain it. It's just . . . Something isn't right. About this house."

"Janie, it's just an old house. I understand wanting to find something to hate, something to blame, but—"

"Stop therapizing me," Jane said. "I told you my mom went all Rambo on the rosebushes, right?"

"Yeah, she was clearly working through some stuff and took it out on those poor plants."

"Well, they grew back."

"Isn't that what plants do?"

"No, like, not this quickly. And also—*all the roses are black now.*"

Salinger made a face. "Oh. That's..."

"Weird."

"Very weird. But there is probably a totally normal explanation for it. Like a plant virus or something. Or a fungus, you know?"

"Maybe," Jane said. She was used to Salinger's calm, rational explanations for things, and it was actually making her feel slightly better. If Jane was the one to overreact, let her emotions get the best of her, Sal was the one to take a step back and analyze things from every logical angle. She was like Greer, in that way. Always practical. Always calm. Basically, the opposite of Jane.

"Try and forget the roses," Sal continued. "How is everything else? How is your mom?"

"She's been fine. Really focused. You know how she has a tendency to kind of throw herself into tasks and ignore everything else?"

"I'm aware, yes."

"So it's been a lot of that. Organizing, cleaning, calling repair people. But today was her first day of work, and she just seems... off."

"I'm sure she's tired," Sal said diplomatically.

"Tired, yeah. But she wouldn't even go look at the roses. And she hardly said a word at dinner."

"Look, I'm just trying to be the voice of reason over here. You've been through a *lot*, and it makes sense that you're feeling all sorts of weirdness because of that. But I think you need to cut yourself a little slack, cut *Ruth* a little slack, chill a tiny bit, and just try and go with the flow for a while."

"I wish I was there."

"Me too."

"So I could smack you in person for telling me to *go with the flow.*"

"Have you considered having some matcha and meditating in a room filled with crystals? It's the Los Angeles way," Sal said, smiling goofily.

"I love you. And I want to smack you still."

"Ditto."

"Thank you."

"You're welcome. Now, go do something relaxing. Make yourself some fucking tea, okay?"

"I will make myself some fucking tea."

"I love you."

"I love you, too."

Jane clicked the red button to end the call.

As soon as Sal's face disappeared, she burst into tears.

Ruth was quiet at breakfast the next morning; they hardly said two words to each other before Susie got there to pick up Jane. Jane moved slowly through her day, trying not to think about roses, trying not to think about Sal, trying not to think about Greer, trying not to think about anything. She was mentally exhausted by the time the last bell rang, and so grateful she almost cried when Susie offered to drive her to Beans & Books for her shift.

"Are you sure?" Jane said, exchanging books at her locker.

"Definitely. Free coffee and a quiet place to do homework. I have twin six-year-old sisters, so my house is *not* a quiet place."

They dropped off Alana first, then drove into town. Susie parked in a tiny lot next to the building and showed Jane a back door that led into a small room with a fridge, a conveyor toaster, and some cabinets and hooks with aprons on them.

"You can put your stuff in here," Susie said, knocking her shoe against one of the cabinets. "And grab one of these." She took a forest-green apron off one of the hooks and held it out to Jane. "Take your time. I'll tell Will we're here."

Susie walked through a set of swinging café doors that led to the behind-the-counter area; Jane could just see the top of Will's head as he walked back and forth taking care of a customer. She put her backpack into the cabinet, then slipped off her jacket and hung it on an open hook. The apron was actually kind of cute; it had a decal on the front of a stack of books with a coffee mug on top. She slipped it over her head and looked at herself in a mirror hanging next to the hooks.

Her hair was messy and loose so she put it into a bun, twisting it around until it was all out of her face. When she was sure it would stay put, she pushed the café doors open slowly. There were a few customers sitting at tables, and Will and Susie were laughing about something behind the register.

When Will saw Jane, he said, "Hate to tell you this, but you're fired. I thought you seemed suspicious before, and now that I hear you've befriended my sister, it's confirmed. You can't be trusted." He tried to pull Susie's hair, but she ducked out of his reach.

"Ha-ha," Susie said. "You better be nice to Jane; she'll tell me if you aren't."

"In that case I will refrain from spilling hot coffee on her to test her commitment to the craft of making lattes," Will said.

"Actually, that sounds like an efficient vetting process," Jane said. "You should have gone for it."

"I changed my mind. I like you again."

Susie rolled her eyes and said, "All right, someone make me a drink. I have homework to do."

"Yeah, yeah, whatever," Will said as Susie went and sat down at an empty table. He turned to Jane. "Welcome to your first day. This is the espresso machine. Those are the tables. Past those you will note the bookcases. Any questions?"

Jane smiled. "Nope. I think I pretty much got it."

"Perfect, you're already crushing it. Think you can make my baby sister an almond milk latte she actually likes? Fair warning; she's a tough customer."

"I can still hear you," Susie snapped from her table.

"Let me give it a shot," Jane said.

She washed her hands in the stainless-steel sink, then rolled her sleeves up to her elbows. It had been a while since she'd made a latte, but she soon found that her hands knew what to do, even if her brain was a little rusty. She ground the beans, fit them into the portafilter, and tamped them down neatly. She steamed the almond milk as the espresso brewed. She even managed a design as she poured the steamed milk over the espresso—nothing fancy, just a little leaf—and Will clucked his tongue in approval.

"That is some nice work," he said.

Jane brought the mug over to Susie's table and made a little bow as she set it in front of her.

Susie cleared her throat dramatically and took a sip. As soon as the liquid hit her lips, her face changed. "Now, *that*," she said, putting the cup on the table again, "is a latte."

Will burst into applause. "Brilliant. You're hired."

"You already hired me," Jane reminded him.

"No, no, remember I fired you? Now you're hired again," he clarified.

"Okay, seriously, leave me alone. I have stuff to do," Susie said.

Will and Jane returned to the counter, where Jane dumped out the used espresso beans and cleaned the portafilter with a towel.

"So I started the book," Will said.

"Oh yeah? *The ABC Murders*? What do you think?"

"I'm only a chapter into it. I like the cast of characters."

"That's pretty typical for Agatha."

"I like that you're on a first-name basis with her."

"Of course. Agatha and I go way back."

"Well, I'm enjoying it so far. It's a lot funnier than I was expecting."

"She's *so* funny. It's that quiet sort of British humor that sneaks up on you."

Will smiled, and Jane noticed that he had the slightest space between his two front teeth, just like his sister.

A tiny bell above the door announced the arrival of a customer.

"Here," Will said, grabbing an iPad and handing it to her. "It's pretty self-explanatory. The password is 2665."

Jane unlocked the iPad as Will took the customer's order. She found the button for Latte and ran the customer's credit card. Will finished making the drink and the customer took it to go.

"Look at you!" Will said.

"Book," Jane replied. "That's cute."

"What's cute?"

"The password is *book*—2665."

Will smiled. "Hey. You got my nerd joke."

"I'm your target audience."

"Great. You're hired." He paused, winked, then added, "Again," and for the first time that day, Jane found that she was able to think of something other than roses.

North Manor was empty when Susie dropped off Jane. The first thing Jane did was turn on strategic lights: the foyer, the upstairs hallway, her bedroom. Then she changed into sweatpants and a T-shirt and made herself a peanut butter and jelly sandwich.

She sat at the kitchen table and spread her schoolbooks out around her and sent a text to Ruth: *Are you still at work?*

Ruth texted back a minute later: *Dinner with coworkers. Sorry I forgot to text! Be home soon.*

Jane put down her phone and took a bite of the sandwich. She started on a calculus worksheet but found it hard to concentrate; the numbers kept blurring in front of her eyes.

You're just tired, she told herself.

The rest of her shift at Beans & Books had passed quickly. Will was fun to work with, and they'd talked the entire time: about books, about coffee, about school. He'd made her a macchiato and she felt buzzy with the caffeine, but still somehow exhausted. She scratched an answer on the worksheet and had another bite of the sandwich.

She was lowering it back down to her plate when she heard it—a weird sound. It was as if someone had dropped something very small on the second floor, right above her, and whatever it was had rolled for a few seconds before stopping abruptly.

She looked up at the ceiling, frowning.

She heard Ruth's voice in her head: *It's these old houses, Janie. They're constantly making noises. It's called* settling; *you'll get used to it.*

She tucked her hair behind her ear, took another bite of the sandwich, and turned her attention back to her homework—

But no sooner had she touched the tip of the pencil to the paper than she heard the noise again. Something dropping. Something rolling across the floor.

Something else like . . . laughter?

Jane stood up. She tossed the pencil on the table; it rolled slowly over the edge and onto the floor.

She looked up at the ceiling again, as if she could somehow see through it.

She picked up her phone. Had Ruth snuck in and made it upstairs without Jane hearing the front door open? She sent her a quick text—*home when?*—and kept listening.

You'll get used to it, she repeated to herself.

Their house in California had been a single story, and every noise had been familiar to her. Comforting. Lying in bed at night, she could pinpoint the second her father got out of bed to use the bathroom, or the morning sounds of her mother making coffee, or the flap of the mailbox when the mail was delivered.

This house was a stranger to her, and every sound it made set her on edge, threw her off a little. Maybe the dropping sound, the rolling sound, had been the upstairs radiators coming on? Her own bedroom's radiator produced so many strange clicking and hissing noises that it woke her up sometimes in the middle of the night. Maybe this was what that sounded like from downstairs?

She sat down again.

Her heart was beating fast, and her hands were clammy and tingly.

"It's nothing," she whispered aloud.

She checked her phone again. Ruth hadn't texted back.

She bent over and picked up the pencil from the floor, and

it happened again—but louder, so loud this time it was as if it had happened right behind her.

She jumped to her feet and whirled around.

There was nothing there. Of course there was nothing there.

The kitchen windows were almost black. She could barely see outside them. Just the shadowy outline of trees and the bright spot of the moon.

Her arms were covered in goose bumps.

She almost sat down again, but something wouldn't let her.

She knew she wouldn't be able to relax until she had gone upstairs and proved that the noise was nothing.

She didn't want to go—her legs felt leaden as she walked to the front of the house, pausing at the bottom of the staircase, stalling.

Should she call the police?

You are not calling the police because you heard a creak in a house filled with creaks.

Halfway up the stairs she froze, listening hard into the silence, but she heard nothing. She held her breath until she made it to the second floor.

She'd left the light on.

The hallway was empty. Her bedroom door was open, as was her mother's. The bedrooms they didn't use were all closed, including the storage room and her grandparents' room.

She stood for a minute in the hallway, forcing herself to breathe, to chill.

It's just an old, creepy house, she reminded herself. *There's nothing about it that can hurt you.*

But then the noise again.

It came from just down the hall.

From the storage room.

Definitely from the storage room—

Like someone had dropped something small . . .

And the rolling sound.

Jane stared at the closed storage-room door until a movement caught her eye. Something tiny had emerged from underneath the door, rolling slowly across the hallway, taking a few seconds before it hit the opposite wall. It rebounded for just an inch or so before coming to a stop.

Her throat had gone dry.

Her heart was pounding so hard it *hurt*.

She wanted to turn and run but she made herself stand her ground, then she made herself take a few steps down the hall, putting one foot in front of the other until she had reached the object.

She bent down and picked it up.

It was a marble.

It was a little purple marble, a deep color with a ribbon of lighter lilac running through it. It was cold against her fingertips. It tugged at a memory, worming its way into her brain, unearthing old secrets.

She was eleven years old, and she had taken a pair of scissors to the ponytail of a girl named Claudia Summers.

Claudia was new in town; she wore ill-fitting jeans and flannel button-ups even when it was ninety degrees outside.

The only open desk in the classroom was the one in front of Jane. Claudia sat down and let her ponytail fall onto the top of Jane's desk. Jane pushed it away angrily. They'd had almost the same hair exactly—the same shade of honey blond, the same tumbling waves, the same length. And almost immediately, they'd hated each other.

Claudia was rude from the start and seemed to target Jane specifically, pushing back against her seat so it hit Jane's desk, causing her to smudge a paper she was writing. Leaving globs of gum on her seat. Passing her mean notes when the teacher's back was to them.

Jane tried to ignore her.

She tried not to get angry.

But it went on for months and months.

One day Jane got to school and opened her desk to find everything gone. Her pencils, her notebooks, her library books. It was completely empty.

And there was Claudia, sitting in front of her, playing with a small purple marble.

Jane's marble.

She kept it in her desk—a present from Sal, who collected them.

All Jane's other things had been thrown into the trash can. When Jane fished them out, they were covered in pencil shavings and used tissues.

"Just ignore her," Sal had whispered into Jane's ear at lunch that day. "I'll give you another marble. Just ignore her."

But Jane couldn't ignore her. She couldn't ignore the way her body felt, almost thrumming with anger. If someone had touched their palm to Jane's skin, they would have felt pure electricity. A palpable vibration.

They would have been scared.

Jane returned to the classroom after lunch and sat at her desk and waited.

When Claudia arrived, she sat down and let her ponytail cascade across Jane's desk. She took the marble out of her pocket and started playing with it, making sure Jane could see.

And before Jane really knew what she was doing, before she had a moment to stop and think about it, she had taken a pair of scissors out of her desk and started hacking at Claudia's hair, just below the hair tie.

It took Claudia a moment to realize what was happening.

The scissors weren't very sharp, and Claudia's hair was thick; Jane had only made it about halfway through the pony-tail before Claudia started screaming and pulling away and flailing her arms, one of her hands hitting Jane's and knocking the scissors to the floor, great chunks of her cut hair falling out of the hair tie and landing on the floor, on Jane's desk, on Jane's hands, everywhere.

She dropped the marble.

And with Claudia still screaming, still flailing, Jane calmly bent down and picked it up.

She held it in her hand now, looking at it.

No, not the same marble.

It couldn't have been the *same* marble.

But it was the exact color, the exact size.

Jane looked at the closed door.

She took a step toward it, then another.

The marble began to warm up in her hand. It felt comforting, perfectly round and smooth, a little worry stone for her to rub her thumb against.

It couldn't have been the same marble.

It wasn't.

She took another step and then she was close enough to reach out and grasp the doorknob. So she did. And she twisted.

Locked.

She felt a draft against her feet, and she looked downward.

The crack under the door was really quite large. Large enough for the marble to roll out from under, and it was a pretty big marble, maybe an inch in diameter.

If she couldn't get into the room, she might be able to at least get a peek of what was inside it.

She lowered herself to her knees, slipping the marble into her pocket so she wouldn't drop it. She put her palms down and inched her chest lower until her belly was on the floor. Then she put her forehead against the door itself and squeezed her left eye shut to focus better. . . .

And she didn't see a single box.

The room was dark, of course. She could see the outline of

long, white curtains at the windows, but barely any moonlight was making its way through them.

But even though she couldn't see much, she could tell that this was definitely no storage room—there was a bed in the corner; she could make out two of the legs and a bed skirt that just kissed the hardwood floor. There was a rug in the middle of the room. Something that looked like a dollhouse on the opposite wall.

But nothing to indicate what might have made the other dropping and rolling sounds.

No other marbles she could see.

She got to her feet slowly and a little sloppily, almost tripping, catching herself on the door handle, getting her balance back.

She felt dizzy, and slightly off balance, like she didn't know which way was up and which way was down and what was real and what wasn't.

Just to be sure, she tried the door again. It was still locked.

She reached her hand into her pocket and felt the marble. It was cool to the touch.

It wasn't the same marble.

That was impossible.

And yet Claudia's face was so clear in her mind, a face she hadn't thought about in years. . . .

It was almost like she'd been sent a reminder.

She squeezed her eyes closed and tried to calm down—

And jumped a mile when the doorbell rang.

Had Ruth forgotten her keys?

Jane made her way downstairs, unlocked the dead bolt, and opened the front door.

There was no one there.

She stepped outside, sweeping her eyes across the front yard, but Ruth wasn't parked in the driveway. There was no one out there.

Faulty wiring, she told herself.

She took a few more steps outside.

It was a mild, peaceful night and the sky was crowded with stars. She had never seen this many stars in Los Angeles; they shone so brightly that she wondered whether some of them might be planets. She picked out constellations she had only ever seen in books. The crooked throne of Cassiopeia. The three stars of Orion's belt. The Big Dipper. The Little Dipper.

She walked out onto the driveway, transfixed by how beautiful it was, by just how many stars there actually were, by how impossibly *big* the sky was.

She tried to imagine what her life would have been like if Ruth had never moved across the country, if Jane had grown up in Maine. Would she have been close with Emilia? Would she know more constellations? Would her body be more used to the cold? Would they have spent holidays at North Manor?

North Manor.

She looked back at it.

It was large and imposing in the darkness.

She had left the front door open.

From the driveway, the house looked like a giant entity, and the front door was like its mouth, and to step inside it was to allow yourself to be swallowed up into the belly of it.

She walked across the front yard, cutting the quickest path to the mouth.

And only when she was a few feet away did she pause.

Only when she was a few feet away did she see it, in the light that spilled out of the mouth from the chandelier in the foyer.

Lying right in front of the door.

So that she couldn't get inside without stepping over it.

A single red rose.

She moved forward and knelt down to pick it up, careful to avoid the thorns that dotted the slender stem.

This one wasn't black like the ones on the rosebushes had been; instead it was a deep, dark crimson, so thick with color that it almost glowed in the moonlight. Jane studied it. Brought it up to her nose and smelled it.

She stepped back into the house and shut the door.

She felt numb—not from cold, from something else. From something too big for her to understand, to wrap her head around.

Where had the marble come from? Where had the rose come from?

Headlights swept across the foyer, and Jane peered outside to see Ruth's car pulling into the driveway. She tossed the rose onto the entranceway table and waited by the door.

There was a mirror hanging over the table.

She caught sight of herself, held her gaze in the reflection. She looked tired. Different. Like the time in Maine had already changed her. Just subtle differences. A shadow underneath her eyes. Slightly darker hair. A sunken look to her cheeks.

But then she noticed something else.

Something else in the reflection.

Something impossible.

She was holding the rose.

Her breath caught in her throat.

She was three feet, at least, from the table. From where she had tossed the rose.

So it was impossible.

She was just tired.

She was just seeing things.

But she moved her hands and felt a sharp prick, and she knew even before she looked down at them what it was.

When she finally let her gaze fall, she was bleeding. She was holding the rose. One of the thorns had pierced the fleshy part of her palm.

She was holding the rose and it was covered in blood.

And when she was good

When Susie picked Jane up for school the next morning, her eyes were rimmed in red, she was quiet and
somber when she backed out of the driveway, and as soon as
they'd made it out to the main street, she told Jane that Alana
wouldn't be coming to school, her cousin had died the night
before.

"Not—Melanie?" Jane asked, shocked.

"Melanie's sister," Susie said. "I don't know if Alana mentioned her. But she was really sick. She's been living in a hospital for a few years."

"What happened?"

"Alana was kind of hysterical on the phone," Susie said.
"But I guess one of the nurses found her last night...." Susie
paused, sniffed loudly. They reached a stop sign, and she dug a

tissue out of the center console and wiped at her eyes. "They're not really sure what happened, but they think she must have gotten something sharp. She had all these cuts on her hands, her arms. That's all Alana told me."

"They think she . . . did it herself?" Jane asked, turning her own palm over and running a finger over the scratch she'd gotten from the thorn. "That's terrible."

"I know."

Jane had thrown the rose into the trash last night, then washed the blood off her palm in the bathroom.

She hadn't told Ruth what had happened.

She hadn't told anybody.

But that couldn't have had anything to do with Melanie. It was just a coincidence, just a weird coincidence.

Alana missed school that day and the next. Melanie was out for longer.

It turned cold, quickly.

A new sort of cold. A cold Jane had never experienced before. A cold so invasive that if she left any part of her hair damp from the shower, it was frozen by the time she reached Susie's car in the morning. She wore jeans and thick socks and flannel shirts and her new winter coat, and she wrapped her neck in a scarf, and she was still cold. She was always cold.

A week after the night with the rose, she let herself into Susie's car and, as usual, pressed herself against the vents, letting the warm air hit her neck, letting it blow down her shirt and over her goose-bumped skin.

"Morning," Susie said.

"Morning," Jane replied, trying to stop shivering.

"It's ridiculous, right? I swear there was snow on the ground this morning."

"How do you deal with it?"

"I wish I had a very good answer for you," Susie replied. "But I don't. You just sort of... try not to freeze. And eventually, it gets warmer. For about two months. And then it gets cold again. And you find ways to take your mind off it."

"That's what I need. Something to take my mind off it."

"Oh! Well I have the perfect thing, actually. Do you like Halloween?"

"I do! I love it. Back home my friend Salinger and I would always wear matching costumes."

"Well—it's next Friday. And they've just announced the theme of the dance."

"You have a Halloween dance?"

"Yeah, and it's actually pretty cool."

"What's the theme?"

"*Haunted Forest.*"

"That sounds promising."

"I know, right?" Susie said. "So... wanna go? With Alana and me?"

"Definitely. Do people dress up?"

"You *have* to dress up. I bet you're just Rapunzel every year, right? With that hair?"

"I've never been Rapunzel," Jane said, laughing.

"Are you serious? A wasted opportunity."

"We'll have to go shopping for a costume. I don't have anything."

"That can be arranged," Susie said seriously.

Jane was excited about the dance, and she, Susie, and Alana spent lunch discussing costume possibilities. Alana was especially enthusiastic, and Jane got the impression she was using it as a welcome distraction from her cousin's death. She hadn't ever been *that* close with Melanie's older sister, she'd admitted to Jane, but she was surprised at how much her death had affected her. She found herself crying at random moments, remembering little things, like going to visit her cousin on her birthday. She couldn't even imagine how Melanie must be feeling.

When it was time for chemistry, Jane got to the classroom just before the bell rang and took a seat at her desk.

It was actually an interesting lesson involving dropping a gummy bear into a tube of molten potassium chlorate (the resulting reaction was fairly violent and fun), and the time passed quickly. When the bell rang. Mr. Barker waved her to the front of the classroom before she could get her things together.

"Just wanted to check in," he said as the rest of the class filed out around them. "See how you're settling into everything."

He was probably around her mother's age, friendly green eyes, black hair peppered with gray. He was one of her favorite teachers so far, and the one who'd waited the longest before throwing any significant homework her way.

"It's been okay," she said honestly. Not great. Not terrible.

"Alana and Susie are good kids. I've seen you around with them."

"Yeah, they're really nice."

"You know, I actually went to school with your mother. Ruthellen and I were good friends, back then. Will you tell her I said hello?"

"Of course," Jane said.

"It was a shame, when she left. I always wondered whether she was okay." He waved a hand, as if brushing away old memories. "Anyway, if you need anything, some advice or just a sounding board, don't hesitate to ask."

"Thanks. I really appreciate it."

"All right, get along, so you're not late."

Jane gathered her things, then started toward her locker to exchange some books, stopping at the beginning of the hallway when she saw Melanie standing at her own locker, staring blankly into it, unmoving.

There was no one else around.

Jane approached her cautiously; Melanie was in her own world and didn't even hear her coming.

"I'm so sorry about your sister," Jane said when she'd gotten close enough.

Melanie turned around slowly, as if moving through water, and when she saw it was Jane, her eyes narrowed. "Don't talk to me about my sister," she said softly, her voice almost a hiss, low and dangerous.

Jane froze, confused—why was there so much hate in Melanie's eyes?

"My father just passed away," Jane continued, "so I know what it's like. I know how you feel, and I'm so, so sorry."

Melanie slammed her locker shut then, in a movement so quick and so unexpected that Jane jumped backward. The crash of metal on metal reverberated down the hallway. The silence that followed was just as loud, just as deafening.

Melanie took a step toward Jane. "You have . . . *no idea* how I feel," she said, her voice steady and even and mean.

"Okay. Chill. I just wanted to say I was sorry."

"Get the fuck away from me," Melanie replied, squeezing her eyes shut. A tear leaked out of the corner of one, trailing a slow line down her cheek. "Get *the fuck* away from me," she repeated, and Jane stared at her for a second, then turned and practically ran down the hallway, her skin prickling uncomfortably. What the fuck was wrong with Melanie? Jane was just trying to be nice, to extend some sympathy, some common ground.

Jane took the long way to her locker and when she finally reached it, she opened it, then angled her body so no one walking past her would be able to see her face.

The anger again—palpable and quick, like it had been waiting just underneath her skin to bubble up to the surface.

Distantly, in the back corner of her mind, she heard the warning bell ring.

She grabbed a random book from her locker. Her English

textbook. She ripped a corner off one of the middle pages. A small piece with nothing printed on it except a page number— 157. It wouldn't be missed. She crumpled it into a tiny ball and set it on her tongue like a pill.

It tasted bitter and greasy. It didn't break down with her saliva.

How many hands had touched that page before hers? How many germs had she just put in her mouth?

She spat it back out into the palm of her hand, then let it drop wetly to the floor.

She took a breath. Her lungs felt insufficient and weak.

The bell rang again. The hallway emptied of voices, of footsteps.

She closed the English book and put it in her locker.

She couldn't move.

She couldn't calm down. She couldn't get enough air to breathe.

She shut her locker but it was more like a slam in the empty hallway, an echo of Melanie slamming her own locker. Jane felt the crash deep in her skull; it thrummed inside her, a heavy vibration.

She'd been twelve, and she had slammed the front door of their house so hard she'd heard something crash in the small foyer within.

She couldn't remember now why she had been so angry.

Hearing the crash had calmed her down, somehow, and she'd opened the door again and stepped into the house.

Ruth had been kneeling on the floor, cradling something

in her hand. The broken pieces of a ceramic figurine, a devil Greer had painted when he was just a little kid. It had been displayed on a shelf in the foyer and the slamming of the door must have been enough to vibrate it off the edge.

"Mom, I'm—"

"Are you pleased with yourself?" Ruth had said, her voice sharp and filled with her own rage.

Jane hadn't been able to respond.

Ruth had gathered up the pieces of the figurine and left the room with them.

And Jane had felt alone. Really alone. And with the realization that you could never go back. Time marched forward. The figurine couldn't be unbroken.

And now, in the hallway, that same bitter truth.

Jane couldn't un-slam the locker door. They couldn't un-move to this terrible town. Greer couldn't un-die.

Jane was grateful for work that afternoon, relieved to have the distraction. Her interaction with Melanie had left her feeling confused and strange and angry, and she'd spent the rest of the day looking over her shoulder, nervous about running into her again.

Susie gave her a ride to the coffee shop, and it was so busy when she arrived that for the first hour of her shift, Jane didn't have a moment to breathe, let alone think. She made latte after latte after espresso after Americano. When she finally got a break, she was hot and a little sweaty, and her hair had started to curl even more by her forehead. She was relieved when someone asked her for help finding a book; walking into the stacks felt like taking a dip into cool water. She led the customer to the history section, then went to mysteries by herself. There'd been a small delivery of paperbacks that morning, and she hadn't gotten a chance to check them out yet.

There were about ten more Agatha Christie books than the last time she'd worked, all vintage paperbacks with the odd, funny covers she loved so much. She picked one up. *Curtains*. The final appearance of Hercule Poirot. Widely considered to be one of Agatha Christie's best works. She picked up another one. *The Mysterious Affair at Styles*. Another Poirot. Then she saw one with a brown spine. She pulled it out. The tagline on the cover read "Hercule Poirot saw DEATH coming!" Two hands held an axlike weapon that sliced a space right through the title: *Mrs. McGinty's Dead*.

It was one of Jane's favorites. The copy she owned had a different cover, and she liked this one way more. She brought it up to the register and set it down on the counter.

Will was sipping an espresso and leaning against the wall.

"That after-school rush will be the death of me," he said.

"I can't feel my fingers," she replied.

"You high-schoolers drink too much coffee. It's going to stunt your growth."

"I think that's a myth."

"You're probably right." He picked the book up and turned it around in his hands. "Well, well. What do we have here?"

"A very underrated book," Jane announced. "It never makes any best-of lists, but it's *so* good."

"I am very into this cover." Will put the book down on the counter. "I have to say, this feels like a bit of kismet."

"How so?"

"Because"—he reached into his back pocket and whipped out the copy of *The ABC Murders*—"I finished it!"

"You did? Finally!"

"It's been, like, a week," Will said, laughing. "That's a perfectly respectable amount of time to finish a book."

"Not an Agatha Christie book. An epic fantasy, maybe, but Agatha's books are *tiny*."

"Well, I liked it. A lot. So I'm taking this one now."

He slid *The ABC Murders* toward Jane and put *Mrs. McGinty's Dead* into his apron pocket.

"Just try and get it back to me in a timely manner," Jane said seriously, slipping *The ABC Murders* into her own apron.

"Fair enough." Will snapped his fingers. "Oh, look! I almost forgot. We got these in." He reached into a cabinet over the espresso machine and pulled out two bottles of syrup. They were clearly hand-bottled, with little corks and watercolor labels. One had a bunch of lavender on it, the other a rose. He set them carefully on the table. "These are from a farm a few miles away. A woman named Madge Delaney makes them. Lavender and rose syrups. For lattes. Did you know roses are edible?"

Jane picked up the bottle of lavender syrup, uncorked it, and breathed it in. It was rich and beautiful; she'd always loved the smell of lavender. "I don't know, aren't most flowers edible?"

"Most flowers are *not* edible, Jane," Will said. "Now I'm a little worried you're going to make me an oleander latte."

Jane rolled her eyes. "Have you tried them yet?"

"Nope. She just brought them by this morning. Want me to make you one?"

Jane handed him the lavender bottle. "Yes, please."

"A lavender latte it is," he said. "They're kind of pricey, these things, but she said a little goes a long way. I think it's time we changed up the menu a bit. I'm getting sick of vanilla lattes."

She watched him make the drink, tamping down the espresso firmly, steaming the almond milk until it was smooth and hot. He added a tiny bit of the lavender syrup to a mug, then he poured the milk in a complicated, fluid motion. When he handed her the mug she saw that he had made an intricate fern. It made her latte designs look childish in comparison.

"That's beautiful," she said.

Will scoffed and swatted a hand in her direction. "It has to taste good, too, or else its beauty is meaningless."

"Isn't all beauty meaningless?" Jane asked as she studied the leaf. A few seconds passed before she realized Will was staring at her with his eyebrows raised. She laughed. "Just kidding."

"You're getting very existential with that latte, Jane."

"It's been a long day." She took a sip. The latte was the perfect balance of smoothness and bitterness. The lavender was subtle but lingered in her mouth after she had swallowed. She sighed and closed her eyes, breathing in deeply as the mug warmed her hands.

When she opened her eyes again, she saw that Will was staring at her with a funny look on his face.

"What?" she asked, suddenly self-conscious.

"Are you okay?" he replied. "You just inhaled enough oxygen for a small village with that sigh."

"I'm fine. The latte is helping."

"It's drinkable?"

"It's perfect."

"Good enough for the menu?"

"Absolutely."

"What should we call it? Lavelatte? Lavenator?"

"How about just lavender latte?"

"I love it," he said. "To the point." Then, serious again, he asked, "Are you sure you're okay? You can talk to me. I know we don't know each other *that* well, but . . ."

"I'm really okay," she said. "Just tired. The usual. Cold. Homesick. Sad."

"Sad?"

Jane bit her lip. Something made her want to tell him. "Did Susie tell you why we moved here?"

"She didn't say anything," he replied, shaking his head.

"I asked her not to say anything. To anybody. But it would have been fine if she told you." She took a deep breath. "My father died. He had a heart attack. There was a lot of money stuff, so . . . we had to move here."

"Jane, I'm so sorry," Will said. He took her hand, just for a moment.

"Every so often it's just like . . . I remember that he's not here anymore." She felt herself tearing up, so she smiled instead, a sad smile. "That's all. I don't really want to talk about it anymore."

"Of course. Well . . . I'm glad you told me. And I'm sorry. I'm so sorry."

"Thanks."

"Okay, so . . ." He reached behind her and picked up a piece of chalk from the lip of the vintage chalkboard that hung over the espresso machine. "Lavender latte. Officially added to the menu. Who wants to do the honors?"

"You have nicer handwriting."

"Years of chalkboard practice," he said with a smile.

Jane watched as he fit "lavender latte" right underneath "vanilla latte." The loops of the *l*'s were perfect.

"You know, if you end up adding the rose latte, too, you'll have to do the entire thing over," Jane pointed out.

"Oh shoot. I forgot about the rose. Want me to make you one of those next?"

"I don't like roses," Jane said flatly. She finished the rest of her latte in one long sip.

When she got home that evening she felt happy and warm with coffee, even though it was already dark and bitter cold as she ran from Susie's car to her front door. She was shivering

139

as she fit her key into the lock and pushed into the foyer. She closed the door behind her and leaned against it for a moment.

She didn't know if she would ever get used to it—how the cold worked its way into your body, forcing its way through you, taking up all the space in your lungs.

She pulled herself away from the door and locked it behind her, then walked toward the kitchen. Even though the house got warmer the deeper into it she went, she still felt heavier and heavier, like the cold was slipping deeper into her, weighing her down.

Ruth was at the kitchen table looking over some paperwork.

"I thought this was supposed to be a part-time job," Jane said.

Ruth jumped a little and looked up, her hand over her chest. "Jesus, I didn't even hear you come in." Her mother held out her arms and Jane walked into them. "I know, I didn't expect to be bringing this much work home. There's just so much to *do*. How was your day?"

"It was fine," Jane replied.

"I totally lost track of time. How's Chinese for dinner? I'll go pick some up."

"Sounds good, Mom. I'm going to go facetime Sal."

"Tell her I said hi."

Jane went upstairs and opened her laptop on the bed. It was four o'clock in California and Sal answered the phone red-faced and panting after a run. She was lying in the grass; Jane recognized the lemon tree that grew in her front yard. It was spotted with bright-yellow citruses. It made Jane's heart ache for Los Angeles.

"Hi!" Sal said, breathing heavily, pushing her sweaty bangs off her forehead.

"You look hot," Jane replied.

"Ugh, it's *terrible* here. I thought I was going to die on my run."

"I'm glad you didn't."

"Me too."

"How far did you go?"

"Five miles. Hey, sorry I missed your call yesterday."

"I didn't call you yesterday, did I?" Jane asked, propping her pillows up behind her and settling back against them.

"Yeah, a bunch of times. I was sleeping. It was pretty late for you. Like, ten here. So one in the morning?"

Jane frowned. She'd gone to bed at nine thirty last night. She grabbed her phone and opened her recent calls. Sure enough, there were the FaceTimes to Sal. Four of them, all around one in the morning.

"Weird. Maybe my phone is broken," Jane said.

"Well, we're here now," Sal replied. "How was your day?"

"It was fine."

"Did you work?"

"Yup."

"How's Will?"

Jane shrugged. "Fine."

"How's your mom?"

"She's fine."

Sal made a face. "Did you call me just so you could answer all my questions with the word *fine*?"

Jane felt a twinge of something in her belly. Discomfort? Irritation? Anger? "No. I'm sorry. I guess I'm just a little tired. But I wanted to call. Tell me about your day."

"It was fine," Sal said, a smile spreading across her face.

"Jerk."

"Love you."

"I love you, too."

"I gotta go shower. Talk this weekend?"

"Yeah. Definitely."

"Bye!"

Sal hung up first, after puckering her lips and kissing the air in front of the camera.

Jane went to kiss back, but the screen had already gone to black.

The conversation left her with a queasy feeling in the pit of her stomach.

The house was quiet; Ruth hadn't gotten back with the food. Jane went into her bathroom and turned the shower on as hot as she could stand it, even though Ruth always said cold showers were better for your skin. She took off her clothes and dropped them on the tiled floor, then stepped into the water.

She let the spray hit her on the chest, warming her up for what felt like the first time all day. When she turned off the water and wrapped a towel around her body, her skin was a dark shade of pink and she felt tired and hungry and happy. She squeezed her hair out over the tub, then wrapped it in another towel and walked back into her bedroom.

She pulled on a pair of flannel pajama bottoms and a T-shirt, then knelt on her bedroom floor and placed her new copy of *The ABC Murders* next to her other Agatha Christie books.

She pulled *The Lion, the Witch, and the Wardrobe* from her bookcase. Just holding it in her hands made her feel relaxed. Calm.

It was hard to explain.

It wasn't even something she thought about that much, during the day.

But on the other hand, it was all she ever thought about.

This moment.

This ritual.

The tug of paper. The gentle rip. The yellowed pages.

And after today, after the confrontation with Melanie, Jane needed something to help her calm down.

So she ate the page.

She took what felt like her first deep breath all day.

When she was finished, she put the book away and stood up, stretching. She removed the towel from her hair and combed her curls out with her fingers. She threw the towel over her bathroom door and was about to peek out the window, to see if Ruth's car was back, when she heard a little thump from down the hall. So Ruth was home. Good. She was hungry now, and on an empty stomach, the paper had left a dry feeling in the back of her throat. Not unpleasant. Just a little scratchy.

She slid on a pair of socks, turned off her bedroom light, and stepped into the hallway.

She'd left the foyer light on, and the hallway was bathed in the soft glow of it. Instinctively, she looked toward Ruth's bedroom door, which was ajar. The light inside was off.

She felt tired. Fuzzy. Something else she couldn't put a finger on.

Afraid?

Yes, she felt afraid.

But why did she feel afraid? Everything was fine.

The noise again.

It was a normal, human noise. The noise of someone walking through a space, bumping their hip against the side of a bed frame, rubbing their skin to ease the pain of it.

Jane's palms itched.

She still stared at Ruth's bedroom door, even though the thump had come from the other side of the hall. Toward the storage room.

Or...no.

Because it wasn't a storage room.

She knew it wasn't a storage room.

And she made herself look.

It was hard to turn her head.

It was like she was turning through air that had suddenly become too thick.

Like turning her head through molasses.

Like turning her head through a heavy current.

And when she finally managed...

The storage-room light was on.

Or no, no.

Because it wasn't a storage room.

She knew it wasn't a storage room.

And the light was on.

Underneath the door. She could see it. A line of warm yellow. Jane stared at it, and even as her heart pounded in her chest, even as all the saliva in her mouth suddenly leached away, leaving her tongue thick and swollen, she pretended it was Ruth.

"Mom," she said, and her voice came out no louder than a whisper. "Mom, what are you doing in there? It's time for dinner. Let's find a movie to watch."

And every single hair on her arms stood up as a shadow passed behind the door.

It was Ruth.

That's what she told herself.

It was Ruth's shadow.

"Mom," she said, but this time her voice wasn't a voice at all, but a scratchy, shaky thing that didn't make it much farther than her own lips.

She took a step toward the door.

"Mom," she said.

But no.

She didn't say it at all. She didn't even whisper it. She didn't make even the tiniest sound.

And then someone put a key into the front-door dead bolt.

Jane heard it as clearly as if she were standing right next to it.

And the front door opened, and Jane heard her mother let out a sigh and dump her key ring in a little bowl they kept on the entrance table.

Such familiar noises. Jane had heard them so many times before.

She would know her mother's sigh anywhere. She would know the jangle of the key ring, how Ruth released it just a little too early, how it clattered noisily against the glass bowl.

And then she couldn't really pretend it was Ruth anymore, in the storage room.

But still—Jane couldn't look away from the door.

She couldn't even blink.

She heard Ruth call from downstairs, "Janie, I'm home!"

But Jane kept watching the storage-room door.

She kept watching.

Kept

watching

Until the light flicked off.

And the doorknob started to turn . . .

Slowly, slowly, the door opened an inch. . . .

Jane could hear her blood in her ears, and she squeezed her eyes shut so firmly that stars danced across the black of her eyelids.

And then Ruth's voice again and the sound of footsteps in the foyer.

"Honey, you ready for dinner?"

Jane's eyes snapped open.

And her feet came unstuck.

And she ran.

She was very, very good

Jane launched herself down the stairs so quickly she almost tripped; she only just managed to grab the railing before plummeting forward, half falling down the last few steps. Ruth wasn't in the foyer anymore, but Jane found her already in the kitchen, holding a plastic bag of Chinese food. Jane ran up behind her, skidding, slamming her hip into the side of a counter.

Ruth jumped. "Jesus, Jane, what's the big rush?" Then she saw her daughter's face, and her eyes narrowed. "Honey? What's wrong?"

"There's...somebody..." Jane couldn't catch her breath; it felt like her lungs were broken, collapsing in on themselves, not holding any air.

"Sweetheart, calm down. Tell me what's the matter," Ruth said, her eyes big now, her expression scared.

"Upstairs," Jane finished finally. "Mom, *there's somebody upstairs.*"

Ruth blinked, unsure. "Honey, we've been through this—"

"Not like before," Jane said, gulping for air. "Not like before. There's someone here. I...I *saw* them."

More accurately, she had seen their shadow, but she *had* to make Ruth believe her. And it worked—Ruth grabbed Jane's arm with her free hand and dragged her deeper into the kitchen. She didn't turn on the light. She walked calmly over to the fridge and set the food inside it, then she pulled her phone out of her pocket and dialed 911.

That small gesture—Ruth putting the food into the fridge—made a manic laugh rise up in Jane's chest. She clamped her hands over her mouth so it wouldn't escape, so she wouldn't end up hysterically laughing while her mother called the police and told them there was an intruder in the house.

But the laughter died away as quickly as it had come, replaced with ice-water terror, a wash of sickly cold that ran through Jane's body like it was in her very veins. She removed her hands from her mouth and wrapped them around her stomach. She felt like she was going to throw up.

Ruth spoke quietly into the receiver, telling them there was a break-in, that someone was still in the house, giving them the address of North Manor in a clear, steady voice that did not shake or waver.

"The back door will be unlocked," she whispered into the phone. "I am getting my daughter out of this house."

And she pressed the End button, put the phone back into her pocket, and calmly grabbed a butcher knife from the knife block on the counter. Jane could not take her eyes off the blade of the knife, how the moonlight that found its way through the windows and into the kitchen glinted off the metal, how her mother's hand tested the weight for one quick second before she whispered, harshly, "Shit."

"What?" Jane asked frantically.

"Go to the mudroom," Ruth said, her voice a low growl.

"Where are you going?"

"The car keys. They're on the front table."

"But you can't—"

"The mudroom, Jane. Go wait for me in the mudroom."

And Ruth picked up another knife, a smaller knife but one just as sharp and glinting, and put it into Jane's hands. Jane felt another panicked laugh rising in her chest as Ruth turned away from her.

"Mom," Jane started, but Ruth hissed *"Shh"* sharply, and Jane was silent.

And then Ruth was gone.

And Jane felt stuck to the floor, unable to move, and a dozen years passed and then a dozen more and then a hundred, and finally, she ripped her feet from the tile floor and ran out of the kitchen, ran into the mudroom, her heart beating a mile a minute, her stomach twisted into knots and her hands already hurting from how fiercely she held the knife.

Only a few seconds passed before Ruth reappeared, the

car keys in the same hand as the one that held the knife. She unlocked the mudroom door and pushed it open and grabbed Jane's arm with her other hand, and they slipped out into the night. Jane couldn't help looking up to the second floor; there were no lights on up there but she swore she saw something move away from the storage-room window. She swore she saw a curtain falling back into place.

"Mom," she tried again, but Ruth didn't reply, only removed her grip on Jane's arm, grabbing her hand, squeezing it as they took off at a run around the side of the house.

Jane saw the headlights flash as Ruth unlocked the car. They hurried to get inside. As soon as Jane's door was closed, Ruth started the engine and threw the car into reverse, pulling out of the driveway so quickly the tires squealed.

"We're safe," she said. "We're safe. We're okay."

She threw the butcher knife into the back seat. Jane did the same.

The car shot into the street, and Ruth threw it into drive and peeled away from the house. Jane looked back again—she couldn't help herself—and this time the light in her bedroom was on.

And then it flicked off.

"Did you see that?" she choked. "That light?"

"We're safe," Ruth repeated.

They reached the main road, and Ruth took a left, barely slowing for the stop sign. "Where are you going?" Jane asked.

"The police station. Honey . . . what happened?"

"I took a shower. And I heard something. A person. Like a person, just walking, and sort of...bumping into something, maybe. I thought it was you, at first. But then I saw a light. In the storage room."

"The storage room?"

"Except it's not a storage room anymore," Jane said. "Did you know that? It's another bedroom. And I think...I think someone has been *living* in it."

She remembered the lights she'd seen in the upstairs window when they first moved into the house, the hand pressed against the glass—that was the storage-room window! She hadn't put it together before, but everything weird happening in the house seemed to center around that room.

"A bedroom?" Ruth repeated. "I don't understand."

"You haven't been in there? Since we got here?"

"No," Ruth said, after a moment's pause. "I don't know. It was always just a storage room."

"Maybe when the house was empty for all these years... Do you think it's possible that someone...moved in?" Jane asked, her words coming faster and faster, a panic rising in her voice, something clawing at her chest.

"I think I would have known if someone was living in our house, Jane," Ruth said, her voice quiet, her hands clenching the steering wheel purposefully, her eyes staring straight ahead at the dark road in front of them.

Jane crossed her arms over her chest, hugging herself to try to stop the shivers that didn't go away, not even with heat blasting out of the vents. She couldn't stop thinking of Ruth so calmly placing the Chinese food in the fridge. She couldn't stop thinking of the kitchen knives, gently rattling against each other in the back seat.

"I almost went and opened the door," she whispered after a minute.

"We're safe," Ruth said, for the fourth time, and Jane found that it lost meaning with every repetition. They were words. Just two words. Three words. Two and a half words. Did a contraction count as two separate words? She put her hands over her face and breathed in deeply.

"I thought it was you," she continued. "I mean, I didn't really think it was you, but it was like my brain was *making* it you. Because the alternative was too scary. Does that make sense?"

Jane thought she would scream if Ruth said *We're safe* again, and she was relieved when, instead, her mother removed her right hand from the steering wheel and set it firmly on Jane's leg. She squeezed.

A flash to Greer driving. Ruth in the passenger seat. Jane in the back seat. Suitcases piled on the seat next to her. Where were they going? A road trip. One of Greer's impossibly long arms stretching into the back seat, finding his daughter's leg, squeezing it just above the knee, tickling her. Her laughter filling the car. Some nonfiction book on tape playing from the speakers. Ruth shushing everyone half-jokingly, turning it up.

Jane put her hand on top of Ruth's hand and she was back,

solidly, in the moment. And Greer was dead. And there would be no more family road trips. And it was freezing, and this wasn't California, and someone had been in their house. And, and, and.

"I'm just glad I got home when I did," Ruth said. But there was something different in her voice, something Jane didn't understand. A hesitation that hadn't been there before.

They arrived at the police station a few minutes later. Ruth let the engine idle for a moment, her hand hovering over the key in the ignition like she wasn't quite ready to leave the safety of the car.

"I'm in my pajamas," Jane said.

"I'm sure they've seen it all," Ruth replied. She turned the car off and got out.

Jane followed her.

Ruth introduced herself to the person at the front desk, a young policewoman in uniform who, when they entered, had been taking a sip from a bright-blue travel mug. She had short, curly brown hair and brown skin and long eyelashes, and she listened intently as Ruth explained who they were, then tapped a few things into her computer and read something on the screen.

"It looks like the patrol cars have arrived at your house, Mrs. North. Please take a seat, and we'll let you know as soon as we hear anything."

She gestured to a row of metal chairs to her right. Her badge said STEVENS. Ruth and Jane went and sat. Jane picked up a copy of *National Geographic* that was five months old.

Ruth chose a *Good Housekeeping* but didn't read it, just flicked through it wordlessly, one page after another after another, her eyes unfocused and unblinking. It made Jane nervous.

Every few minutes Ruth looked up from the magazine and over at her daughter—quick, fleeting glances that Jane tried to meet but kept missing.

Fifteen minutes passed. A half hour. And then the front door to the police station opened and a few cops walked in. Jane saw her mother sit up a little straighter. One of the cops, a man about Ruth's age, started for the front desk, but saw the two of them and walked over.

"Ruthellen North. I almost didn't believe it," he said. Ruth stood up and shook his offered hand.

"Freddie," she said. Then: "I'm sorry. Officer Elton."

He waved his hand: *Don't bother with the formalities.* "We checked it out. Every inch of that place. Nothing out of the ordinary at all. Can you tell me what happened?"

They sat down again, and Officer Elton swung one of the metal chairs around so it was facing them.

"I was out getting Chinese food," Ruth said. "My daughter was home. Freddie, this is Jane."

Freddie turned to Jane and stuck out his hand. They shook, then he hesitated, his eyes studying her face in a way that made her vaguely uncomfortable. He took his hand back and exhaled.

"Wow. You look exactly like her."

"Like who?" Jane asked.

"Like me," Ruth said pointedly. "When I was your age."

"I do?"

Jane had only seen a few photographs of Ruth as a teenager, but her mother had always had short hair and a different nose, straighter and narrower. Jane didn't think they looked that similar at all.

"People have said it," Ruth said. "Freddie, maybe we could talk privately? I don't want to upset my daughter further. It's been a stressful night."

"But I have to tell him what happened," Jane said.

"I'll tell him, Jane," Ruth replied. "That's okay, Freddie?"

But she said it in a way that gave Freddie no other choice. He nodded and stood up, and they left Jane alone, feeling uncomfortable, feeling a bit like she was left out of a joke everyone else was a part of.

She pulled her phone out of her pocket. It was just after eight. She had a text from Sal.

Ok? weirdo

Jane narrowed her eyes at the text. It had popped up on her home screen, so she couldn't see what had come before it. Had she texted Sal after they'd gotten off the phone? What was Sal replying to?

She opened her messages and read the one before it, what she'd sent to Sal:

Everything is so good. Everything is perfect. I love it here.

And the one Sal had sent before that:

Sorry I had to get off the phone so quickly. Going out to dinner with fam. Ily

Jane's hands were shaking just a little. She couldn't tell if it was from the cold or from her nerves. Probably both.

She hadn't sent that message. Had she sent that message?

She looked at the time stamp. Just ten minutes or so after they'd hung up from FaceTime. Jane would have been in the shower.

I love it here.

She hadn't sent that message. She *wouldn't* have sent that message.

But she was so tired. She had probably sent it off without even thinking about it, meaning to be funny, lighthearted. She couldn't worry about it; she couldn't worry about *anything*, because her head was pounding and there wasn't room in her brain for anything other than the headache that was slowly blossoming behind her eyes. She brought her knees up to her chest and rested her forehead on them, closing her eyes to block out the harsh fluorescent lights of the police station.

She kept seeing the shadow pass in front of the storage-room door. But with every repetition of the vision, it got vaguer and vaguer, until she hadn't actually seen anything, until she'd made the whole thing up.

It felt like a long time before Officer Elton and Ruth came back.

Ruth looked tired. She stopped in front of Jane and put a hand on her cheek. "Come on, honey. Officer Elton is going to follow us home and make sure we're all settled in."

Officer Elton followed them outside and got into his cruiser as Jane folded herself into the passenger seat of their car. Ruth started the ignition and backed out of the parking spot. She waited a minute or two, then cleared her throat.

"Honey—"

"Do you think I made it up?" Jane asked, but what she meant was probably closer to *"Did* I make it up?" because she honestly had no idea, and having no idea felt even scarier to her than if someone *had* been in the house. She just wanted to know, one way or the other, and not knowing made her feel weird and untethered and scared.

Ruth took a deep breath. "I don't know. Of course I don't think you made it up, honey, but I do believe Freddie, and he says they searched every inch of that place. No windows open, no doors unlocked, nothing taken or out of place." Ruth paused. "I don't know, Jane. I don't think you made anything up; of *course* I don't. But sometimes our minds play tricks on us. Especially at night, especially when we're alone. And, Janie…it's been a very hard couple of months. I believe without a doubt that you heard and saw something. I just don't think I believe that what you heard and saw was actually real."

"So I'm seeing things."

"I think that's oversimplifying it," Ruth said. "I think you've had a tremendous loss. And grief manifests itself in unpredictable ways."

"Okay," Jane said, because she didn't know what else to say. Because there *wasn't* anything else to say.

They got to the driveway, and Jane glanced behind her to see the cruiser pull in after them.

The cops had left the entranceway chandelier on, but other than that, the windows of the house were dark.

"Why did you want to talk to the officer in private?" Jane asked suddenly, not knowing where the question had come from.

I don't want to upset my daughter further.

Ruth looked over at Jane. She looked tired, sad. She sighed and rubbed at her eyes.

"I don't know, Janie. I don't know what to do anymore. Every time I make up my mind one way or the other, I always end up doubting myself."

"I don't know what you mean."

Ruth laughed softly. "I'm just trying to figure it all out. This new life. This loss. Greer... I know I'm the mom here, and I'm trying to keep everything together, to be there for you, but... I'm worried that I'm failing. That I'm not doing a good enough job. I don't know, honey. I don't know how to do this."

Of course, Jane thought, because she wasn't the only one who'd lost someone. Greer had been her father, but he'd also been Ruth's husband. They had both lost him in different ways.

Jane reached over and took her mom's hand. "I'm sorry," she said.

"Oh, honey. I'm the one who's sorry," Ruth replied, squeezing Jane's fingers. She smiled—weakly—then opened her door and met Officer Elton in front of the car. Jane waited a minute and joined them.

"How are you holding up?" Officer Elton asked Jane.

"Fine," Jane said, even though she felt about as far from *fine* as humanly possible.

Officer Elton clapped his hands together softly. "All right, then. Shall we?"

They went inside.

Officer Elton led the way, turning on lights as he went, talking loudly. Jane got the impression that he was trying to fill up the house with light and noise in an effort to make them feel comfortable. He made a show of opening doors and cabinets and even the silverware drawer. Jane saw the missing knives from the block on the counter and realized they'd left them in the back seat of the car.

Officer Elton pushed on, from kitchen to living room to sitting room to piano room to Chester's study to the mudroom, then finally back to the foyer of the house, where the chandelier was blazing brightly above them. Jane looked up at it. She wondered how much it was worth. A plane ticket to Los Angeles, at least.

"Let's head to the second floor," Officer Elton said, pointing his chin up the stairs.

"I'm sure Jane is starving," Ruth said. "Honey, why don't you go warm us up some of that Chinese food. Freddie, can we make you a plate?"

"No thanks, Ruth, I'm okay."

"I'll come upstairs with you," Ruth said.

Jane watched them walk up the staircase, then shrugged to nobody in particular and went back to the kitchen. Every light in the house was on. She turned off a few as she went.

She got the Chinese food out of the fridge and made two plates. She didn't feel hungry at all, just tired and a little scared. She kept getting the sudden desire to look over her shoulder, to check behind closed doors. But she didn't let herself. She put one plate into the microwave and ate it while the second one warmed up. The food seemed tasteless in her mouth—even the fried rice, her favorite. She choked it down like it was made out of cardboard.

Something was nagging at the back of her mind, something that couldn't have possibly been true....

Melanie had been to her house once before.

Melanie had thrown a rock through the window.

But vandalism was one thing.... Would Melanie really have broken into North Manor?

Jane put her face in her hands. She couldn't tell what was real anymore; she couldn't tell what was reasonable and what was impossible. Her brain felt overloaded, unsure of whom to trust, including herself. Had she sent that text message to Salinger? It must have been her—it was her phone.

But why couldn't she remember sending it?

It was an unsettling feeling.... Was it possible someone else had used her phone? If it *was* Melanie, had she come into Jane's bedroom to send those messages?

But *why*? Why would Melanie take Jane's phone only to send a fairly benign text message to Sal? And what about the FaceTime calls?

No, something had to be wrong with her phone. She would look it up in the morning, find some glitch in the software.

She took another bite of her dinner and made herself chew and swallow.

She heard Freddie and her mom walking around upstairs, creaking floorboards announcing wherever they went. The noise was directly above the kitchen now, so Jane guessed they were in the storage room.

Ruth had seemed surprised when Jane told her the storage room wasn't actually a storage room, but she had also hesitated, as though she'd been trying to choose her next words carefully.

The microwave dinged for the second plate of food just as Ruth and Freddie walked into the kitchen.

"We can't thank you enough, Freddie," Ruth said.

"Just doing my job," he said, then turned toward Jane. "I was telling your mother: I'm going to have the night shift make a few rounds by the house tonight. Just to make sure everything's quiet over here. Hope that'll ease your mind a little."

Jane forced a smile. "Thanks."

"You ladies try and get some rest. I'll call you tomorrow, Ruthellen."

"Let me walk you to the door," she replied.

She was gone only a minute. In the silence of the house, Jane heard the dead bolt slide shut with a resonant *clank*.

Ruth came back and got her plate of food and sat across from Jane.

"What a night," she said quietly.

"We left the knives in the car," Jane said.

"Very dramatic, in hindsight," Ruth observed. "But the adrenaline kicked in."

"Do you think you would have actually stabbed someone?"

"To protect you? I wouldn't think twice."

A moment, then: "I'm sorry," Jane said.

"You have nothing to be sorry for."

"But nothing happened. I made the whole thing up."

"Let's talk about it tomorrow. Let's just get in bed and watch a movie until we fall asleep, okay? We can put the bureau in front of the door."

"You want to do that?"

"If it would make you feel better," Ruth said.

"I'm going to be so tired tomorrow."

"Then stay home."

"I can't. I'm still catching up."

"That's where we're different," Ruth pointed out. "If Emilia ever gave me the option of staying home from school, I wouldn't have given her a chance to change her mind. PJs all day. Wouldn't have even brushed my teeth."

"Did you not like school?"

"Hated it," Ruth replied. "I was always getting into trouble."

"What kind of trouble?" Jane asked, leaning her elbows on the table to get a little closer. Ruth rarely talked about herself as a young girl, and Jane didn't want to miss a word.

"Oh, for silly things," Ruth said. Her eyes were glazed, like she was a million miles away. "I could be kind of a punk back then."

That word. *Punk*. Greer's word. Jane could almost hear his voice now, echoing around them in the kitchen.

"What do you mean? What did you do?" Jane asked.

Ruth shook her head and blinked. She tapped the side of her plate with her fork. "This sure hits the spot, huh?"

Jane smiled sadly. She knew by her mother's tone that Ruth was done reminiscing. They finished their food in silence, put the dishes in the sink, then walked around, turning off all the lights Officer Elton had turned on.

They met again at the bottom of the stairs.

"So what do you think?" Ruth asked. "Want to sleep with me tonight?"

"I'm okay," Jane said. "I think I'll just stay in my own bed."

Ruth smiled—a tired smile. "You've always been that way, you know. Even as a kid. Never crawled in bed with us."

They let the word *us* have a wide berth. They let it explode into fireworks above their heads. Jane missed her father more than she had ever missed him yet, a great, huge tsunami of missing him that made her physically sway where she stood.

Ruth misinterpreted. She saw the sway and put a hand on Jane's elbow.

"You look exhausted, baby. Let's go get some sleep."

Once she was in her room, alone, Jane locked the door and paused for a moment before dragging her bookshelf in front of it. Then she took *The Lion, the Witch, and the Wardrobe* and sat on the floor. Just one page. The familiar medicine of ink and paper dissolving in her stomach.

She started to cry.

She removed her phone from her pocket, opened up her messages, and found Greer's listing. The last message he'd ever sent her. A stab of pain in her gut as she read that one word.

She clicked his name and hit Call, then held the phone to her ear, hands shaking as it went straight to voicemail.

"Hiya! Greer here. Leave a message and I'll get back to you when I can."

She clicked End.

She didn't know when Ruth would get around to canceling Greer's cell phone. Maybe her mother kept it active for just this reason—so she could call and hear her husband's voice whenever she wanted.

Jane held the phone tightly in her hands, shutting her eyes, feeling the tears drip hotly down her cheeks.

Would she ever feel safe again?

Would she ever feel safe, without her father?

She listened into the stillness of the house, knowing she wouldn't sleep a wink that night, and thought, *No.*

She was predictably exhausted the next morning, moving through her routine sluggishly: shower, clothes, breakfast. Ruth was practically drowning herself in coffee when Jane reached the kitchen. There was a pot of oatmeal bubbling on the stove; she got herself a bowl and sprinkled brown sugar on top. It was something she had never had before moving to New England, oatmeal and brown sugar, but it had become a staple in their mornings now. She poured herself a cup of coffee and joined Ruth at the table. Ruth grunted a greeting.

"Ditto," Jane said.

"How are we going to get through this week?" Ruth said, almost to herself, almost to Jane, then she pulled herself up a little straighter in her seat and saw the oatmeal. "Oh yeah. I forgot about that."

Jane pushed the bowl over to her mother and got up to make herself another one.

"I made you lunch," Ruth said.

"How long have you been up?"

"Since yesterday morning."

"You didn't sleep?" Jane asked, sitting back down.

"I gave it my best try. But nope. Instead I've been going through my dad's old things, trying to clear out his study. Say what you want about my father, but that man was *diligent* in his record keeping. It's really excellent stuff for someone who can't sleep. I found a receipt from a root canal he had done *twenty-five years ago.*"

"I'm assuming you're putting that in the 'keep' pile?"

"Oh, I'm keeping plenty. Dental records aren't making the cut." Ruth had a bite of oatmeal.

"You work today, right?"

"Just a few hours. I'm going to call it a half day. You?"

"Yup."

"Are you working too much, Janie? How's your school-work going? Not falling behind at all, right?"

"Not yet. Oh yeah—do you know Tim Barker? He said to say hi. How come everyone here calls you Ruthellen?"

"Tim Barker," Ruth repeated. "Wow. I guess I underestimated how long I could fly under the radar here. Two weeks seems to be my limit."

"Ruthellen?"

"Oh. God, I know. That was an Emilia thing. Ruthellen was a family name. A great-great-aunt or something. And Emilia could not abide nicknames. Practically clutched her pearls into dust when I told her I was naming you Jane."

"She didn't like my name?"

"Oh, honey. She had an opinion about everything. And her opinion about *Jane* was that it wasn't a big enough name for a North. I said, 'Well, she isn't a North, Mama. She's a North-Robinson.'" Ruth chuckled. "She didn't like that answer very much."

"Did she like Dad?"

Ruth sighed. "That's a little complicated. I mean, everything is a little complicated with Emilia. But she didn't like that I left Maine. She didn't like that Greer lived in California.

She didn't like that I never visited. She always blamed him for that. Even though I told her, again and again, he had nothing to do with it. In the beginning, he was constantly suggesting we take a trip back east. He wanted to see where I grew up. But I kept saying no, and he finally stopped mentioning it."

"You kept saying no because..."

Ruth smiled. "You live in this house now, Janie. Why do you think I never wanted to come back?"

Jane couldn't think of a suitable answer to that.

She finished her oatmeal and washed her bowl, setting it down to dry just as Susie texted.

The first thing Susie said when Jane climbed into the car was, "Did you hear all the sirens last night?"

Jane's skin prickled uncomfortably. She settled her backpack at her feet and adjusted the air vents. "I heard them, yeah."

"They sounded close."

Susie backed out of the driveway as Jane wondered whether to tell her. She hadn't thought about it yet, but she couldn't really see any reason not to.

"They *were* close. They were at my house."

"Wait—really? Is everything okay?"

"Everything's okay. It was all just a big, weird...I don't know what it was," Jane said truthfully. "My mom went out to get Chinese food and...I heard something. I thought someone was in the house."

"Oh my gosh, Jane, that's so scary. What happened?"

"They didn't find anything. The cops. There was nobody there."

"But you did the right thing," Susie said firmly. "Either way. Better safe than sorry."

Jane paused. She chose her words carefully. "I'm not convinced they're right."

"What do you mean?"

"I just...I don't know. I have this terrible feeling. About that house. I know, I'm probably just..."

"Look—we haven't known each other that long, Jane, but you don't seem like an alarmist to me," Susie said. "Otherwise, you probably wouldn't have agreed to move into that house in the first place."

Jane laughed. "Why, because it's creepy?"

Susie shot her a quick sideways look and said, after just a moment's hesitation. "Yeah. Because it's creepy."

Jane bit her bottom lip. "Can I tell you something?"

"Of course."

"I'm wondering...if maybe Melanie had something to do with it...."

"Melanie?"

"I just...I had this super-weird interaction with her yesterday, and...I don't know. It's probably nothing."

Susie exhaled. "I don't think Melanie would do something like...like break into someone's house."

"I don't know," Jane said. "I'm not saying she did...."

"But you're not ready to say she *didn't*, either," Susie finished.

"Yeah. I'm not."

Susie didn't have an answer for that.

Jane moved through the morning half-asleep, and when she got to lunch, Susie took one look at her and said, "Okay, we have to get this girl a coffee."

"Field trip?" Alana said, perking up at once.

"Field trip," Susie confirmed. "Meet me at my car in five. I'll sign you guys out."

Susie headed to the office, and Jane and Alana walked to their lockers together.

"How are you doing?" Jane asked when they were alone.

"Oh," Alana said, shrugging. "I'm okay. It's really sad, obviously. But I feel sort of...I don't know. Like an outsider. I mean, I'm not as sad as Melanie, because it was her sister. And I'm not as sad as my mom, because it was her niece. I feel like I'm almost on the periphery. Like if I'm *too* sad, I'm, like, embellishing my sadness or something." She paused and made a face. "Does that make any sense?"

"I've had all those same thoughts," Jane admitted softly. "Even though he was my dad, I kept wondering—does my mom get to be sadder? Does *his* mom? Does his brother? I think the important thing to realize, to try and remember, is that grief doesn't have a rule book. You're allowed to feel every emotion under the sun. You're even allowed to invent new ones. I think I've done that a few times."

Alana smiled weakly. "Thanks, Jane. That's actually really helpful."

"I saw Melanie yesterday," Jane said cautiously. "I didn't expect her to be back already."

"I know. I guess her mom tried to get her to take more time, but . . . maybe she needs the distraction or something."

"Sometimes the longer you take, the harder it is to get back to a normal life," Jane said. "Or . . . the new normal."

Jane wanted to tell Alana about how weird Melanie had been, how strangely volatile their exchange had been, but for some reason she didn't. Melanie was in pain. Didn't Jane herself understand exactly how much pain she was in?

Alana grabbed her jacket from her locker, then they walked to Jane's locker together. And although nothing huge was out of place, although the door was shut and it was locked, Jane paused. The number dial was on 15. The last number of her combination. Jane always put the dial to 0 after she closed the door.

"What's wrong?" Alana asked.

"Nothing," Jane said. But she put in her combination more slowly than usual, turning to each number at a snail's pace.

When she finally opened the door, a cascade of fabric and papers and broken bits of pens and pencils spilled out onto her feet. Everything that had been in her locker was torn to shreds, destroyed. Jane picked up a swatch of fabric—her jacket, cut up into tiny pieces. She removed the lifeless spine of a hardcover book, her chemistry textbook, all the papers ripped out and tumbling out of the locker.

"What the fuck?" Alana said, taking the piece of cloth from Jane. "Is this your jacket? Jane, what the hell is all this?"

"Yeah," Jane confirmed, slamming the locker door so suddenly and violently that Alana jumped and dropped the fabric she was holding. "My jacket. My books. My things. *Everything.*"

"Jane...Who...?"

"Melanie. *Obviously* this was Melanie."

Jane closed her eyes. She tried to hear Greer's voice in her head, the voice of reason, one of the only voices in the entire world that could calm her down when she felt like she might explode. But Greer was gone; Greer didn't have a voice anymore.

Alana was still talking, but Jane couldn't tell what she was saying. It sounded like her words were coming from underwater, a stream of senseless syllables that meant nothing.

Jane could hear the blood rushing in her head, pulsing in her ears.

She was going to kill her.

She was going to kill her she was going to kill her she was—

"Jane!" Alana's voice cut through the chaos of Jane's internal monologue and Jane's eyes opened, surprised. "It's okay," Alana continued. "I'll get her to replace it. All of it. I'll talk to my mom. I don't know why she would do this. I honestly think...I mean, I don't want to make excuses for her—I know she's just so, so sad, this whole thing...She was really close with her sister."

Maybe it was the shock of hearing Alana raising her voice when she was usually so calm and chill that snapped Jane out of it, but it worked....Jane breathed in slowly. She felt herself returning to her body. The sound of blood rushing in her ears dulled to a gentle background noise.

"Are you okay?" Alana asked quietly. "You turned bright red."

"Just a little angry," Jane replied, struggling to keep her voice calm.

"I totally understand. I'm so sorry."

"You don't have to talk to your mom. It's fine. I don't want to get anyone else involved. I just want to ignore it. Ignore everything. Until it goes away."

"Okay," Alana said, nodding. "Okay, I get it. I won't say anything. But if you change your mind..."

"I'll let you know."

"Are you okay? Do you still want to get a coffee?"

"Yeah. Definitely." She made herself smile. She gestured at the floor, at everything that had fallen out of her locker. "What about this?"

"Here," Alana said. She took her own jacket off and spread it out on the floor, using it to collect all the pieces. Then she poked her head into the nearest empty classroom and dumped everything into the trash.

"Thanks," Jane said.

"I'll talk to Rosemary," Alana promised. "I'll get you new

books. And here—do you want to wear this? I'm fine." She held out her jacket.

"No, thanks. That's sweet." Jane smiled.

"Okay," Alana replied. She seemed unsure of what to do next, filled with a nervous energy.

"Let's go. Susie's waiting for us," Jane said, still smiling.

She was getting really good at making herself smile.

They told Susie what had happened as they drove to Beans & Books, and Susie, after launching into an impressive stream of expletives aimed at Melanie, finally quieted down and let out a hiss of air. "What is *wrong* with her?" she asked. Then, a moment later, "I mean...aside from...you know."

"There's no excuse for doing that to Jane's things," Alana said, her voice even and calm. "No excuse."

"I have to ask," Susie said. "Are we *sure* it's her? I mean, it's probably her. But are we sure?"

"We're not sure," Jane admitted. "But...I just know."

"Melanie once cut the feet off every single one of my Barbie dolls," Alana said flatly. "We're sure it's her."

"Damn," Susie said. "What an *asshole*."

Just the way she said it—so earnestly and simply—made Jane burst out laughing, and pretty soon they were all laughing, which felt really, really good, and served to vanquish any remaining anger in Jane's body. Alana laughed the longest, burying her head in her lap and shaking uncontrollably in the front seat, and Jane wondered if it felt just as good for Alana as it felt for her—to laugh that much.

"Okay, okay," Susie said. "So we're all in agreement: It was Melanie. Jane, what are you going to do about it?"

"Nothing," Jane replied without any hesitation.

"I want to tell my mom," Alana said, finally pulling herself together. "Or Mel's mom."

"It's just not worth it," Jane continued. "Especially not with everything she's going through. I'm just going to ignore it and hope she doesn't do anything else."

"In that case, we need to do something to take your mind off it," Susie said. "What about a movie night at my house Friday? My parents are taking the twins out of town. You can both sleep over, and we'll order pizza or something. Jane—we haven't even hung out outside of school yet," she pointed out.

"Sounds great!" Alana said.

"Sounds fun," Jane echoed. "Should we watch a scary movie? For Halloween?"

"Absolutely not," Alana said. "I hate scary movies."

"But don't you love Halloween?" Jane asked.

"Love Halloween, *hate* scary movies," Alana clarified.

"Well, sorry, but you're outnumbered," Susie chimed in. "I have to side with Jane on this one."

"Ugh, *nooo*," Alana said, and for the rest of the car ride, she kept up a nonstop barrage of romantic-comedy movie suggestions, of which Jane and Susie rejected every single one.

Jane avoided Melanie for the rest of the week, keeping her

head down when they passed each other in the hallways. Alana came through with a new set of textbooks, and Susie insisted on giving Jane a half dozen spiral-ring notebooks and a handful of new pens.

Ruth remained busy with her new job and came home tired and quiet; most nights, Jane cooked herself dinner and ate alone and did her homework at the kitchen table.

North Manor was quiet, too. There wasn't so much as a strange creak of the floorboards. No unexplained shadows. No marbles. No rose petals. Nothing.

On Friday, Jane worked at Beans & Books after school, then went home to shower. She'd been looking forward to movie night, partly for the selfish chance to see what Susie's house was like. Was it as big and creepy as North Manor? Did it make the same strange noises, the same sounds of settling Ruth kept telling her she'd get used to?

She hadn't told her mother about her coat. She had saved enough from working that she could replace it on her own, and Susie had agreed to take her to the mall that weekend to get it. She just didn't want to bother Ruth about it. She had enough on her mind. She'd sent a text that afternoon saying she'd had another busy day and worked right through lunch. She was getting dinner with a coworker after work, though, so at least she was making friends.

Making friends! Jane had replied.

Making money, Ruth responded, adding a winky face.

Jane took a quick shower, dried herself off, and walked

over to her window. She moved aside the curtain and looked out at the front yard. It was already so dark, and the sky was a menacing deep gray. The weather people had been warning about snow flurries for a while, but so far there had been nothing more substantial than frost. Maybe tonight would finally be the night.

She heard a buzzing on her bed and found her phone on the covers. A message from Susie to her and Alana.

Terrible news. My parents canceled their trip last minute, and the twins have already claimed the basement for the night.

Another message popped up from Alana: *Noooooooo*

Jane let the phone drop while she toweled off her hair and slipped into her sweatpants. When she picked it up again, there were five new messages.

Susie: *Alana, can we do it at your house?*

Alana: *Negative. My cousins are here from New York. Barely room to turn around in this house.*

Susie: *Should we go to the movies?*

Alana: *Still closed for renovations remember?*

Susie: *Ugh, great. Well, I guess we reschedule?*

Jane hesitated before sending a message back. *We can do it here? My mom is working late. No pressure though. We can reschedule.*

Did she *want* the girls to come over to North Manor? Not particularly, but she also didn't want to be alone right now. And with Ruth out of the house, it made sense.

Susie: *I'm down! Are you sure?*

Alana: *Yes I'm in!*

Jane: *Yeah, totally. Come over whenever.*

Jane tossed the phone down again and finished getting dressed, slipping on a T-shirt and pulling a zip-up hoodie over it.

It took about fifteen minutes before she began to wonder whether this was a terrible idea—but by then, Susie had already texted to say she was on her way to pick Alana up, so Jane sucked it up and called the local pizza place. She ordered some pies and waited in the kitchen, holding her phone, looking at the last messages she'd exchanged with Sal.

Sorry I had to get off the phone so quickly. Going out to dinner with fam. Ily

Everything is so good. Everything is perfect. I love it here.

Ok? weirdo

Reading them over made her stomach knot up in a strange way.

Why couldn't Jane remember sending that message? Was something wrong with her phone, or was something wrong with *her*? And why hadn't she talked to Sal since the night of the suspected break-in? Jane hadn't even *told* Sal about it. She used to tell Sal *everything*. So why was she keeping this from her?

Maybe because she knew Sal would try to rationalize it, try to convince Jane that nothing had happened. And Jane didn't need to hear a lecture on what she already knew.

When the doorbell finally rang a few minutes later, Jane made her way to the foyer and let Susie and Alana in. They were each holding an armful of snacks and wearing pajama pants.

"Hi!" Susie said.

"I never thought I'd see the inside of this house," Alana whispered, staring straight up at the ceiling. "Susie, look at that chandelier. Do you see it?"

Susie laughed. "Yes, I see it, Alana."

Jane closed the door behind them. "I ordered pizza."

"Great, I'm starving," Susie said. She took her jacket off and dropped it by the door with her backpack. "Where should we set up?" she asked, holding up the food.

"Oh, living room is this way," Jane said. She couldn't help noticing Alana, still looking around, her eyes wide and strange. "You okay, Alana?"

"Sorry. It's just a little . . . I never thought I'd be in here. It's a little sad."

"Sad?" Jane repeated. "What do you mean?"

Jane saw Susie shoot Alana a look, and Alana responded by shaking her head and forcing a smile. "Just that it was empty for so long, you know. That's all."

"Well, now Jane's here and all is well," Susie said, a cheerfulness in her voice that sounded just slightly forced.

"Yeah. Here I am," Jane said, holding out her hands awkwardly.

"Sorry," Alana mumbled. "I'm just hungry."

"No worries," Jane replied. "This way."

She led them through rooms, stealing glances behind her to see how quiet they both were, how wide-eyed they seemed as they looked around at everything they passed. Was that how she'd acted the first time she walked around this house? Probably. And it wasn't that much of a stretch to get a feeling of sadness, either—after all, Emilia *had* died here.

Trying to lighten the mood, she turned around suddenly and put on her best tour guide voice: "If you'll look to your left, you'll see original wallpaper from the 1800s. This paper was shipped over from Paris, where it was hand-painted by local artisans."

She'd expected her friends to laugh, but instead they just looked so fascinated that she ended up laughing instead.

"Wow, that's amazing!" Alana said earnestly.

"I totally made it up," Jane admitted.

"Sorry, are we being weird?" Susie asked. "It *is* really… I mean, this is a pretty famous house. Even outside of Bells Hollow."

"I get it," Jane said. "Do you guys… want a tour?"

"Absolutely!" Alana replied, and Susie nodded just as enthusiastically.

"Okay. Well, the living room is just through here, so you can drop the food off." She led them through one more set of pocket doors and they made a pile of snacks on one of the couches, then she showed them around the first floor, through the fancy dining room to the kitchen, back around past Chester's study, rooms that she honestly hadn't even been in since their first few days in the house.

Susie and Alana drank in everything, moving slowly. When they got to the piano room, Susie put a hand on the polished wood of the instrument and breathed out loudly.

"This is a 1925 model B Steinway," she whispered.

"How did you *know* that?" Jane asked.

"Susie is an amazing piano player," Alana said. "Play something, Susie."

"I think I'm going to pass out," Susie said. "Can I? I mean, am I allowed...?"

"Go for it," Jane said. "I don't think that thing's been touched in years."

Susie sat down on the bench slowly, almost reverently. She lifted the fallboard to reveal the keys underneath, and Jane had to stifle a laugh when she audibly gasped.

She began to play.

The song started out quiet at first, but gradually rose to a brilliant crescendo. The music seemed to fill North Manor in a way Jane had never experienced before. With sound, with light... It was beautiful.

She finished the song just as the doorbell rang. It could have been five minutes or fifty minutes; Jane was too transfixed to notice.

"Susie, that was..."

"Thanks," Susie said, getting up from the piano. "My parents gave me money for pizza. To apologize for making us change our plans."

They walked into the foyer and Susie dug her money out of

her backpack as Jane opened the door and took the pizzas from a girl their age.

"Oh, hey, Nettie!" Susie said, straightening up and handing her the cash.

Nettie didn't reply. Her eyes were wide and unblinking. She took the money and shoved it into her pocket without counting it.

"Nettie?" Alana said.

"When the address came up, I was like . . ."

But Nettie didn't say what she was like. She just stared into the house like she couldn't believe it was real.

"Is something wrong?" Jane asked.

"You guys are, like, staying here?" Nettie continued.

"I live here."

"Oh, I know," Nettie said. "I just mean, like, they're staying here . . . voluntarily?"

"No, I'm keeping them tied up in the basement," Jane snapped, annoyed. "I just let them out because I needed help with the pizzas."

Nettie looked at Jane finally, her eyes focusing, narrowing. "I heard this house makes people crazy," she said. "You guys should be careful."

"Okay," Susie said loudly. "Thanks for the pizzas, Nettie. See you at school."

She closed the door so quickly Nettie had to jump backward to avoid being hit.

"Well, I'm starving," Alana announced awkwardly.

"What the hell is her problem?" Jane asked.

"Nettie's weird," Susie said, taking the pizza boxes from Jane. "Honestly, who knows."

"This house makes people crazy?" Jane repeated. "Is she talking about my fucking dead grandmother?"

She felt the anger rising in her body. Her vision went to black.

"Um, are you going to beat Nettie up?" Alana asked, and her words seemed to wake Jane up a little—her hand was on the doorknob, she'd already pulled the door back open a few inches.

Jane looked at her hand. She couldn't even feel it. Had she opened the door?

She pushed it closed again. "Sorry. No. I don't...I was just trying to be funny."

"Oh, good!" Alana said. "You definitely looked like you were going to go beat her up."

Jane forced a laugh. "No! Gosh. You should see the looks on your faces. Let's eat, okay?"

"Yeah, sure," Susie said.

Jane swore she saw them exchange a look right before they turned around and walked back to the living room, but she tried not to let it bother her.

"Let me just get plates and napkins," she said when they reached the living room. She mostly succeeded in keeping her voice light, carefree. "The remote is in that drawer if you want to start looking for movies!"

She left Alana and Susie in the living room and made her way to the kitchen, where she put both of her palms on the cool granite countertop and took big, steadying breaths. It felt like Nettie's comments had sunk deep into her skin, unsettling and enraging her in a way that made her fingers tingle.

She needed to go upstairs. Just one page, that was what she needed. This had been a terrible idea, inviting Susie and Alana to this house.

She slipped out of the kitchen and took the back way to the foyer, moving quickly. She could be upstairs and back in just a few minutes; the girls wouldn't even notice.

She reached the foyer and put a hand on the banister—then she heard it.

Delicate piano music coming from the Steinway. A quiet, haunting melody.

She paused to listen, and as she did, she could feel her anger unwinding, loosening. She closed her eyes and let the music wash over her in gentle waves. Each individual note seemed to sink into her body, enveloping her, calming her.

She stepped away from the stairs and walked toward the piano room. She'd never heard this song before; it was so lonely, so *sad*, it almost brought tears to her eyes.

But when she reached the doorway of the room, she stopped dead in her tracks, the calm in her body replaced with a cold rush of fear.

Nobody was sitting at the piano bench.

Nobody was playing the piano.

The fallboard was closed; the keys were hidden.

Jane fell sideways a few inches, leaning her weight against the wall, suddenly cold, shivering.

No, no. That was impossible. It was Susie; it had to have been Susie. She'd just finished and gone back to the living room before Jane had gotten here.

Her brain was cloudy. She walked to the living room slowly. Susie and Alana were already eating; the pizza boxes were spread out on the coffee table.

"Hey, what song was that?" Jane asked, and she could hear how weird her voice sounded but she couldn't make it stop, she couldn't make it sound natural.

"What song?" Alana asked, her mouth full.

"The song you were playing on the piano just now."

"Oh, before? 'Clair de Lune.' It's Debussy."

"No, not before. Just now," Jane pressed.

"Just now I was playing the song of stuffing my face with pizza," Susie said, laughing.

"No, I mean, on the piano," Jane said, but she couldn't make her voice work the way it was supposed to; her words were just a whisper.

"Girl, are you okay?" Susie asked. "You look super pale. Come sit down. I'll get the plates."

"Just hungry," Jane whispered. Or maybe no words came out at all. She sat down in an armchair. She could feel Susie and Alana looking at each other again. She could feel them looking at each other, judging her. She could *feel* them—

"Here, got you some water," Susie said, suddenly kneeling in front of her, holding a glass of ice water. How had she gotten the water so fast? How had she gotten the plates and napkins?

"Thanks," Jane said. She took the glass and had a sip of water. "I think I just . . . didn't have enough to eat for lunch."

"I've been there," Alana said. "Your blood sugar tanked. Do you feel better after the pizza?"

"Yes," Jane said.

She'd eaten a slice of pizza. The dirty plate was resting on the arm of the chair. There was an aftertaste in her mouth, of cheese and tomato sauce.

The water was ice cold and felt good in her throat, in her stomach. It seemed to return her to the present, to clear the remaining cobwebs from her mind. Susie and Alana were being a little delicate with her but were otherwise normal. Alana was eating another slice of pizza, and Susie was scrolling through movie options. Things were normal. Things were okay.

Jane pulled her phone out of her pocket. She had meant to text Ruth before it got too late, to give her a heads-up that she had people over. She opened her messages and started to type before realizing they'd already texted.

Ruth had said, *Just finishing up dinner sweetie*

Jane had said, *Take your time, mama. I have friends over. We're having so much fun!*

Ruth had said, *haha, since when do you call me mama? Love you honey, glad you're having fun!*

Jane checked the timestamps. Just about five minutes ago.

But she was okay now. She felt better now. She just hadn't had enough to eat at lunch. Like Alana had said, her blood sugar had tanked.

She slid off the armchair and got herself another slice of pizza.

Susie picked a rom-com Jane had already seen before, but she pretended she hadn't.

It didn't escape Jane—that Susie had said she wanted to watch a scary movie, but she picked a romantic comedy now without acknowledging that she'd changed her mind.

This house was scary enough on its own, Jane thought.

Why would anyone want to add to that?

"Can you turn it up a little?" Jane asked a few minutes into the movie.

Susie turned it up.

"Thanks," Jane said.

But even though it was pretty loud, probably a little louder than it should have been . . .

Jane could still hear it.

Every few minutes, rising to a delicate resonance.

Piano music.

Susie and Alana slept together in one of the spare bedrooms, and Jane slept in her own bed, grateful to be alone. Her nerves were a wreck by the time she finally crawled underneath the covers. She removed a page from *The Lion, the Witch, and the Wardrobe* and ate it under the sheets, her hands quivering with every breath she took.

In the morning, Ruth got up before them and had pancakes waiting, and although Susie and Alana were perfectly polite and seemed fine, Jane knew they'd probably spent the entire night whispering about how weird she'd been, about how creepy this house was, about how they'd never step foot in there again.

She'd slept terribly, anyway, and she tried to engage in the morning conversation and be present, but she just kept yawning.

"Thanks, Mrs. North," Alana said when she finished.

"Those pancakes were honestly just as good as Sam's Diner," Susie added, walking her plate to the sink.

"The highest praise, Susie," Ruth replied, beaming.

"I should probably get going," Alana said. "My mom's making me spend time with my cousins before they leave."

"Same. I need to start that essay for English, otherwise I'll never finish by Monday," Susie added. "Jane, I'll text you later and we can run to the mall?"

"Sounds good."

"Thanks for everything, Jane!" Alana said, giving her a quick hug.

"Of course."

"That movie was kind of awful, but other than that it was fun," Susie said, hugging her, too. "Thanks, Mrs. North."

"Nice to meet you girls," Ruth said.

Susie and Alana left the kitchen, and Ruth raised an eyebrow at Jane.

"What?" Jane said.

"Shouldn't you walk your guests out?"

"They don't want me to, trust me."

"What are you talking about?"

"They're dying to get out of this house. Can you blame them?"

Jane got up from the table in a huff, leaving her untouched plate and storming out of the room. She just missed Alana and Susie leaving; the front door closed right as she reached the foyer and pounded up the stairs. She walked into the spare bedroom where they'd slept and started ripping the dirty sheets off the two twin beds, throwing them in a pile on the floor.

She started crying as she stripped one of the pillows of its pillowcase, and before she knew it, she felt arms wrapping around her from behind. She turned and let Ruth envelop her in a hug.

"Honey," Ruth whispered into her hair. "You want to tell me what's going on?"

"I hate this house," Jane sobbed. "I hate this town. I hate everyone here."

Ruth guided Jane over to one of the bare mattresses, and they sat down next to each other.

"I hear you, honey, and trust me, this isn't my favorite place in the world, either. But I'm not sure I'm following. Those girls seem like sweethearts. It sounds like everyone had a great time last night. So what's happening now?"

"They're lying. They're lying because they just wanted to get out of here as soon as they could."

She was crying so hard now her words were barely decipherable. Ruth put a hand on her face and paused, then moved it to her forehead.

"Oh, honey. You're burning up. We gotta get you in bed."

Jane let herself be pulled up and led across the hall to her own bedroom, where Ruth moved the covers back and gently guided her under the sheets.

"I'm fine," Jane protested weakly, still crying, her face hot and wet with tears. "I'm fine."

"You are not fine, baby. You're on fire, big-time. You must have caught a virus or something. God, I hope it's not the flu. We should've gotten flu shots before we left California." Ruth put her hand on Jane's forehead again and frowned. "Fuck, I don't have a thermometer or anything. Okay, I'm going to run into town quick, get you some Tylenol and a thermometer. Stay in bed. I won't be long. Got it?"

Jane nodded, and Ruth kissed her quickly on the forehead before leaving.

Jane rolled over and buried her head in her pillow. She felt a little better now that she was lying down, and she was worried she'd been really rude to Alana and Susie. She felt on her nightstand for her phone but it wasn't there. Where had she seen it last? At the kitchen table, maybe.

Her ears were thrumming with blood, a steady, oceanlike whoosh that drowned out all other noise. Maybe she really *was* sick, and everything that had happened last night was because of a fever she hadn't been aware of. She put her hand to her forehead now and her skin *did* feel hot.

She needed to text Susie and Alana and say sorry. She should have walked them out. She should have been a better host. She would tell them she hadn't felt well, that she was sick, and it would all be fine.

She sat up. Her head felt dangerously light. How long had Ruth been gone? How long would it take her to get back? She should just wait for her, she knew it, but she felt terrible about how she'd acted that morning. She would just run downstairs and run back up. It wouldn't take more than a minute.

She swung her legs over the side of the bed and stood up slowly, testing her weight, gently pushing herself upright.

The room swayed around her. She closed her eyes and took a deep breath, then started walking, putting one foot in front of the other slowly. She reached the doorway and put a hand on the wall for support, then pressed onward, down the hall, down the stairs, through the foyer, back to the kitchen.

Her phone was lying on the kitchen table. She picked it up and wrote a message in the group chat.

Thank you for coming over—I'm sorry if I was out of it. I have a fever. I think I didn't realize I was sick.

She slipped the phone into her pocket and put her hands on the back of a chair, steadying herself.

Thirty seconds passed. A minute. She closed her eyes and breathed in and out, in and out.

Her brain turned off, her legs buckled.

She gasped and tightened her grip on the chair.

Had she fallen asleep standing up?

She pulled her phone out of her pocket. It had been five minutes since she'd written the message. No one had replied yet. She needed to get back into bed.

It was a dark, gray morning. The house was cool and shadowy.

She had the chills.

She started walking.

And every step she took, it was like a heaviness was settling itself around her shoulders. Almost like something with weight and shape, something she could brush off.

Except she *couldn't* brush it off.

But her feet kept working.

Up and up.

Even as a little warning bell went off in the back of her head—

Stop stop stop.

But she didn't stop.

She kept going.

She reached the second-floor hallway.

All was quiet. All was normal.

And nothing was normal.

Jane knew that, too.

Nothing was normal. Nothing was normal about this house, about this town, about anything in her life.

Her head was pounding. Her skin was burning.

Nothing was normal.

She felt numb. A wave of delicate pins and needles, like coming out of anesthesia.

But still, she pressed on. She walked down the hallway. She opened her bedroom door. She turned on the light.

And she screamed—

Her room was trashed.

The bookcase was overturned, the sheets were ripped off her bed, one closet door hung forward on its hinges, the drawers had been pulled out of the bureau, and her clothes had been scattered everywhere. And on the floor in front of her, written in rose petals, arranged carefully, one next to the other next to the other, were the words: *do books taste like roses?*

Jane screamed again.

And from some corner of her brain, she heard pounding behind her—

Pounding, pounding, pounding—

Like running feet.

And then someone grabbed her from behind.

And she felt her knees buckle.

And she went limp—

And everything went dark.

But when she was bad

She woke up in a dark place.

A dark, bad place.

It smelled of earth and roses.

And she couldn't turn her head.

And she couldn't move her arms.

And there was a weight on her chest. The weight of something heavy. Pressing her down. Down into the earth. Down into the dirt. Was she in dirt? Her nose and her mouth were clogged with it. Yes, dirt. She was in dirt, in the rosebushes, buried. She'd been buried. She opened her mouth to scream but only let in more dirt. Choking with it. Sliding down her throat, grainy and dark.

And she couldn't turn her head.

And she couldn't move her arms—

Until she could.

And she came up kicking and flailing.

do books taste like roses?

"Whoa, whoa, Jane—calm down, calm down. It's okay. You're okay."

A familiar voice. A man's voice. A friend's voice.

She opened her eyes.

And everything was fuzzy at first, but then it slowly came into focus.

Will.

It was Will.

Hi, Will.

Her head hurt. She closed her eyes again.

One second, Will.

She tried to say something, but it just came out as a moan.

"Take your time," Will said. "No rush. Just breathe for a minute."

So she wasn't buried? She wasn't in the dirt. She tried to feel her mouth, to make sure it was clear, to make sure she could breathe, but she overshot it and hit herself in the head.

"Ow," she said.

"Just relax," Will said.

"The piano isn't right," she whispered.

But no. That had come out wrong. He wouldn't understand her. She tried again:

"Somebody is here. Be careful, Will. Be . . ."

Her room, ransacked.

The rose petals on the floor.

do books taste like roses?

Her eyes shot open again.

"Someone was in my room," she said. "We need to call the police."

"You saw someone in your room?"

"Look at it. Look at it, it's trashed. She ruined it. How did she know? How did she know about the books?"

"How did *who* know? Who ruined it? Who ruined *what*?"

"Don't you see it? The whole thing..."

"Jane, just take a deep breath. I'm not sure what you're talking about. What am I supposed to be seeing?"

"My room. I want to get up."

"Are you sure? Do you need another minute?"

"I'm fine. I want to get up."

So he helped her up.

Her arms and legs felt wobbly and weird, like the feeling was still coming back into them. She let Will support her, leaning into him because she knew if she didn't, she'd end up right back on the ground.

"You passed out," he said. "Jane, you feel... You feel really warm. Are you sick?"

She hadn't looked into her bedroom again. They were both in the doorway now; she pressed her back against the door-jamb for support.

"What are you doing here?" she asked suddenly.

"Susie left her phone," Will explained. "I guess she got all the way to Alana's and remembered we were supposed to go over to our grandparents' house this morning. They live near Alana, so she didn't want to have to drive all the way back here. She asked me to grab it on my way."

"But how did she call you if she didn't have her phone?"

"She used Alana's phone," he said, raising an eyebrow.

"How did you get in here? You just came in?"

"Jane, I heard you screaming. The door was unlocked. Are you . . . accusing me of something here?"

"Sorry." She squeezed her eyes shut for a moment. "I'm sorry. Thank you for coming in. I mean—you scared the shit out of me. But still. Thank you." She opened her eyes and made herself smile. Will looked worried.

"You're sure you didn't hit your head? I tried to catch you, but . . ."

Jane tapped her temple. "I feel okay."

"Is your mom . . . ?"

"At the store."

"Should we call her?"

"Let me just . . . think for a minute, okay?"

She straightened herself up a little. The feeling was returning to her fingers, to her toes. Her head didn't feel so airy.

She still hadn't looked at the room.

She put her hands on either side of her head, like blinders.

She knew what she'd see when she looked.

She could tell by the way Will was acting.

"I think you need to lie down," he said gently.

She nodded.

She made herself turn her head.

She made herself look.

Not a thing was out of place. Not one pillow on the floor, not one torn curtain, not one open closet door.

She rubbed her forehead with the palm of her hand. She felt a wave of fatigue pass over her, a rush of light-headedness. Will put a hand on her arm.

"Jane? I think you should get in bed."

She nodded and let him lead her over to it, crawled underneath the covers slowly, laid her head down on the pillow. He sat on the edge of the mattress.

"What happened?" he asked softly.

"The fever," she said. "I think I'm . . . seeing things."

He nodded. "You need some rest."

"Her phone should be in the kitchen."

"I'll find it."

"I'm sorry," she whispered.

"Don't apologize."

"You didn't see . . . any rose petals. Right?"

"Rose petals? In here?"

She nodded.

"No rose petals. Nothing weird," he assured her.

"Okay. Thanks, Will."

"Text me later, okay?"

"I will."

"Bye, Jane."

She pulled the covers over her face as he stood up from the bed and left the room. Her head was on fire, pounding. She felt like she was on a boat, like the bed was gently rocking back and forth, tossed among huge rolling waves.

She uncovered her face and rolled onto her side, staring at the wall, willing herself into stillness.

She'd seen the room, torn apart and wrecked. Was it the fever? Was it making her hallucinate?

She'd seen the rose petals, dozens of them, arranged to spell out the words....

What were the words?

She couldn't remember. Something about books. Something about roses.

But there were no roses; there was nothing wrong.

She was sick. She was seeing things.

She rolled over again; she couldn't get comfortable. She sat up in bed and hit her pillow, fluffing it, then arranged the covers around her.

And when she lay back down, when her head hit the pillow again...

A small puff of bright-red rose petals floated up around her.

Her fever broke on Sunday night but she stayed home from school on Monday, at Ruth's insistence. She spent most of the weekend in bed, with Ruth bringing her soup and toast and endless glasses of water. She finally got up Monday afternoon to shower and change into fresh pajamas and venture outside of her bedroom for the first time in over forty-eight hours.

The house was quiet as she made her way slowly down the hallway, then step by step to the first floor. Her legs felt shaky and weak, like they didn't quite belong to her. She wandered from room to room and finally found Ruth in Chester's study, sitting cross-legged on the floor surrounded by little piles of paperwork.

"Is there some method to this madness?" Jane asked, looking down at her mother.

"The optimist in me says yes," Ruth replied. "The pessimist in me says, why am I even bothering?"

"I think just toss it all. That's your best option."

"You may be right. How are you feeling?"

"Like a new woman."

"Well, two days in bed will do wonders for a person."

"What are you looking for, anyway?"

Ruth sighed and let her shoulders droop. "I don't know. Honestly, honey, I don't know. It started as something I thought I needed to do, look through my father's things before I got rid of them, but now I think I'm just procrastinating."

"I don't think you're going to find anything in here that you need."

"You're probably right."

"So I'll get some trash bags and we'll clean this up, okay?"

"You're not doing anything strenuous, young lady."

"Mom, I'm fine. I've been lying down for two days; I need to do something."

"All right," Ruth said, half-defeated and half-relieved. "Go get the bags."

Jane went to the kitchen and grabbed the box of trash bags from the cabinet under the sink. She brought them back to the study.

"I'm gonna pee," Ruth said. "Anything on the floor is fair game."

"Got it."

Ruth slipped out of the room, and Jane began scooping up piles of papers and dumping them in the first trash bag. She filled it quickly and opened up another. She stopped to look at a few of the papers and found useless receipts for old furniture, typed minutes from meetings held twenty years ago, and invoices for various jobs done at the house. None of it was important, and soon she had two trash bags full and the floor was cleared. She got out a third bag and pulled open a drawer of Chester's desk. Ruth hadn't been in here yet; it was overflowing with stuff.

Jane picked up a handful of receipts and deposited them all into the trash bag. Underneath them were some old greeting cards. She picked up one with a stuffed bear on the front. The bear's fur was made of a velvety material and it held up a brightly colored banner that said THANK YOU! Jane ran her thumb over the bear's fur before she opened the card. The neat handwriting on the inside said: *Dear Grandpa, Thank you so much for my new dollhouse. I am so excited to play with it and I love the dolls and the furniture and—*

"What's that?"

Ruth, from the doorway. Jane jumped a mile.

"Jeez, Mom, you scared me."

"What is that?" Ruth repeated, and before Jane could even blink, Ruth had crossed the room and snatched the card out of Jane's hands.

Jane watched her mother's lips move as Ruth read it to herself. Her hands were shaking a little. The card vibrated gently in her grasp.

"That's not from me, is it?" Jane asked. "I mean, I don't remember Grandpa ever giving me a dollhouse."

"It's from me," Ruth said quickly. "The card is from me."

"But it says *Grandpa*."

"It was a joke. I called my father *Grandpa*."

"Why?"

She only hesitated a moment. "I didn't know my grandparents. All my friends had grandpas and grandmas, and they'd buy them presents and take them to get ice cream. So I asked my father if he could be my father *and* my grandpa."

Ruth's hands were still shaking, and she wouldn't meet Jane's eyes. She closed the card purposefully, then shut the drawer Jane had pulled it from.

"Thank you for helping me clean up," she said. "But I really think you should still be resting. I need to go to the grocery store. What would you like for dinner?"

"Wait, so that's *your* room? The room with the dollhouse?"

"What room with the dollhouse?" Ruth asked. Her voice was even and icy. She still wouldn't look at Jane.

"The storage room. The room you *thought* was a storage room. There's a dollhouse in it. But you said another room was your bedroom."

"The storage room was my playroom. When I grew up, my mother filled it with boxes. I don't know why it's not a storage room anymore. I don't know what she did with the boxes. She must have taken them to the dump."

"But the room had a bed in it," Jane insisted. "Why would your playroom have a bed in it?"

"Enough, Jane!" Ruth said sharply, finally meeting her daughter's gaze. "Do you want a written history of every change of furniture in this house? I don't know why there's a bed in that room. It was never a bedroom. It was my playroom. Do you see how many beds there are in this house? Maybe my mother was obsessed with beds. Maybe she went so batty in her old age, living here without my father, that all she could think about was beds, okay? How the fuck am I supposed to know why she did the things she did? I barely knew the woman."

Jane didn't breathe. Ruth, on the other hand, breathed too much; her chest rose and fell rapidly. Her cheeks were spotted with red (*like roses*, said a voice in Jane's head). As Jane watched, Ruth put her hands over her face and took a deep, steadying breath. When she let it out, she uncovered her face and said,

"I'm going to get us food. I'll be back soon. Come out of this room, please."

So Jane followed Ruth out of the study, and Ruth took a key out of her pocket and locked the door behind them.

Jane didn't speak. She didn't know what to say. She just followed Ruth quietly into the foyer and watched as her mother slipped on her shoes and coat and walked out the front door.

Ruth had still been holding the card.

The card addressed to Grandpa.

A gust of cold evening air had squeezed in through the briefly open door, and it swirled around Jane as she stood motionless, thinking.

Why had Ruth reacted so bizarrely when Jane had seen the card? The change in her demeanor had been palpable, alarming.

Was that what grief did after it had a chance to cool? Did it turn into something like rage, something that festered underneath the skin and caused irrational bursts like the one Jane had just witnessed from her mother?

Rage was something Jane could understand.

The house creaked around her, a sound that Jane was now almost used to: the sound of settling.

Would a house like this ever be fully settled? Or would it ache and moan until the end of time, until all the newer, shoddier houses had fallen to ruins around it?

A flash of the earth with everything destroyed except this house, the last building standing, and Jane within it, trapped inside its walls, not really caring anymore whether she made it out or not.

She turned and looked into the mirror that hung above the entranceway table.

She looked pale. There were deep circles underneath her eyes. Her hair was loose and tangled. It had been a while since she'd gotten it cut. The ends were dry and split, and there was a sizable chunk of new growth that had started near the center of her forehead, a two- or three-inch piece of hair that curled more vigorously than the rest because it was so short. It fell to a stop just between her eyebrows. She would have to clip it out of her face later.

Something had happened in this house.

She wasn't sure where the thought came from, when exactly it had been born, but it arrived now like a force, like a storm.

Something had happened in this house. Something wasn't right here. Something had happened.

She went upstairs.

She walked to the end of the hallway, past the playroom with the bed in it, and opened the door to her grandparents' bedroom.

She felt around on the wall for the light switch. She clicked it on and stepped inside the room.

It smelled like something in here.

Like roses.

But it wasn't like the roses in the backyard; this was just a touch of fragrance, a delicate hint of flowers.

Jane crossed over to her grandmother's vanity and saw a vintage glass perfume bottle, the kind with an atomizer. She picked it up and sniffed. Rose water. Emilia must have made her own rose water from the plants in the garden. All these years later and it was still strong enough to give off a perfume.

There was a door against the right wall that led into a master bathroom. An empty soap dish. An empty toothbrush holder. An empty towel rack. The toilet bowl lid was closed.

Jane found herself fixating on the empty toothbrush holder.

When had Emilia's toothbrush been thrown away?

Someone must have come through and cleaned the house. Had the nurse who'd found her grandmother's body taken the time to throw away the toothbrush, take out the trash, put all unnecessary clutter into drawers?

Had Ruth thrown away Greer's toothbrush?

Had she picked it out of the ceramic toothbrush holder and dropped it into the trash can?

And what about his shampoo, his razor, his shaving cream?

Had she thrown everything out, one by one?

A few days after Greer died, Jane had woken in the middle of the night, one or two in the morning, and noticed the hall light was on. The crack underneath her door was illuminated with the pale yellow glow of it. She got out of bed and crossed her room, opening the door and peering out, blinking.

There were trash bags in the hallway, a handful of them all lined up in a row. As Jane stood there, her eyes adjusting to the light, Ruth came out of her own bedroom dragging another one, lining it up with the others. She pushed her hair away from her forehead, turned around, and—seeing Jane—jumped.

"You scared me," she said. "Was I being too loud?"

"What are you doing?"

"Nothing. Cleaning. I couldn't sleep."

Jane took a few steps into the hallway and peered into a trash bag. It was filled with Greer's clothes, neatly folded and piled one on top of the other.

"Oh," Jane said.

"You never think about these things," Ruth whispered, and when Jane looked up, she saw that her mother had started crying again. Or—continued to cry—because in those first weeks after Greer's death, had either of them really ever *stopped* crying?

"What are you going to do with them?"

"There's a shelter," Ruth said. "I found it online. They need donations."

Jane removed the top item from the bag. It was an old sweatshirt, fraying around the collar and cuffs, the perfect faded gray. She brought it up to her nose; it still smelled like him, and her stomach twisted painfully, aching as she hugged it to her chest.

She had taken the sweatshirt, packed it with the clothes she brought to Maine, but she hadn't yet worn it. She hadn't even unfolded it, just removed it carefully from the box and placed it into her closet. She didn't want to touch it too much. She didn't want the smell to fade.

Now, in her grandparents' bedroom, she crossed to the bureau and pulled open a drawer to reveal nothing inside. Empty. Another drawer—empty. All of them, empty.

Who had cleaned these out? What had they done with the things inside?

Jane felt tired suddenly, and a wave of sadness threatened to put her off her feet. She swayed a little, took a step back into the bedroom, and sat down on the edge of her grandparents' bed.

Who had slept on what side?

How did people decide things like that, who slept where?

How had her parents decided what side of the bed they would each take?

Where did her mother sleep now?

Did she stay on the same side, or had she moved toward the middle, spreading out so she wouldn't notice the empty space, so she wouldn't feel the absence of Greer so distinctly?

Jane felt that same absence now, that same familiar ache in the pit of her stomach.

But it wasn't sadness.

It was anger.

A comforting, all-encompassing anger.

It wasn't fair, that he'd left them. It wasn't fair that he'd lost all their money. It wasn't fair that they'd had to move here, to this terrible house. None of it was fair.

She pushed herself up from the bed and went to her own bedroom, closing the door behind her. Her fingers were tingling as she sat on the floor and pulled *The Lion, the Witch, and the Wardrobe* from the bottom shelf of her bookcase.

She opened the book and tore out a single page.

The house creaked around her. The house was always creaking. It was a living thing, the house. It was just as alive as anyone.

She ripped a corner from the page and put it into her mouth.

The house creaked again.

She imagined the paper re-forming in her belly. She imagined the words dissolving off the paper and sinking into her bloodstream. She imagined her body filled with words. Made up of them. Words instead of blood, words instead of organs.

And the creak grew louder, and Jane put another piece of paper into her mouth, and the creak grew louder, and Jane looked up suddenly and there was Ruth, standing in the doorway, her hand over her mouth, and the creaking had been the creaking of the door, and Jane had been too distracted to even notice.

She swallowed before the paper was really soft enough. It stuck on the way down, it scratched her throat and made her cough.

"What are you doing?" Ruth asked, her voice strangely quiet, strangely even.

"We *knock*, Mom," Jane said.

"What are you doing?"

"You need to knock!"

"You don't tell me what to do; I'm the grown-up here, I tell *you* what to do. Now, answer me. What were you doing?"

Jane looked down at the book in her hands. No one had ever known. No one had ever seen her. The book, half-eaten, was also alive. It trembled in her hands.

Ruth took a step toward her. "Give that to me," she said.

"No..."

"Jane, hand me that book."

And something in Ruth's voice made Jane do it, even though everything in her body was screaming *no no no no no*—

She held it out, and Ruth took it.

"This whole thing?" Ruth whispered.

"It's not a big deal."

"You did this? You..."

She couldn't bring herself to say the word *ate*.

Jane still held the page in her hand, just one little corner ripped off and eaten. She could feel it worming around in her belly. It didn't feel comforting, for once. It felt strange and sour.

"It's not a big deal," Jane repeated. "It's just a thing... It's just, I don't know. It's just a thing I do sometimes."

"You do...sometimes?" Ruth said, and her eyes moved from the book she was holding to the books on Jane's bookshelf, to the row of journals all made from other books.

Made from other books Jane had consumed.

"Mom..."

"You can't do this," Ruth said, and Jane looked up at her, because it was both Ruth's and not Ruth's voice that came out of her mother now. It was Ruth but it was also a sadder, younger Ruth, like her words were drifting through time and space, like she'd somehow said them before. "You can't eat things that aren't food," she continued, and her eyes were unfocused and glazed over, and she held the book in her hand like it was something much more fragile than it was.

Something like a flower.

Something like a rose.

"You can't put things into your mouth that aren't food," she whispered, and then she stepped backward until her legs hit the edge of the mattress and she sat down, heavy, on top of the bed.

She started to sob.

Jane held the page in her hands and watched her, unable to move, unable to speak. Her whole body was frozen, because when Ruth had sat down, a dozen rose petals had lifted from the bed and floated up around her and then dissolved in the air into nothing. . . .

"Mom?"

Ruth covered her face with her hands, and she sobbed loudly and frantically, and Jane just sat there and stared at her; and even if she had wanted to get up and do something, get up and comfort her, she couldn't make herself move.

Finally, Ruth stood up and left the bedroom quickly, taking the book with her, and Jane heard her walk into her own bedroom and shut the door and still Jane didn't move, and still her hands shook a little and her throat itched, and she tried to stand up but couldn't, and she tried to uncross her legs but couldn't, and she tried to do anything but couldn't, couldn't...

Ruth couldn't have that book. She couldn't take that book. That wasn't okay; that wasn't okay.

Jane was still on the floor; she crumpled into a ball and tucked her head in between her knees, breathing heavily. She couldn't get mad. The book was gone. But she couldn't get mad, because the book was gone. And if the book was gone, she couldn't get mad, because there would be no way for her to combat her anger.

She started to cry. She let her body fall sideways until she was lying on the plush carpet. She kept both her hands pressed against her face, blocking out the light.

She felt like her hands didn't belong to her, like her skin didn't belong to her. Like the only thing real and true in her body was the anger that Greer had so methodically taught her to overcome.

But it was the only thing she had left now. She leaned into it gratefully, letting it fill her, letting it wash over her in a warm embrace.

With it, she was not alone. She was never alone.

She let it carry her into darkness.

Hours later, days later, years later, she opened her eyes.

The light in her bedroom had changed, gotten darker. Her

arm was asleep where she'd lain on it. Her head was pounding and her body was cold.

She pushed herself to a seat.

She was still holding the page she'd had in her hand when Ruth took the book. It was ruined now, damp and wrinkled. She crumpled it into a ball and let it drop on the floor.

She put a hand to her forehead. The fever hadn't come back. She was hungry and sore. She found her phone and checked the time—almost midnight.

She got up quietly, avoiding the spots on the floor she'd come to know as the creaky ones, opening her bedroom door and peeking out into the hallway.

Ruth's bedroom light was off; Jane could see only darkness coming from the crack underneath the door.

She went downstairs.

It looked like Ruth hadn't made it downstairs to cook, so Jane got herself a bowl of leftover soup from yesterday and warmed it up in the microwave.

She ate it standing up, methodically taking bite after bite, then put the empty bowl into the sink and paused, her eyes trained on the back door of the kitchen, the one that led to Chester's study.

She walked over to it.

There was her grandfather's closed study door. In the darkness she could see only the doorknob, flashing in the tiny bit of moonlight that made it here from the mudroom entrance.

She knew it was locked, and she knew Ruth had probably taken the key with her.

What was the truth behind that greeting card? What other secrets would Jane find, if she were able to get behind that door?

She turned and took one step back into the kitchen, then froze as she heard it—

A surprisingly loud *click*.

Like the turning of a lock.

And another noise, like the turning of a doorknob.

And another noise, like the opening of a door.

The house was suddenly so dark and so narrow and so twisting that it felt like it was moving around her. Was she standing on the floor or the ceiling? Was the floor pulsating beneath her feet?

She reached out her free hand and pressed it against the wall to steady herself, but the wall was moving, too, and she lurched forward, almost falling, barely catching herself.

Silence.

She counted ten breaths, twenty breaths, and there was no sound.

It felt terrible, having her back to the door. It felt like having her back to a monster that was just waiting to swallow her whole.

She turned around.

The study door was open just a few inches. A crack of blackness—like a doorway to another world. A world that was darker than this one could ever be. So dark it looked wrong.

She moved toward the blackness before she could really

decide if it was a good idea. She wouldn't let herself think about anything—why had the door opened? *How* had the door opened?—she just made her legs move until she was close enough to the door that she could slip a hand inside, feel against the wall until her fingers found the light switch.

She flicked it on, then pushed the door open another few inches, enough so that she could stick her head into the room and see that it was empty.

It is amazing how quickly fears will quiet in the light. She stepped into the room and closed the door behind her, holding the doorknob open so it wouldn't make a sound. Already her heart was beating slower. Already she felt foolish for how scared she had been. Already she felt herself not caring how the door had opened. It was open now, wasn't that all that mattered?

She crept around to the front of her grandfather's desk and lowered herself into the oversize chair. The old leather was soft and quiet as she sank into it.

She didn't know what she was looking for, but she pulled open the drawer she'd found the card in and stared at the mess of papers it contained. She removed a bill for a piano tuning, then a dozen others like it, twice a year every December and June first. She piled them on the desk. Underneath them, she found a neat stack of oil-change receipts, held together by an old paper clip. Underneath them, a yellow legal pad filled with her grandfather's cramped, barely legible writing.

She replaced everything in the drawer, closed it, and opened the next one down. This one was entirely filled with office supplies: rolls of tape, a decades-old stapler that probably belonged in a museum, a pair of scissors with one handle broken off. She closed the drawer and moved on to the next one, the bottom drawer on the left side of the desk. When she went to pull it open, it stuck, and looking closer, she realized it was the only drawer in the desk with a keyhole in it. Locked.

She sat back in the chair for a moment, disheartened but not giving up. She knew, somehow, that whatever it was she was looking for *had* to be in that drawer. She had to get in there.

She opened the drawer of office supplies and fished around in the bottom until she found a paper clip. She uncurled it so it was a wobbly line of metal, then inserted it in the keyhole, wiggling it around until she found purchase, trying different angles when nothing happened.

After a few minutes of digging around, just seconds away from giving up, she felt something give, and the drawer opened about an inch. She withdrew the paper clip, set it on the desk, and took just a moment to be surprised that it had actually worked.

She opened the drawer.

It was stuffed with hanging files, each with a little label at the upper corner, things like HOUSE and CARS and DOCTORS and MISC.

And near the back was one labeled RUTHELLEN.

Jane slid this one out and laid it on the desk, then opened it carefully. The first few pages were childhood art projects. A smudgy pastel still life of a bowl of fruit. A charcoal hand. A crayon self-portrait that actually wasn't half-bad. It showed Ruth with long, messy, curly blond hair. Jane smiled; Ruth had always had short hair, dyed dark. Jane hadn't known it used to be longer.

Some of the pictures were signed: *Ruthellen, age 8. Ruthellen, age 10.* The back of the self-portrait had a crayon written message:

happy birthday daddy
I love you
love Ruthie

Jane had never heard anyone call her mother *Ruthie* before. She doubted her grandmother would have approved; it must have just been between Ruth and Chester.

After the artwork, there was a report card from kindergarten. The teacher had handwritten a paragraph at the bottom of a row of stickers meant to denote how Ruth had done in various subjects like Listening and Story Time.

> *Ruthellen remains a bright and shining spot*
> *among our class. She is always volunteering to help*
> *with cleanup, she is an excellent listener during free*
> *play, and she is almost always in a happy mood. Still*
> *having some issues with her temper, however, as we've*
> *previously discussed. When she feels like she's been*
> *"wronged" in some way, it is very hard to calm her*
> *down and get her back to that happy Ruthellen we all*
> *know and love. Please continue to speak to her over the*
> *break about managing these mood swings!*

Jane smirked. It was funny to picture her mother as a moody kindergartner. She let the report card fall to the desk and picked up the next paper, another report card, this one from the end of first grade. It was similar in structure to the kindergarten one, with bright, happy stickers next to categories such as Counting and Spelling. Ruth had gotten happy faces and stars for almost every category. Next to Listening and Cooperation, however, there were small frowny-face stickers. The note at the bottom of the page was written in black ink:

> Ruthellen is such a strong-headed little girl. We loved having her in class. We had many conversations, as you know, about the importance of being kind to our classmates. Please continue to talk to Ruthellen about the importance of keeping her hands to herself, and not touching other people without their permission. We need to get that little temper under control before we enter the second grade! We are also still trying to break Ruthellen's pesky habit of chewing on the ends of her hair. Such beautiful, healthy hair she might have if she would just stop putting it into her mouth!

Jane frowned.

What a weird thing to put in a report card, that Ruth chewed her hair.

Jane felt a little uneasy, but she couldn't quite pinpoint why.

The next paper she picked up was a memo from a teacher at Ruth's school.

Mr. and Mrs. North,

Forgive the note, but you have proven quite difficult to get in touch with over the last several months. I understand you are both very busy individuals, but having rescheduled our meeting now for the fourth time, I find it necessary to reach you in other ways. I would have much preferred discussing this in person, but here we are.

Your daughter's behavior in school has become unwieldy. She does not respond to any normal means of punishment for her actions, nor does she seem to care much about positive reinforcement, either. She is instead an island, operating according to some internal set of guidelines I cannot begin to understand.

I implore you to escalate this matter with the highest level of urgency. I have included the business card of a child psychiatrist, a personal friend of mine and someone I trust implicitly in these matters.

Yours,
M. Quatrano

Nothing on the paper gave any indication of how old Ruth might have been when it was written, and it left Jane with an unsettled feeling in her stomach, like she'd stood up too quickly.

What had her mother done to warrant such a serious note? From the sound of it, it was multiple events, but Jane had never known Ruth to be anything but levelheaded and calm. But clearly, something in the note had struck a nerve with Chester, because the very next piece of paper was another note, this one from a psychiatrist:

Mr. North,

At your somewhat unorthodox request, I agree to see your daughter, Ruthellen, without the knowledge or support of her mother. I have to tell you, what you've shared with me about Ruthellen troubles me greatly, which is the reason I'll keep our arrangement quiet, for now. You may bring her by next Thursday the 10th at 4 p.m.

Yours,
Lyle Graves

Why would Chester have wanted to keep something like this from Emilia? Jane flipped through the next few papers quickly, finding nothing of interest until her hand landed on a note from Bells Hollow High School. It was a notice of a five-day suspension. Jane skimmed the page until she found a description of the incident.

Ruthellen North and Elizabeth Brooks were witnessed engaging in
physical violence by member of faculty J. Knowles. Knowles attempted
to intervene in the altercation between the two individuals; Ms. Brooks
immediately desisted while Ms. North struck Knowles in the face, caus-
ing Knowles to suffer a bloody nose and bruising.

Jane's hand shook slightly as she lowered the paper to the
desk.

The rest of the papers were more of the same. Notes from
the psychiatrist, Graves. Notes from the school. Two more suspensions. Countless detentions. And then, at the very bottom
of the stack, an ultrasound. Ruth must have sent it to her father
when she was pregnant with Jane. Why he would have kept it
in this drawer, with all these much-older papers, she couldn't
understand.

She put everything back in the drawer. Her eyes burned
and she felt suddenly exhausted, like the very bones in her
body had turned to lead. She couldn't look any further tonight.
She had to get some sleep.

She made sure everything was back in its proper place, then
she slipped out into the hallway, closing the door behind her.
There was no way to lock it without the key, so she left it open,
and walked into the kitchen to pour herself a glass of water.
She'd just taken the glass from the cabinet and set it next to the
fridge when the house settled. A long, slow creak.

And then something else.

Not the house.

A small thing, dropping and rolling.

A marble making its way across a bedroom floor.

And before she could really think about it, before she had a chance to change her mind, she walked toward the front of the house.

She climbed the stairs slowly, stepping lightly, so she wouldn't make any noise.

The hallway was dark except for the room that wasn't a storage room. The dollhouse room's light flickered on and off as she watched, on and off and then stayed off.

But she didn't feel scared.

She didn't feel anything.

So she walked up to the door and opened it—

It was locked one minute and not the next, exactly as Chester's study had been, exactly as if someone on the other side had unlocked it for her.

She slipped inside and closed the door behind her, then waited to see if Ruth had heard. But the house was quiet.

Her eyes adjusted to the light.

It was a little girl's bedroom.

There was a small twin bed, a white wooden headboard painted with vining roses. A matching bureau. A tiny little vanity with a stool and mirror. A soft pink, round rug. A jar of marbles. The dollhouse.

There was a smell in the room, the same smell the house had when Ruth and Jane had first arrived. The smell of disuse. Nobody had been in this room for a long, long time.

Jane walked over to the bureau. There was a wooden

jewelry box on it. She opened it and tinny music filled the room as a plastic ballerina spun around.

She closed it quickly, listening. . . .

Still nothing from Ruth.

She opened the top drawer of the bureau.

It was filled with little-girl clothes. Lacy white tops and turtlenecks with flowers embroidered onto them, long-sleeved cotton shirts with fake pockets and ruffles at the sleeves.

But Ruth said this hadn't been her bedroom. . . . Was she lying?

Jane shut the drawer and opened another one.

Little pairs of white cotton shorts and striped linen pants.

Another drawer.

Socks and underwear.

Another drawer.

Tights and stockings.

She walked over to the closet and opened it.

There was a light bulb hanging from the ceiling with a string attached to it; she pulled on it gently and the closet was bathed in a dull yellow glow.

Perfect rows of fancy dresses, all a little too formal, a little too perfect. But all clearly worn—this one had a slight stain on the elbow, this one had a tear at the seam.

A shelf at the top of the closet held patent-leather Mary Janes, brown low-heeled oxfords, white party shoes with delicate pink bows instead of laces. One ratty, old teddy bear sat propped against the corner, its fur dirty and matted, its eyes two vacant, unseeing beads.

Jane ran her hand over the dresses and tried to imagine her mother small enough to fit in them. She thought they might be for an eight-year-old, maybe nine.

But why would all her mother's things still be hanging here? Where were her clothes at ten years old, eleven, twelve?

Jane kept the closet light on but turned back to face the room again. She walked over to the vanity and knelt down before it. There was a small crystal atomizer—rose water, she was sure—and a pink plastic comb and matching hand mirror. Jane picked up the mirror and looked at herself. The curl was right in the middle of her forehead. She pinched it with one finger, pulled it straight, let it bounce back up.

She put the mirror down.

There was one drawer in the vanity, and she pulled it open.

It contained a pale-pink rosary coiled neatly around itself, a half dozen hair clips, a small silver compact.

And a Polaroid picture, facedown.

Jane picked it up and turned it over, and it took her a moment to really see it, to really process it....

Because it was her.

It was her as a little girl.

But it wasn't her.

Because she was standing in front of North Manor, and Jane had never been to North Manor before, not until a few weeks ago.

And she was wearing a pink frilly dress with buttons up the front, and Jane had never worn a dress like that.

But she was Jane.

A perfect copy of Jane.

Or—almost.

Her face was almost, almost Jane's....

But not quite.

But her hair.

It was Jane's hair completely.

Long and blond and a little unruly, even though someone had clearly done their best to tame it.

There was writing on the white part of the Polaroid. Faded ink that was hard to read in the half-light.

It said:

Jemima Rose, Eighth Birthday.

Jane's hands were trembling.

Jemima Rose?

She put down the photograph on the vanity and let out a long, shaky breath.

It fogged the little hand mirror.

And as she watched, a word appeared.

As if someone was writing it in the fog with their finger.

Letter by letter.

And it said—

Sister.

And then, underneath—

Hi.

She was horrid

Jane scrambled back from the vanity, overturning the small stool as she did. The slap of it against the hardwood floor was so loud she was sure Ruth would wake up, and she pressed herself against the opposite wall of the bedroom, her heart pounding, her eyes squeezed shut, her hands clamped over her mouth so she wouldn't scream, and she counted to ten, then twenty, but she heard nothing to indicate Ruth was awake.

She had never felt quite so scared before.

Not even when she had heard (thought she'd heard?) someone in the house. Not even when she'd seen her trashed bedroom. This fear was icy and immediate and dangerous. She could feel her pulse beating in each of her wrists. It was hard to swallow. She wanted to open her eyes but her motor skills weren't working. She couldn't get her eyelids to cooperate.

Finally, she removed her hands from her mouth and she pressed them against her stomach, squeezing herself into something like a hug, just trying to breathe and not pass out. She didn't want to pass out in this room.

But what *was* this room?

Who was Jemima Rose?

The dress she wore in the photograph was one of the dresses still hanging in the closet, washed and pressed and untouched for years.

Jane opened her eyes.

The room was quiet and still and unmoving.

She had almost expected... Well, she didn't really know *what* she had expected, but it was nice to find the room empty. It was nice to find herself alone.

The hand mirror was resting innocently on the vanity, and Jane made herself take a step toward it, then another step, then another until she was close enough to see that it was unfogged and normal, just a cheap plastic thing you gave a kid until they were old enough to have a nicer one.

Jemima Rose.

Jane had never heard that name before.

But—*sister*.

Her mother had a sister?

Had she been older or younger than Ruth?

And what had happened to her?

Surely nothing *good*?

You didn't preserve an eight-year-old's bedroom if they had turned nine, ten, eleven.

You didn't keep their eight-year-old clothes hanging in the closet if they were sixteen and still living in the house.

So something had happened to Jemima, something bad, and this room was tidied up and left alone, the bed made and the dollhouse furniture neat and in its proper place and the vanity set as if, at any moment, a little girl might sit down at it and comb out her long, blond hair.

Jane had always thought she looked like Greer, only like Greer, but here was evidence that she also had some North in her. Here was a little girl with long, tangled hair clipped deliberately out of her face. Here was a little girl with something in the mouth Jane couldn't quite pinpoint, a certain line or shadow that Jane could see mirrored in her own face.

Here was her aunt, and Jane looked so much like her that she felt light-headed.

So much like a dead girl.

So much like a . . .

She didn't want to say the word, didn't want to even think it, because it was silly. She had made the whole thing up. The shock of seeing the photograph, of realizing Ruth had a sister . . . Her imagination had run away with her. Her brain had made the connection, the obvious conclusion, and her eyes played tricks on her.

Because there was no such thing as . . .

She wouldn't say the word.

But there was no such thing as dead little girls who could write words on fogged-up mirrors.

It just wasn't possible.

Her breathing was returning to normal.

She wanted to get out of this room.

This wasn't a good room; this was a time capsule of grief.

The air was heavy with it. Jane could feel it now. Like a stickiness that settled onto your skin, like something invisible that crawled around on the back of your neck.

She backed up toward the door, felt behind her for the handle. She didn't want to turn around, to take her eyes off the room—just in case.

She had made the whole thing up, of course, but just in case...

Her hand closed around the doorknob, and she twisted it open and stepped out of the room noiselessly. She closed the door slowly, slowly, and it didn't creak, and it didn't make even a whisper as she shut it and released the knob.

She turned around and yelped at the shadow of a person standing in the hallway—

The light flicked on.

It was Ruth.

Her eyes were awake and clear.

She looked calm—an unsettling calm.

"Why did you go in there?" she asked.

"I just wanted to know," Jane replied, and it was the truth.

"And what do you know now?"

"You had a sister. Jemima Rose."

Ruth was quiet for a long time. Then she nodded her head slightly. "Yes. A sister."

"How come you never told me?"

"It was a long time ago."

"Did she die?"

Ruth pressed her lips together. "Yes."

"How?"

"An accident. A terrible accident."

"What happened?"

"I don't want to talk about it," Ruth said. "It's in the past, Jane, just let it be in the past."

"But she was my aunt."

"She was never your aunt. She was never anything to you. It was a long time ago."

"Is that why you never came back here?" Jane asked, realizing. She knew she was right by how long it took Ruth to answer.

She had her arms crossed over her chest.

She let them fall, and Jane saw that she was holding a set of keys in one hand.

"Please, just let her be," Ruth said. "Just let her rest."

"You won't tell me anything about her?"

Ruth stepped past Jane and fumbled with the key ring until she found the one she was looking for. She stuck it into the doorknob and Jane heard it lock.

"Not tonight, Jane. It's late. She was just a little girl. Okay? There isn't anything to tell. She was just a little girl, and she died, and it was a long time ago."

"I'm sorry," Jane said.

"Just let it go. Please."

Ruth stepped closer to Jane and wrapped her arms around her, and Jane felt that her mother was shaking a little, like she was crying without the tears, a gentle vibrating as she held on to her.

When she pulled away, Ruth's eyes were dry but faraway, and when she looked at Jane, it was like she was seeing someone else.

"I'm sorry. Please go to bed," she said. She kissed Jane on the forehead and went back into her bedroom.

Jane stood in the hallway for a few minutes, then went into her own bedroom.

Something had happened in this house.

She knew it.

Something had happened.

Someone had died.

Ruth was already gone when Jane woke up the next morning.

She hadn't slept well. The night had felt endless, one of those nights when it seems like you're lying awake for eight hours straight, but you've also dreamed, strange dreams that don't make much sense, dreams made up of images and sounds and feelings but no real storylines.

She made herself oatmeal and coffee and wished she didn't have to work after school. She wanted to sleep more. She wanted to come home after last period and crawl back into bed and sleep for the entire afternoon and night.

She put the bowl into the sink when she was done with the oatmeal, then she took a quick shower and dressed in jeans and a shirt Salinger had given her. It was vintage: a faded blue wash with white smoke letters that said *Genie* as they rose up from a magic lamp.

Salinger.

This was the longest they had gone without talking or texting that Jane could remember.

The house was quiet and the upstairs hallway, which didn't have any windows, was semi-dark and still. Last night—the Polaroid, the plastic hand mirror, the rows of frilly dresses— felt like just another dream in a night full of dreams. It felt like a dream in the way that morning felt like a dream. But when Jane raised her hand and gripped a chunk of her hair and pulled it gently—it hurt.

"So I'm awake," she whispered.

Her mother had locked the storage room door.

Jemima Rose's bedroom.

Jane's aunt.

She watched it, for a moment, the door...

But nothing happened.

No lights, no marbles dropping on the floor, nothing.

She almost went and tested the doorknob, but her phone buzzed in her hand. Susie was outside.

They hadn't been able to go to the mall that weekend because of Jane's fever, so Jane still didn't have a winter coat. She threw a sweatshirt over her shirt and ran out to the car.

"Are you feeling better?" Susie asked.

"Much better," Jane replied.

"What happened?"

"I'm not sure. Right after you guys left on Saturday, I just got so sick. My fever was 102."

"Damn, girl. Well, here. You need this." Susie reached into her back seat, grabbed a jacket, and handed it to Jane.

"Susie, I can't take your jacket from you."

"One thing you need to know about East Coast girls, Jane. We each own one thousand jackets. I haven't worn this one in years. At least borrow it until you get a new one, okay?"

Jane nodded and slipped it on. It was dark blue, thick, and puffy, and she felt instantly warmer. "This is really nice of you."

"Don't mention it," Susie said.

"But now you'll have to make do with only nine hundred and ninety-nine jackets."

"It will be a struggle," Susie said, nodding seriously. "But I'll figure something out."

It was a long day. Jane was tired and slow and couldn't

concentrate in any of her classes. She somehow made it through the morning and lunch and was a few minutes early to her first afternoon class, chemistry. She paused just inside the door when she saw that the only other person in the room was Melanie. Her heart caught in her chest, and she felt a cold rush of anger run through her body. But her desk was on the opposite side of the room, so she made herself take a breath and sit down.

She pulled out her chemistry textbook and looked over what they were currently studying. She couldn't concentrate on the words; they blurred in front of her eyes when she tried to focus on them. She heard a quiet shuffle, and a shadow fell across her desk a moment later. She clenched her hands into fists and looked up to see Melanie, her face blank of any discernible emotion.

"You look tired," Melanie said. Her voice was quiet. "Did you not get enough sleep?"

Jane looked back down at her textbook, closed her eyes, and took a long, slow breath. Just like Greer had taught her to do. She pictured him next to her now, standing over her, his hand on her shoulder as her heart started to race. She didn't say anything.

"Were you sick?" Melanie continued. "You look like you might be a little sick."

"What do you want?" Jane asked. Her voice shook just a little. She hoped Melanie hadn't noticed.

"I'm giving you a chance."

"A chance?" Jane looked up, genuinely curious, genuinely confused. What the hell was she talking about?

"To get the fuck out of Bells Hollow," Melanie said, her voice a low hiss as she leaned even closer to Jane. "To pack your bags and move back to California before you really start to regret it."

Jane squeezed her eyes shut. They were still the only two people in the classroom, and the warning bell hadn't even rung yet. Why hadn't she turned around when she saw her in the room? Why hadn't she gone to the bathroom, waited outside until other people had gotten there?

"What is your problem?" Jane asked, struggling to keep her voice steady. "I haven't done anything to you."

"Don't act so innocent." Melanie snorted. "Don't act like you don't know."

"Know *what*?"

"That terrible things happen in Bells Hollow."

"What things?"

"People get hurt. People die."

People die. . . .

Melanie's sister. Jane's grandmother. Jane's aunt. Jemima Rose.

"Just leave me alone," Jane said, her voice low. "Just *please* . . . leave me alone."

"I'm trying to help you," Melanie said. "I wouldn't want something to happen to you. Or to your mom. I mean, that would be terrible. Can you imagine? Your family's been dropping like flies lately. You really can't afford to lose another one."

And one moment, Greer was standing next to Jane, his hand on her shoulder, steadying her.

And the next moment, he was gone.

And one moment, Jane was inside her body—

And the next moment, something curious happened.

The next moment, she was sort of above herself, and she was watching Melanie turn away from her. Everything seemed red—red skin, red hair, red clothes—like she was wearing glasses with crimson lenses in them. And time had slowed down. Melanie moved in slow motion. And Jane watched herself twitch and then she watched herself stand up and then she watched herself launch her body across a row of seats.

And then she was inside her body again.

She landed on top of Melanie, knocking her to the ground. They came to a hard landing on the floor. Jane raised her arm; her hand was clenched so tightly into a fist that she could feel her fingernails digging into her skin, drawing blood. The first punch landed squarely on Melanie's nose, but Jane was unbalanced, not quite ready, there wasn't enough power behind it. She pulled her hand back again, winding up, but before she could throw the second punch, someone had grabbed her wrist and was pulling back her arm sharply, lifting her to her feet with a strength that seemed unnatural when she finally rounded on whoever it was and saw—

"Susie," Jane said, panting, out of breath and filled with an antsy adrenaline that coursed through her veins faster than blood.

"What the *fuck*?" Melanie said. She pulled herself half-way to her feet, wobbled, fell down again on her knees. "Are you a fucking *psycho*?" Her nose was bleeding. She touched it with the back of her hand and pulled away a long, thick line of blood. "Are you fucking *insane*?"

"I didn't...I didn't..." But Jane couldn't finish her sentence, because *I didn't mean to* couldn't have been further from the truth. She *had* meant to. She *still wanted to.*

Susie hadn't taken her hand off Jane's arm. She tightened her grip and pulled her to the door.

"Jane, come *on*. Move it, before Mr. Barker gets here."

"She's fucking insane! She fucking attacked me!" Melanie screamed.

"Oh, and I'm sure you were just sitting here minding your own fucking business," Susie snapped. "Go clean yourself up, Melanie, you look like you got the shit kicked out of you."

Susie kept pulling Jane's arm, and finally she managed to drag her out of the classroom. There was a bathroom right across the hall, and they burst into it just as the warning bell rang.

"What the hell was that about?" Susie said, letting go of Jane's arm, moving between Jane and the door like she was afraid Jane would storm right back out and go find Melanie.

"I didn't...I don't know. She said...She said something about my family.... And I just snapped...."

"Jesus," Susie said. "Put some water on your face or something, you're beet red."

Jane went and looked in the mirror. Her face was red and splotchy, and she realized as she struggled to turn the tap on that her hands were shaking.

She backed away from the sink, backed up until her shoulder blades hit the stalls.

"I just got so mad," she whispered.

"Yeah, I definitely picked up on that," Susie said, and laughed a little—a short, anxious laugh that didn't help to break the tension in the room. "You looked like you were going to kill her."

"She's going to tell Mr. Barker....I'm going to get expelled...."

"Melanie won't tell anyone. She threw a rock through your window, remember? Now you both have shit on each other. She's an asshole, but she's smart enough to realize that."

"I guess."

Susie laughed. "You really just walloped her. Right in the nose. Boom."

"Did you just say *walloped?*"

Susie laughed again, louder this time, and then Jane laughed, and finally they were both cracking up, doubled over and holding their stomachs.

Jane felt the anger leaving her, like a tiny tap had been opened in her body and it was all seeping out—the dark, hot rage turning into steam when it touched the air. When she went back to the sink, her hands had stopped shaking. She looked in the mirror, and the red was gone from her face.

"What did she say?" Susie asked, not really laughing anymore, coming to stand next to Jane.

"She said my family was dropping like flies."

Susie took a sharp intake of breath. "That's so fucked up. I'm sorry." Susie paused and touched Jane's arm. "Are you okay?"

"I think so. And thank you. For helping me. You could have just walked away."

"Walked away, no. What I almost did was take out my cell phone and start filming. But I figured this was the better move."

Susie winked, then held the bathroom door open for Jane to slip out.

Melanie wasn't in Mr. Barker's class when they got back, and Jane didn't see her again for the rest of the day. She was oddly unsettled by that; she found herself peering around corners before she rounded them, constantly feeling like she was being watched.

Susie drove her to Beans & Books after school, and Jane's stomach twisted uncomfortably when she saw that Will was there, loading coffee mugs into the dishwasher. She hadn't seen or talked to him since Saturday morning, since he'd come into the house and found her absolutely losing it.

When he saw her, he greeted her cautiously, like he was worried she might spontaneously collapse.

"Hey," he said.

"Hi."

"Feeling better?"

"Yeah. I was out all weekend."

"I wanted to text you, but I didn't know if you'd want to be bothered," he said. "I'm really sorry, Jane. That I just came in like that. I keep thinking about it and...It was totally inappropriate."

"No, no, I'm glad you did." Jane reassured him. "It's really fine. Obviously, you hear screaming, and the door is unlocked, you're going to come in."

"I'm just sorry. But I'm glad you're feeling better."

"Thanks. Me too."

She almost told him. What had happened between her and Melanie that afternoon. About Jemima Rose, her dead aunt. She almost told him everything, but he went back to loading the dishwasher and she decided she didn't want to burden him, she didn't want all that baggage sitting between them. She didn't want to ruin anything.

She grabbed a rag and started cleaning the counters. Since her last shift, Will had done a bit of decorating for Halloween. Just a few things to keep it festive: some fake spiderwebs and decals on the window that made up an elaborate graveyard scene.

She couldn't believe it was only three days away. And she had to admit—there was something different about Halloween on the East Coast, something the West Coast could never hope to achieve. The grayness of the sky, the crispness to the air, the evenings that grew so dark, so early.

"It looks great in here," she said when Will finished loading the dishes.

"You think?"

"Yeah. Very creepy."

"Speaking of creepy, I'm almost done with *Mrs. McGinty's Dead*."

"Really? What do you think so far?"

"It's great. Better than *The ABC Murders*."

"Do you know who did it yet?"

"No idea. Give me a hint."

"No way!"

"A tiny hint."

"Are you one of those people who reads the Wikipedia summary before you watch a movie?"

Will rolled his eyes. "Just a *little* hint, Jane. A little hint never hurt anyone."

She paused, thinking, then said, "Okay, well . . . The reveal is really genius. It all hinges on this one piece of knowledge that everyone in the town knows except Hercule Poirot. And nobody's told him because they all assume he knows, too. It's called a *secret de Polichinelle*."

"A *secret de Polichinelle*," Will repeated. "I like that. And I know I said this before, but I keep being surprised by how funny it is. I never knew Agatha was this funny."

Jane smiled. "Hey, now you're on a first-name basis with her, too."

Will laughed. "I guess I am. You've rubbed off on me, Jane."

He reached out and touched the sleeve of her flannel shirt. He looked like he wanted to say more, but the door of the café opened and a customer walked in. Will let go of her shirt and smiled a bit sadly. It was nonstop the rest of the day, and whatever he'd been wanting to say, he never got a chance to actually say it.

On Thursday, Jane went to the local thrift store with Susie and Alana and found an old prom dress to wear for her Rapunzel costume. She bought blond hair extensions at a beauty shop in the next town over. She added purple ribbons to the bodice of the dress, then hand-washed it in the bathtub and hung it up to dry.

Melanie hadn't come back to school after their altercation. Alana said she was taking more time off, that she'd rushed back to school because she thought she needed the distraction, but really she'd needed just the opposite. To *not* be distracted. To fully feel her grief.

And although Jane doubted she'd ever forgive Melanie for what she had said, still . . . she felt sorry for her.

The morning of Halloween arrived gray and chilly. Jane dressed in jeans and a flannel shirt, her standard uniform these days, and threw her hair up in a messy bun.

She paused in the hallway and looked at the closed door of Jemima's childhood bedroom.

What happened to you? she wondered for the thousandth time since Monday night.

And she paused a moment—as if, what? As if Jemima might actually answer her?—then went downstairs to make herself some oatmeal.

The vibe at Bells Hollow High was chaotic and excited. The Halloween dance was the only dance that was open to every grade, and Susie said it was always packed. They were selling tickets at lunch, and Alana grabbed money from everyone and volunteered to stand in the long line.

"I'll pick you up around eight," Susie said as Alana made her way across the cafeteria.

"What?" Jane asked, not looking.

"Jane? Eight?"

"Sorry. Yeah. Melanie's still not here. Do you think she's going to be at the dance?"

"Oh. I don't know. Alana hasn't said anything."

Jane nodded and rubbed at the back of her hand. There was the faintest shadow of a bruise still spanning two of her knuckles.

"Ouch," Susie said, pointing. "Have you ever hit anyone before?"

Jane tried to keep her expression light. "No. Never."

"Me neither," Susie said. "What was it like?"

"It hurts," Jane answered. "I don't recommend it."

Ruth wasn't at North Manor when Jane got home from school, but Jane was used to that by now. The part-time job had quickly turned into a full-time job, one whose hours stretched longer and longer each day. It was almost as if Ruth was trying to spend as much time away from the house as possible— whether consciously or unconsciously. Jane couldn't blame her. She took as many shifts at Beans & Books as she possibly could these days, saving every penny she earned for a trip back to California.

Alone in the house now, Jane made her way down the hallway that led to the mudroom and let herself outside.

It had been so cold lately that she hadn't come into the backyard in a while. But the weather had turned warmer that week; it was chilly but almost nice. The air smelled like fallen leaves and something spicy. Like a distant bonfire, maybe.

And something else.

Yes—roses.

Always like roses.

Jane had gotten so used to the smell that it took her a moment to even pick it out. It was like how, if you lived by the sea, you eventually stopped smelling the salt.

Unless a particularly bad storm had disturbed the water enough.

And then you smelled it again.

Just like how, if the roses had suddenly taken over half the backyard . . .

You smelled them again.

And there they were.

Jane walked closer to them.

They had spread considerably since the last time Jane had been out there. They were at least twice, three times what they had been. The rose arbors were completely hidden from view as the plants tumbled over them and around them, spilling out across the yard, eating up anything in their way.

Jemima Rose.

Roses...

What was the connection?

Jane walked to the fountain, dry for so long now, and paused, resting her elbow on it, just looking at the vivid spots of reds and pinks and oranges that stood out against the grays and blues and dull greens of the rest of the yard.

And the spots of black.

Because so many of the roses were black now, a thick, unyielding black.

There had been several frosts in the past few weeks and surely these plants were not supposed to be like this now?

Jane pulled out her phone and took a photo of them.

The picture came out surreal, almost like an oil painting, and Jane composed a message to Sal without giving herself a chance to second-guess whether she should even send it. She attached the photo and wrote: *Is this normal?*

She watched as the message went through and was marked *delivered*. Sal was definitely still at school, but her reply came just moments later.

Is what normal?

These plants. They keep growing. But it's winter. They're supposed to be dead by now, right?

I don't know anything about plants, Janie. I'm sorry.

And Jane knew the *I'm sorry* meant two specific things:

I'm sorry I don't know anything about plants.

and

I'm sorry for whatever's going on between us.

Jane wrote back: *I'm sorry too.*

They look a little out of season. Especially if it's been so cold.

I know. They just keep growing.

It's like something is keeping them alive.

Jane stared at Sal's text for a minute or two then typed—

Or someone.

And hit Send.

Like who? Your mom?

Jane didn't respond right away. She walked back toward the house, let herself in the mudroom door, and shut and bolted it. She turned back around and looked out the window, through the pane of glass that had to be replaced when Melanie had shattered it.

She wrote a reply to Sal.

Probably my mom, yeah.

And she hit Send, even though she didn't really believe that at all.

Ruth got home around six thirty and changed into her Halloween costume, a flannel shirt with a pair of ripped jeans and a straw hat. She had a small bag of craft hay that she put on the counter. She made dinner while Jane sat at the kitchen table, watching her.

"I think this is the first time I've ever seen you dressed up for Halloween," Jane observed.

"Hmm? Oh. Frank insisted," Ruth replied, shrugging. "I think it's not a bad idea. For me to get out of the house."

"How come?"

"Just so I'm not alone."

"I could stay home with you," Jane offered, and meant it.

"No, honey, go to the dance. You're going to have so much fun."

"Are you sure?"

"Positive," Ruth replied.

"Well, you look cute. You should let me do your makeup."

"How do scarecrows do their makeup?"

"With stitches on their mouth, and patches."

"Oh. Yeah, I guess you should."

Ruth brought two dishes of risotto to the table and they ate quietly, then headed upstairs to Ruth's bedroom. Ruth brought the bag of hay, and Jane opened it and took out a fistful. She arranged it so it was sticking out of Ruth's collar and the cuffs of her sleeves.

"Perfect," Jane said.

Ruth reached out and touched Jane's hair, the little piece of new growth that had annoyingly come to rest on her forehead. "I'm so proud of you, Janie. For everything you've accomplished here. Making friends so quickly, getting a job. You've really made the best of a shitty situation."

Jane shrugged. "Thanks, Mom."

"And you need a haircut," she said.

"I know."

Ruth still held the little curl. She pulled it gently and let it go.

"I want to tell you something," she said after a minute.

"Tell me what?"

There was a long pause, during which it seemed to Jane that Ruth didn't breathe, didn't even move. But then she looked up and inhaled and smiled and said, "I'm just so proud of you."

"You already said that," Jane replied, and somehow she knew that wasn't what Ruth had meant to say at all. Somehow she knew her mother had really started to say something else entirely, but had changed her mind at the last minute.

"It's worth repeating."

"Come into the bathroom," Jane said. "Where's your eyeliner?"

So Ruth sat on the toilet's lid and closed her eyes as Jane carefully traced a scarecrow's smile on her mother's cheeks. She used orange eye shadow to create a patch on Ruth's forehead, and another one on her chin, and eyeliner to trace delicate stitches around them both. Then she stepped back to admire her work.

Greer had always been the one to help Jane with her costume.

Ruth hated Halloween; she didn't take her daughter trick-or-treating or decorate the house, and she would have even refused to give out candy, had Greer not insisted. Jane and Salinger would go out around Jane's neighborhood, checking back in with Greer every so often to let him know they were safe, to let him slip extra candy into their pillowcases, to let him fix their witch or cat or princess makeup if it had smudged.

Ruth would spend the night in her bedroom, watching movies on her computer, romantic comedy after romantic comedy, an endless stream of happiness in ninety-minute chunks.

And then—a sudden memory. A conversation Jane hadn't thought about in years.

She had asked her father about it.

She had asked Greer one Halloween, as he carefully traced whiskers on her face for a puppy-dog costume when she was eight or nine. Why did Ruth hate Halloween so much?

Greer had sighed, put down the eyeliner, and looked carefully at his daughter. He'd always been a straight shooter, and Jane could tell he was trying to find the truth now, in a way that was appropriate for his daughter.

"It isn't my story to tell," he said after a moment.

"Did something happen?" Jane asked.

"A long time ago."

"Something bad?"

"Yes, Janie. So it's hard for your mother to enjoy Halloween, when there's always this thing hanging over her head."

"Will she tell me what it is?"

"When you're older, she'll tell you."

Jane blinked and she was back in North Manor, holding the eyeliner, standing in front of her mother, feeling the phantom cool trace of whiskers on her cheek as Greer worked his magic.

"Does it look okay?" Ruth asked.

And instead of answering, Jane said, "It happened on Halloween, didn't it? That's when Jemima died."

Ruth blinked. Jane didn't think she would answer. She thought her mother might even get upset enough to leave, storm away, but to Jane's surprise, she didn't. To Jane's surprise, she said, "Yes. It happened on Halloween."

"And that's why you don't like Halloween."

"That's why I don't like Halloween."

"I'm sorry."

"It's all right. It was a long time ago."

"And it happened in this house?"

"Yes."

"And that's why you never came back here?"

Ruth nodded.

Jane could feel her mother slipping away from her, mentally checking out of the conversation. Jane touched a hand to the cuff of Ruth's flannel shirt.

"Where did you get this hay, anyway?"

"From the craft store."

"Well, you look adorable."

"Thanks. I feel itchy."

Jane touched up a spot on Ruth's cheek, then found a hand mirror in the top drawer of the vanity and handed it to her mother.

"Voilà," she said.

Ruth examined herself in the mirror, nodding appreciatively. "This is pretty good, honey."

"You're gonna have fun."

"I hope so," Ruth said, even though the expression on her face made it seem like she didn't much care either way. "When are you heading out?"

"Susie is picking me up around eight."

"Text me if you need anything. And keep me posted about how late you'll be, okay?"

"The dance is over at eleven, so I won't be much later than that. Susie mentioned maybe going to Sam's after."

"We used to go to Sam's after our dances, too," Ruth replied, smiling, remembering.

"You and your friends?"

"Mmm. After dances, after bowling, after anything." She laughed. "Emilia hated it."

"How come?"

"She thought it was improper for a girl to be out so late. But I was your age; I had a car and a job. She couldn't really say much."

Jane remembered the stack of papers she'd found in Chester's desk. Her mother's suspensions, her countless detentions, a string of terrible behavior Ruth had never once hinted at.

"What did she think was going to happen?" Jane asked carefully.

"What any parent fears will happen, I guess. That the life they have so carefully prepared for their kid will be rejected by them when they're old enough to make their own decisions about it."

"And you rejected it?"

"I did. Not on purpose, really. But maybe a little bit."

"What do you mean?" Jane pressed, trying to keep her voice light, aware of how delicate it was to talk to Ruth about the past, how Ruth could shut down at any moment, how one wrong word from Jane could ruin everything.

"I don't even know where to start," Ruth said, shrugging. "Besides, I better finish getting ready."

"Can we talk about this later?"

"Sure, Jane." Ruth reached up and rested the palm of her hand on Jane's cheek. Jane got the impression that when her mother looked at her, she wasn't really seeing Jane at all. It made Jane feel a little weird, but she didn't pull away, like she wanted to.

"I love you so much," Ruth said.

"I love you, too, Mom."

"Be safe, okay?"

"Always."

Ruth pecked Jane on the cheek and left her alone in the bathroom.

Jane turned toward the mirror. She felt like she always felt with Ruth—like she came so close to understanding something about her mother, but at the very last moment, it was taken away from her, snatched out of her fingers before she could get a good look at it. Trying to picture her mother at the age Jane was now, going to Sam's with her friends, was impossible. The only Ruth who Jane knew was the Ruth she'd grown up with: a secretive, quiet mother who'd always been there for her but at the same time had never been fully, *completely* emotionally available.

There but not *fully* there.

Always just a tiny bit checked-out.

Always with something sad, something heavy around her eyes. Like a darkness that circled her irises.

It gave Jane the creeps now and admitting that it did only made her feel guilty and strange.

She met her own eyes in the mirror, and for a second she was nine years old, with eyeliner whiskers and a brown sweatshirt and Greer standing behind her, smiling at his handiwork.

"Well, you're certainly the cutest dog *I've* ever seen," he said, but then the doorbell rang and he was gone and Jane was seventeen again, and the past was in the past and her father would never do her makeup for Halloween again. Jane blinked and shook her head and went downstairs to get the door, assuming Ruth had locked herself out of the house. But it was Alana and Susie, grinning wildly, already in costume.

"Trick or treat!" they yelled at the same time.

"Oh shit, you just reminded me—we didn't even get any candy," Jane said, holding the door open to let them in. "We should have left a bowl out."

"No offense, Jane, but I don't think you're going to get many trick-or-treaters here," Alana said, so earnestly that Jane couldn't help laughing.

"Okay, fair," she replied. "You guys are early."

"We were bored," Susie said. "You're not even in your costume yet?"

"I was helping my mom get ready. You look amazing."

Alana did a little spin. She wore black leggings, a long-sleeved black shirt, knee-high black boots, and a sparkly cat-ear headband.

"Dang. Sexy cat," Jane said.

Susie gave a curtsy next, and flashed her teeth. She was wearing an old wedding dress she'd gotten at the thrift store. She'd poured fake blood down the front of it, and glued two vampire teeth over her own canines. She'd drawn a line of fake blood from one corner of her mouth to her chin.

"Very spooky," Jane assessed.

"You better get moving, Rapunzel," Alana said. "It's already seven forty-five."

"Okay, okay." Jane hesitated for just a second—it felt weird to have Alana and Susie back in North Manor, after their sleepover. But it wasn't like she could ask them to wait outside. "You guys want to come upstairs?"

They both nodded, and Jane led them upstairs and into her bedroom. She had her hair extensions laid out carefully on her bed. Susie touched one and said, "Like you need any more hair."

"This is for length!" Jane replied.

"Hello, your hair already touches your butt," Alana pointed out.

"But Rapunzel's hair drags on the floor," Jane countered.

"So this won't quite make it, but at least it will be long enough to put into a braid and swoop over my shoulder."

She grabbed the hair extensions and went into her bathroom. She changed into her dress first, then she carefully clipped the hair extensions in. She put them pretty low, attaching them to sections of her own hair with invisible elastics. When they were all in place, she started on a chunky French braid that incorporated all the pieces and made them look like they were actually part of her own hair.

She stuck little stems of baby's breath into the braid, then admired the finished product. It was pretty impressive, she had to admit. She looked almost *exactly* like the animated movie version of Rapunzel.

She came out of the bathroom and twirled around dramatically for Susie and Alana, who were sitting on the bed.

Susie whistled, and Alana said, "Damn, girl. You look hot."

"Thank you, thank you."

"All right, let's go," Susie said.

Jane turned out lights as they made their way downstairs, then locked the front door behind them. She couldn't help looking back at the house as she slid into Susie's car, but North Manor was dark and quiet behind her.

Susie backed out of the driveway and they were on their way. In the back seat, Alana pulled out a little silver flask. When she opened it, the entire car was filled with the scent of cinnamon. She took a swig and handed it to Jane, who sniffed it.

"What is this?"

"Goldschläger!"

"Gold *what*?" Jane replied.

"It's cinnamon schnapps! It has real gold in it!" Alana gushed.

"You want me to drink gold?" Jane asked.

"Where did you even get that?" Susie added.

"In the very back of my parents' liquor cabinet. I don't think they've touched it in years. The bottle was covered in dust."

"They haven't touched it in years because people aren't supposed to drink *gold*, maybe," Jane insisted.

"Just try it. It's really good."

Jane took a hesitant sip. "Oh wow. This *is* really good." She felt the warmth spread instantly down her chest. It was *really* good.

"You're lucky I don't like cinnamon, or I'd feel very left out right now," Susie said.

"Thank you for being our DD, Susie," Alana said.

"Thank you, Susie," Jane echoed.

"You're welcome," Susie replied.

The school looked different in the dark; Jane had never seen it after three o'clock before. The brick façade was imposing in the moonlight, and someone had replaced the light bulbs over the front door with black lights. Everyone who walked underneath them was washed in a spooky, dark glow.

"Look at my teeth," Susie said gleefully, baring her fangs, which were currently glowing. "Do they look cool?"

"Very cool," Alana said. "Say cheese." She pulled out her phone and snapped a picture.

They walked into the entranceway and up to a folding table that had been placed outside the doors to the gym. Rosemary, the receptionist who had greeted Jane on her first day, was taking tickets. She was dressed like a clown, complete with an orange, curly wig and a red nose.

"Hi, girls! Don't you look amazing?!" she exclaimed.

They handed over their tickets and she stamped the backs of their hands.

"Thanks, Rosemary!" Alana said. "Lovin' the nose."

Rosemary beamed and waved them all through the doors and into the gym—

Which had been completely transformed.

"Holy *crap*," Susie whispered.

It looked amazing. The bleachers had been pushed back and were completely covered by enormous trees strung with orange fairy lights. Bats and spiders had been attached to the branches, and cobwebs stretched from treetop to treetop. They had hung a disco ball from the ceiling and all the lights were low, plus some of the bulbs had been replaced with black lights here, too, giving the whole gym a slightly glowing, surreal feeling. An enormous banner hung from the ceiling: WELCOME TO THE HAUNTED FOREST.

It was really impressive.

The gym was already crowded with people dancing to the music. Someone had built a small raised platform at the far corner of the room, and there was a DJ standing there in front of an elaborate computer setup. She was dressed like a unicorn with an enormous, lit-up sparkly horn.

"Check her out," Susie said, pointing.

"I'm in love," Alana replied.

"This is really cool," Jane said.

They took a slow lap through the gym, making their way around the outer edge of the room, taking everything in. There were two long tables of refreshments in front of a section of bleachers, and Jane grabbed a mini Twix bar from an enormous cauldron filled with candy. She unwrapped it as they walked and shared half with Susie, who was making grabby hands.

The closer they got to the DJ platform, the more crowded the dance floor became. There was hardly space to move toward the center, so they stayed on the outside, just observing. Alana pulled out the flask again after surreptitiously checking for chaperones, and she and Jane each had a sip. There was hardly enough in there to get any of them really buzzed, Jane thought, but then Alana reached down her shirt and pulled out a tiny bottle of vodka.

"Did you have that in your bra?" Susie asked, impressed.

"One on each side," Alana confirmed. "It has to be even, you know."

She twisted off the top of the bottle and had a swig, then handed it to Jane. Jane took a tiny sip and felt it go right to her head. She really didn't drink that much, aside from an occasional half glass of wine at dinner, and the schnapps and vodka had combined efforts to make her feel a little light-headed and tingly. In a nice way. She finished the bottle.

"All right, girl, get it," Alana said appreciatively.

"Let's find pizza," Susie said. "There's supposed to be pizza somewhere."

"Let's *dance*," Alana argued.

"Let's get pizza, *then* dance," Jane offered.

That was agreeable to everyone, so they pushed back out of the throng of dancers and found the pizza table. They made themselves plates and took them over to a corner of the gym that had been set up with café tables and chairs. They found an empty table and crowded around it.

Jane felt good: The pizza was amazing, the music was loud, the energy in the room was high. She bobbed her head to the music as she ate, and when they were done, they cleaned their table and made their way back onto the dance floor.

Dances at her old school had been nothing like this. She'd gone to junior prom with a boy she'd been sort of dating at the time, and it was held in the ballroom of a fancy hotel. They'd rented a limousine and exchanged corsages and boutonnieres and had a stuffy dinner and danced to music just slightly out of date. The whole thing had felt a bit like kids playing at being adults, and she couldn't really say that she had *fun*. At least, nothing like the fun that everybody was clearly having here. There were no slow songs, just music you could dance to, and kids were huddled in big groups, jumping up and down to the beat.

Her own group wasted no time in getting into the swing of things. Susie was an amazing dancer, and for a second Jane just watched her, transfixed as she swung her hips around in perfect time to the music. Alana, on the other hand, was laughably bad, but knew it, and played up her two left feet by dancing wildly and without reservation. Jane was somewhere in the middle, not horrible but not great, and she found after a few minutes that she didn't even care what she looked like, she just cared that she was with friends and having fun and not at home in the creep house.

They danced for at least an hour—until Jane was hot and thirsty and the line of blood at Susie's mouth had smudged and they had all laughed so much their throats ached.

"Let's get some water, I'm dying," Alana said finally, and the three of them made their way off the dance floor to the refreshment tables, where Jane poured herself a cup of water from an enormous cooler, and they all stood around breathing heavily and drinking.

Jane pulled out her phone and sent Ruth a text that said, *At the dance! So much fun, hope your party is great!* Then she saw that she had a message from Will, so she clicked over to read it.

I just finished the book. I don't know how to say this, but I just have to ask . . . do you not know?

Jane stared at the text for a moment, reading it over again to see if she'd missed something. She wrote back: *Do I not know what?*

The little speech bubble that indicated Will was typing a

response popped up, then disappeared, then popped up, then disappeared, like he kept deleting whatever he was writing. Finally he sent back a simple: *Never mind, let's talk later.*

No no, what do you mean?

"I have to pee!" Alana exclaimed suddenly. "What bathrooms are we supposed to use? The locker rooms?"

"Probably," Susie said. "Come on, we'll all go."

Someone grabbed Jane by the forearm and led her across the gym to the bathrooms, where the line to pee was at least ten girls deep.

"I can't wait this long," Alana said. "Can we use the ones in the science wing? Are we allowed to leave the gym?"

"Rosemary will let us," Susie replied, so they made their way back to the entrance, where Rosemary was reading a book in lieu of anything else to do.

"Hey, girls!"

"Rosemary, we have to pee," Alana said. "It's an emergency. Can we use the bathrooms by the science wing?"

"Sure, but right there and back, okay? No detours."

"We promise," Alana said. She was currently jumping up and down on the balls of her feet.

Rosemary laughed. "Go on, you're welcome."

Jane still held her phone in her hand but Will hadn't texted anything back, hadn't even typed anything.

What did that mean? *Do you not know?*

"Jane, come on!" Susie said, tugging Jane's arm.

Jane let herself be led to the science bathrooms. The noise

of the gym died away almost completely as soon as they turned the first corner past the main office. The corridors were dark and a little spooky, and the bathroom light was off. Alana flicked it on, then dashed into the nearest stall.

"Somebody sing something! It's too quiet to pee!" she demanded.

Susie launched into a pretty good rendition of "Single Ladies" while she stood at the sink reapplying her line of fake blood. Jane stood near the door, staring at her phone.

She sent Will a text that just said: ???

He still didn't write back.

She put the phone into her purse.

Alana finished peeing and washed her hands while Susie ended her song with an impressive howl. Then Alana seemed to realize Jane hadn't moved in a solid three minutes, and with a hand full of paper towels she said, "Jane? Are you okay?"

Jane's brain was whirring a mile a minute. She still felt the warmth and gentle fuzziness of the alcohol swimming around in her stomach.

"A *secret de Polichinelle*," she whispered.

"Come again?" Alana said.

"It's from an Agatha Christie book. It's a secret that everybody knows," Jane said, her voice getting louder as she started to realize something.

"What are you talking about?" Susie asked.

"And because everybody knows the secret, nobody talks about it, because everybody just assumes that everybody else knows it, so there's no reason to ever bring it up," Jane continued.

"You've totally lost me," Alana said.

"Your brother," Jane said, turning to Susie. "Your brother asked me, *Do you not know?*"

"What don't you know?" Alana asked.

"Something that everybody else knows," Jane said. "Something you all know but you don't talk about in front of me." She watched as they caught up, as their expressions changed from confused to understanding. Alana's mouth actually fell open slightly. She looked horrified. "What don't I know?" Jane asked.

"You don't know about..." Susie trailed off. Alana took a tiny step back. Her hands were clasped over her chest so tightly they were turning white.

"Susie, tell me what I don't know," Jane said, and maybe it was because her voice was so calm and unshaking, but Susie finally nodded and took a deep breath.

"You don't know about what happened in that house, do you? About what happened in North Manor?"

"Is this about Jemima Rose?" Jane asked.

"You have to know about Jemima," Alana blurted out. "Everybody knows about Jemima."

"What happened to her?" Jane asked.

"She died," Alana whispered.

"How?"

"It was a freak accident," Susie said quietly. "She was playing in the garden with a friend. Hide-and-go-seek. They had been doing gardening back there. Planting rosebushes. Putting up arbors for the roses to vine up. She wasn't supposed to go back there. There were open holes, all this loose dirt. And nobody really knows exactly how it happened. But…"

Susie's voice became so low that nobody could hear her anymore, and finally she just stopped talking altogether.

Alana bit her lower lip, hard, then continued, "There was a big hole. She fell into it. And when she tried to climb out, all the dirt that was piled up fell on top of her. She suffocated."

"She was buried alive?" Jane asked, her fingertips suddenly cold, her mouth suddenly dry.

"It was really sad," Susie continued. "She was only eight. Her friend ran to get help, but when they found her, it was too late."

"It happened on Halloween," Jane said.

"Yeah," Susie said. "Your mom took it really badly. That's why she moved to California."

"But—years later," Jane said. "I mean, she didn't leave Bells Hollow until she was in her twenties. It must have been, like, twenty years later."

"Twenty years? No, it was just a week after Jemima died," Alana corrected. "She was there for the funeral, and she was gone the next day."

"A week?" Jane repeated. "That doesn't make any sense. Jemima died when they were kids."

"Jane…," Susie said, her voice faltering. She cleared her throat and started again. "Jane, who do you think Jemima was?"

"My aunt," Jane replied immediately. "Jemima was my mom's sister."

"Oh no," Alana whispered.

"What?" Jane asked. There were warning bells going off in her brain. She felt light-headed and woozy. She took a step back, then another, until she felt the wall behind her. She leaned into it. "What?" she repeated.

"Jemima wasn't your aunt," Susie whispered.

"Jemima was your sister," Alana said.

Jane heard all this, but she heard it as if it were happening at the end of a very long tunnel. She heard her friends' voices as if they were warped and wiggling. She saw stars in front of her eyes. A gentle lightening of her vision. She slid down the wall until she was seated on the bathroom floor with her knees pulled up to her chest.

"Jane?" Susie asked.

Jane put her forehead down on her knees. She took big, gulping breaths.

Sister.

She was going to pass out.

No, she was fine. She was sitting down. She was breathing.

"Jane?"

She tried to hold up a finger, *one minute*, but her hands weren't working the way they were supposed to work. She couldn't even feel them anymore. There were tears stinging at her eyes, and her chest was moving up and down, up and down, but she wasn't getting any air. Everything was going black.

"Jane?" A voice very close to her. A hand on her shoulder. Susie, kneeling down in front of her. "Jane, just breathe. I'm right here."

Gradually, the whooshing noise in her ears faded and the feeling returned to her fingers and when she lifted her head from her knees, there was Susie, a calm but concerned look on her face. Behind her, Alana had tears on her cheeks.

"I'm okay," Jane said.

"Do you want to stand up?" Susie asked.

"Yes."

So Susie helped her up. They went slowly. Jane had a flashback to Will helping her in the doorway of her bedroom.

Will. He knew, too. Everybody knew.

"Everybody knows," she whispered. She was standing now. Susie let go of her hands and Jane realized she was holding her phone. She must have pulled it out of her bag. Her hands were shaking. She held on to it tightly, gripping it hard enough that it hurt, concentrating on the pain to wash the cobwebs out of her head.

"Jane, we're so sorry. We didn't think you would want us to talk about it. We all just assumed you knew," Alana said.

"Everybody knows," Jane repeated. "Right? Sorry. I'm just trying to wrap my head around it."

"It's sort of . . . town legend," Susie said, her voice soft and gentle. "Everybody knows, yeah."

Jane nodded, grateful for the honesty. All she wanted now was honesty.

A flash—

Greer, telling her the reason Ruth didn't like Halloween was because something bad had happened on that day, years ago.

He knew.

Why hadn't he told her?

Why hadn't any of them told her?

It wasn't Greer's daughter, said a small voice in the back of Jane's head. It had been years before Ruth met Greer. So who was Jemima's dad? Just some kid Ruth had met at Sam's Diner after a night out with her friends?

"Would you drive me home?" Jane asked Susie, her voice quiet. "I think I just want to go to sleep."

"Jane, I'm so sorry," Susie said. "I feel terrible. I feel like I should have said something. But it never seemed like the right time to bring it up. And it never would have occurred to me to ask if you knew. . . ."

"*Hi, welcome to Bells Hollow, do you know you had a sister who died here?*" Jane said, nodding. "I understand. I'm not mad at any of you. Can you please just . . . ?"

"Of course. I'll drive you home. Let's go."

"You should stay," Jane said to Alana.

"We could all come over," Alana offered. "This dance is kind of boring anyway."

Jane smiled. "No, it's not. It's really fun. And you should stay, and Susie will come back after she drops me off. It's only nine thirty. Please stay. I'm just going to get in bed."

"Are you sure?" Alana asked.

"A hundred percent," Jane insisted.

"Okay. But text me. If you need anything."

"I will."

They walked back down the hallway together and Alana went into the gym. Susie spoke to Rosemary quickly, explaining that she'd be driving Jane home but coming back to the dance, and Rosemary agreed. She glanced at Jane, a look Jane thought was filled with sadness and pity.

She knows, Jane thought.

Everybody knew.

The ride back to North Manor was quiet, but not uncomfortable. Jane stared out the window at the darkness of the night rushing past her. One word kept repeating in her brain, over and over, a sloppy rhythm that had no real beat.

Sister. Sister. Sister.

Jane had always wanted a sister.

And now she both had one and didn't have one.

Now she had both found one and lost one, all in the span of a minute or two.

When they reached Jane's driveway, Susie put the car in park and sighed heavily.

"I can't imagine what you must be feeling," she said quietly.

"Just a little numb," Jane responded.

"I am *so* sorry you had to find out like that."

"She should have told me."

"Yeah. She should have."

"But I'm glad I know now."

"I'm so sorry."

"Thank you for driving me home," Jane said, turning to face Susie. "You're a good friend."

"Are you sure you don't want me to come in?"

"It's fine. I'm tired. I'm just going to go to bed. I'll text you in the morning."

"Okay. I'll wait until you get inside."

"Have fun," Jane said. She leaned over and they hugged quickly, then Jane pulled away and got out of the car and walked up to the front door of North Manor.

She unlocked the door and pushed it open, then turned around and waved at Susie, who waved back and began reversing out of the driveway.

Jane stepped inside the house and shut the door behind her.

And she knew she wasn't alone the second it latched shut.

How did she know?

It was a few things.

The tiny hairs on the back of her neck stood up straight. She felt goose bumps crawl up her arms, from the back of her hands to her shoulders. And there was a buzzing in her ears. A deep tinnitus that momentarily blocked out any other sound.

She couldn't move.

The house was the darkest it had ever been, the darkest any place in the world had ever been. She couldn't move, she couldn't breathe.

And then the lights came on.

Jane blinked, suddenly blinded. The chandelier blazed above her, and she spun around quickly, but there was no one beside her who could have turned it on.

But there were two places you could turn the chandelier on.

She looked up the stairs, to the top of the enormous, winding staircase, and there was her mother, sixteen and pregnant, a prisoner in this house, just a child carrying a child, with nowhere to go, no options but to stay under Emilia's roof, in this house she hated, in this town she couldn't wait to leave.

Jane blinked and her mother was just her mother again, still in her scarecrow costume, her makeup smudged, her hat missing.

"I got your text," Ruth said.

In the quiet of the house, her words almost echoed.

"My text?" Jane repeated.

Ruth took a few steps forward, a few steps down the staircase. She was holding her phone. She clicked something on it and read, *"I hate you, I've always hated you! You never wanted me, you just wanted HER. Well, now I know everything. And you can't have her and you can't have me, you can't have either of us."*

"I didn't . . . But I didn't . . ."

Jane fumbled with her purse, pulling her own phone out of it, and clicked into her messages with her mother.

Sure enough, there it was. Sent twenty minutes ago. From Jane's phone to Ruth's.

"I don't even know what this means," Jane said, her voice coming out in a whisper, her chest twisted and tight.

"I can't tell you how many times I told my mother I hated her," Ruth said. She took another few steps down the staircase, until she was on the landing.

"But I don't hate you," Jane said, dropping her purse on the ground. "I don't even remember sending this!"

"Who told you?" Ruth asked.

"I..."

"Who told you about Jemima? This is about Jemima, isn't it? Who told you?"

"Mom, I didn't..."

"It's not important. It was only a matter of time."

"You said she was my aunt," Jane said. "You lied to me."

"Do you have any idea how many times I tried to tell you, Jane? In that endless fucking car ride across the country, how many times I tried to tell you what had happened in this house? Why I never came back here; why I never brought *you* back here? I tried."

"You should have tried harder," Jane said, her voice rising, so that by the time she finished, she was yelling. "You should have told me! You should have told me *years* ago! That I had a sister!"

The word *sister*.

An enormous word.

A word too big for Jane to fully comprehend.

"She wasn't your sister," Ruth said sadly. "She was barely my daughter, Jane. I was sixteen, just a kid, just a *baby*. Jemima was my mother's child, her perfect child. The child I never was. The child who would wear pinafores and lace and pink ribbons and white, spotless stockings. Don't you see?"

"No," Jane said. "No, I don't see anything. I don't understand *anything*."

Ruth nodded. She took a deep breath. She sat down on the landing. "Okay. I'll tell you. But it's not a good story, Jane. It's not a good story."

"Okay," Jane said. "I want to know, though. I need to know."

Ruth nodded again. She looked up for a moment, like she was searching back through time, putting everything in order. Then she looked back at Jane and started talking. "I was a tough kid. Angry at everyone. Resentful. Growing up in this house, living under Emilia's rules... Everything had to look a certain way, everything had to present a certain way. Including me. There was no room for compromise, no room for who I was. I don't actually think she cared much. It wasn't about having a child, for her; it was about rounding out the family portrait. You didn't *not* have kids, back then, especially not someone like Emilia. So she had me, and she wished I was a boy, and she passed me off to nannies, and she took me out when she needed a good prop." Ruth paused. "I hated her."

"She wished you were a boy?" Jane said.

"Oh god, yeah. Someone to pass on the family name, to take over the business from my father; all that typical, old bullshit."

"And you didn't want it?"

"I didn't want any of it. I think I was a normal enough kid, you know? I wanted to get dirty, play with my friends, run around. But Emilia kept me inside. I was grounded all the time. She stuffed me in party dresses and made me practice the piano and take French lessons—all these things I couldn't care less about." Ruth paused. She bit her lower lip, thinking. "Then I turned thirteen, fourteen, fifteen, and things changed. I changed. I was getting into a lot of trouble at school. I think Emilia just checked out. She wouldn't sign my detention slips, my report cards. She didn't care about trying to make me someone I wasn't anymore. I don't think she cared about *me* anymore. She just...left me alone."

"What about Chester?"

Ruth softened. "He was living under Emilia's roof, too. He worked a lot. Stayed in his study most nights. But he tried. I do think he tried. But by then, I was too far gone. I was doing things just to spite her. Just to get her attention. And then, of course, I got pregnant."

"What did she do?"

"A full one-eighty," Ruth said, doing a little spin with her index finger. "She yanked me out of school, hired private tutors, let me eat and do whatever I wanted. She was my mom again. She was attentive, kind...I wanted to give her up. The baby. That was the plan, the entire time. But then I went into labor...I delivered her right here, you know. In this house." Ruth looked upstairs, and Jane followed her gaze, as if they both might see her, sixteen-year-old Ruth and her newborn child. "They took her away. I thought I would never see her again. I was sad, but I knew it was the right thing to do. I went to sleep, and I woke up the next morning and I thought it was all over. My body was sore and my emotions were wrecked, but I thought that was it."

She paused again, her mouth a straight line, her eyes wet and faraway. "And then a nurse brought her into the room. She was dressed in a pink bodysuit. With two little bows right here and here." Ruth pointed to either side of her chest. She laughed, but it was less of a laugh this time and more of a choke, a sob, and Jane saw that she'd begun to cry. "The nurse lifted up my shirt. I was too shocked to protest, to say anything....I thought she was gone. I thought it was over. The nurse pressed the baby into me, helped her latch. And she said, 'Her name is Jemima Rose.' And she sat down in a chair and waited until I was done, then she took her away again."

"She named her?" Jane asked, her voice a whisper. "Emilia named your baby?"

"I think it was her way of saying, *This is mine*. I was hardly ever alone with her. I was kept out of school. We were cloistered here, secluded. After the birth, something in me just... broke. All this anger, all the resentment that had been building up inside me for so long, it was gone. Like I'd pushed it out with Jemima. I didn't leave the house for two years. I hardly even left my room."

"For two years?"

"Emilia went back to ignoring me. It was all about Jemima. She was Emilia's shining, bright new baby. And she was a good baby. She slept well, she hardly ever cried. She was beautiful.

She was everything Emilia wished I had been. I don't even think she minded that it was another girl." Ruth took a long breath and wiped the tears from her cheeks. "But I knew something was wrong with her. I knew it from the beginning."

"Something was wrong with her?"

"I became obsessed with the idea. I would sneak into her room and watch her sleeping in her crib. I'd watch her do everything Emilia asked her to do, play her part like a perfect little doll, then turn around and snarl at me, this look in her eyes like..."

"Like what?"

"Like all the anger and resentment that had left my body had gone right into her."

Jane shivered. It was suddenly cold in the foyer, like the temperature in the house had dropped a few degrees. Ruth was still crying, silent tears that fell down her cheeks and dripped off the side of her chin.

"Do you think that's what happened?" Jane asked.

"I was just a kid," Ruth said. "Just a scared, fucked-up kid with a mother who didn't know what I needed. It's all fuzzy now, you know? What I saw. What I didn't see. The truth versus whatever twisted reality my brain was inventing. Jemima grew up. Sometimes she called me *Mama*, sometimes she called me *Ruthie*. It was never hidden from her, that I was her mother. She called Emilia *Grandma*. Emilia never pretended to be anything other than that. And Jemima was...different. I know she was different. And then she died. And it was like a spell had been broken. I left after her funeral. I'd never set foot outside this town before, but I had enough money to get myself to California. Bus after bus after bus. And when I finally saw the ocean, I cried. I sat down in the sand and cried and missed her and mourned her but...felt finally free. From all of it. It was over. It was like a nightmare I was waking up from."

"How did she die?" Jane asked softly, wanting to hear Ruth's version of events, to compare it to Susie and Alana's.

"Another day, Janie," Ruth replied. "I can't think about it anymore tonight."

"I just...I need to know," Jane pleaded. "Just a little more? Just...What happened to her?"

Ruth nodded. "There was a terrible accident. They were digging these little trenches out back, installing new arbors for my mother's prized roses. Jemima was homeschooled; she didn't have many friends, but one of the housekeepers had brought her daughter to work with her one day. Emilia was furious, of course. The housekeeper couldn't find a sitter; she was in tears. I watched this whole screaming fight between them.... But Jemima took to the little girl right away. Annie. Annie Cansler. They started playing together. And suddenly Annie was coming with her mother once a week. She was Jemima's first real friend."

"Cansler," Jane repeated.

"She was a beautiful little girl," Ruth continued. "She had this stuffed teddy bear. Simon. She carried him everywhere. For all the years I knew her, she always had that bear.

"They were eight years old. Annie came over; they were

going to go trick-or-treating together. My father was going to take them. Annie's mom dropped her off. They went to play out by the rosebushes, even though they knew they weren't supposed to, and...Jemima fell into one of the holes. It was just big enough that she couldn't get out. Annie tried to help her, Jemima tried to climb out, but...She was covered by dirt. She suffocated."

"Why does that name sound familiar?" Jane wondered aloud.

"I need to go to sleep, Janie. I'm so sorry. For everything. For keeping this from you for so long. I hope you don't hate me." Her voice caught, and she rubbed her eyes with her fingers. The house felt colder still, like a chill had worked its way through the windowpanes, through the walls, up through the floorboards.

"I could never hate you," Jane replied automatically, and it was the truth.

She hadn't sent that message. She hadn't told Ruth she hated her. She hadn't sent that message.

I hate you, I've always hated you! You never wanted me, you just wanted HER. Well, now I know everything. And you can't have her and you can't have me, you can't have either of us.

She didn't understand. She didn't understand what it meant.

"Mom..."

"Do you really think I never wanted you?" Ruth asked. She stood up, gripping the banister with her hand so tightly that Jane could see the skin at her knuckles turn white.

"No, I don't, I didn't..."

I didn't write that message.

"It destroyed me when she died," Ruth continued, her eyes vacant now, a million miles away. "I was too young to have a baby. I didn't know the first thing about having a child. I wasn't even emotionally capable of taking care of myself, let alone another living thing, a *baby*. I kept her at arm's length. I wouldn't let myself get too close to her. If she called me Mama, I...Sometimes I corrected her. But I loved her. Of course, I loved her; she was my child. I was devastated when...when it happened. But I was also set free."

She took a hard, scratchy breath that turned into a sob halfway through. "I know how that sounds. It's something I've wrestled with my entire life. Whether I'm a monster for even admitting that I felt some sort of relief when she died. I'm not proud of it. The opposite. It mortifies me, it *kills* me. And I swore I would never have another child...."

"But then I met your father. And we fell in love. I'd never been in love before. I wasn't in love with Jemima's father; I barely spoke to him after I got pregnant. He tried to call me a couple times. He even showed up at the house once, but my mother made it clear that his role was done. And as the years passed, and the distance and the time worked to soften the terrible tragedy of her death...I decided I was ready to have another baby. So we tried, and you were born, and..." She was really sobbing now, harder than Jane had ever seen her cry before. Jane wanted to go to comfort her, but she couldn't move, she couldn't make her legs work. "So you can't say I didn't want you. You can never say I didn't want you."

"Mom, I—"

"Please don't ask me anything else tonight, Jane. Please. I can't. I can't."

Still gripping the banister, Ruth turned and walked up the stairs, one step at a time, slowly, and she didn't turn around at all. She reached the top floor and disappeared down the hallway and Jane couldn't move, she couldn't make her feet move. The chandelier was blazing above her, beating down its harsh, yellow light.

She was still holding her phone. The message was on the screen, the message she hadn't sent. But if she hadn't sent it, who had?

I hate you, I've always hated you! You never wanted me, you just wanted HER. Well, now I know everything. And you can't have her and you can't have me, you can't have either of us.

If Jane hadn't written it . . .

She looked up the stairs.

Dimly, in the back of her consciousness, she heard Ruth's bedroom door shut.

If Jane hadn't written it . . .

You never wanted me, you just wanted HER.

The text message to Sal: *Everything is so good. Everything is perfect. I love it here.*

And the message she'd written to Ruth when Alana and Susie had stayed over: *Take your time, mama. I have friends over. We're having so much fun!*

And the FaceTime calls she couldn't remember.

And and and . . .

Jane's fingers were numb.

Was she ready to admit, now, that she believed in . . .

The word was still so hard to say. It was silly and childish. It was white sheets with eyeholes cut out and grainy pictures of disembodied heads and bumps in the night when you're home alone, all tucked in bed and frozen with fear.

Ghost.

Sister.

Were they one and the same?

She put her hand on the banister and took a deep breath.

Had she known this was going to happen? Had she known this was how tonight would end? Had she felt the inevitability of it, even before they'd left California, even before she'd ever stepped foot in this state, this town, this house?

She went upstairs.

She didn't feel frightened, not really.

What she felt, instead, was a sort of resolve. A calmness that radiated from her heart. A warmth that spread out to the tips of her fingertips. A sort of happiness . . .

A sister.

She had always wanted a sister.

She reached the top landing. The upstairs hallway stretched long in front of her, dark and shadowy and, perhaps to some, a little creepy.

But not to Jane.

She wasn't creeped out anymore.

She was just curious.

She closed the distance to her sister's room.

Her *sister.*

And the light was on. Of course the light was on. Hadn't she known the light was on as soon as she had heard Ruth's bedroom door close? Hadn't she known the light was on when she was underneath the too-bright chandelier?

She reached the door. And she let her hand sit on the doorknob for just a moment. It felt warm and soft underneath her grip.

She turned it.

She pushed the door open.

And there she was.

A small, delicate-looking girl wearing a stuffy dress with white stockings and white patent-leather shoes. Sitting on the bed. Her long, curly hair tumbling over her shoulders and down her back. One single misbehaving lock falling right in the middle of her forehead. A face that looked so much like Jane's. A face that looked up at Jane now, and smiled, so big, so wide...

Don't worry. She won't wake up.

Jane couldn't breathe, couldn't move, couldn't blink—

Someone's coming. Do you want to have a little fun?

It wasn't possible it wasn't possible it wasn't.

I'm really happy you're here.

But no no no.

Jane blinked and there was no girl, there was just an empty bedroom.

Jane blinked and something crashed downstairs.

Jane blinked and the bedroom light turned off.

And voices...

There were voices.

There were two voices and laughter and the sound of fumbling as whatever had been knocked over was set right again.

"Watch where you're fucking going." A girl's voice.

"Can't believe they left the front door unlocked." A guy's voice.

"Sort of disappointing. I was looking forward to smashing another window."

"And you're sure nobody's home? I mean, why is this light on?"

"Nobody's home. She's at the dance. Courtney saw her. And her mom is at Frank's party. My cousin is there. I don't know why the light's on. My mom leaves lights on, too. But trust me—nobody's here."

Jane couldn't help it; she smiled. This town really *was* small. Melanie had eyes everywhere.

Because of course it was Melanie. Melanie and her boyfriend, Jeff. But what were they up to?

Jane looked back at the bed. It was empty. The room was dark. It was easy to admit, now, that there hadn't been a little girl on the bed at all.

Because there was no such thing as—

Footsteps on the stairs.

Jane ducked into the closet, pushing aside rows of stuffy party dresses until she was totally hidden. She'd left the door to the room open, so she could hear Melanie and Jeff clearly when they reached the upstairs hallway.

"This one," Melanie said. They were the right distance away; they were going into Jane's bedroom. "Let's start in here."

"And why are we here again? The Halloween dance is the only dance that doesn't totally suck."

"Because they're both gone. And we needed them out of the house, so we can look for it."

Jane listened intently, every cell in her body given over to the act of listening, and as she listened she felt her skin start to itch with the familiar heat of her anger.

She told herself it was fine. It was fine. She didn't know what they were doing here, what they wanted, but they couldn't stay long. They wouldn't. It would be fine.

But what if it isn't fine?

A small, childlike voice. A dark, scratchy, dangerous voice. Jane whirled around in the closet so quickly she almost lost her balance. But she was alone. Of course she was alone. Because there was no such thing as—

What if they touch your things? Your books, your journals? I know how much you love them. I've seen you with them.

On the other side of her—

Jane spun back around so quickly she *did* fall, but she caught herself on the back wall of the closet before she crashed into anything.

The closet was empty. She was all alone. She was alone and safe.

Safe, yes, but not alone anymore. And isn't that nice? You never have to be alone again. We have each other now.

Jane covered her face with her hands, pressing her palms against her cheeks, squeezing her eyes shut. From far away, she heard a crash that might have been her bedside lamp. There was no way Ruth was sleeping through this. She would wake up, she would help Jane....

She won't wake up. I told you she won't wake up. She's deep, deep asleep, it's just you and me....

She was alone, she was alone, there was no such thing as ghosts....

I never meant to scare you, Jane. But you kept not seeing me. I just wanted you to see me.

It was hard to breathe. Jane opened her mouth and tried to get enough oxygen. She felt light-headed and strange and scared. She was making it up, she was making it all up....

How come Mama never grew her hair long again? Did she not want to look like us anymore?

Ruth had always had short hair.

No, it used to be long, like ours. Grandma was always yelling at her to get her hair out of her mouth. Do you know the doctors had to cut into her stomach and take away all the hair she'd eaten? It was in a big ball inside her.

Jane's ears were ringing. A high-pitched, angry scream.

So Grandma went into her bedroom one night when she was sleeping, and she cut it all off. She cut off all her hair so she couldn't put it into her mouth anymore.

Jane's eyes opened underneath her palms.

I know you eat things you're not supposed to eat, too. I know what it's like to love something so much you have to eat it.

She knew when she took her hands away she would be alone and not alone. She knew when she took her hands away she would see her sister. She could *feel* Jemima now, close to her, so close the hairs on the back of her arms felt electric.

"What do you mean?" Jane whispered, careful to keep her voice quiet enough so it wouldn't leave the safety of the closet.

I ate things, too. Things I wasn't supposed to eat. Mama would get so mad at me.

"What things did you eat?"

The roses. I loved roses so much that Grandma planted more for me. Did you see all the roses in the back? The petals are so soft. Whenever I felt angry or mean or sad or scared, I would eat them. They would always make me feel better. Is that how it works with you, too, Janie?

Jane took her hands away from her face and there was her sister, kneeling on the floor of her closet, her hands clasped together on her thighs, her hair wild and curly, her skin slightly glowing and slightly transparent, her eyes bright and happy and just a little bit mean.

But she wasn't really there at all. Because she wasn't real, and Jane could both see her and not see her. If she squinted,

Jemima was clearer. If she opened her eyes, she was alone in the closet.

"You ate the roses," Jane whispered.

A flash to her mother: *You can't eat things that aren't food,* she had said, and Jane had known, even then, that she had said those words before, that she'd had those exact words said to *her.*

They taste yummy, and they don't make you sick. They make me feel better. Sometimes I get so angry, angry, angry, but the roses always help.

Jane opened her eyes and Jemima was gone. She squinted and she could see her again, the blurry lines of a sister who was long dead. The blurry lines of Jane's own imagination. Because ghosts weren't real. Because none of this was happening. . . .

Jemima looked past Jane and it was like she was seeing through the closet wall, down the hallway, through the walls of Jane's bedroom. Her eyes darkened. Jane's breath caught in her throat when she saw how similar she and Jemima looked when they were angry.

She's going to touch your things, Jemima said, her voice a razor. *She's going to touch your special books.*

Then she smiled, and her little white teeth seemed to glow, and her smile wasn't the smile of a nice eight-year-old girl; it was the smile of something wrong, and not good, the smile of someone who had done bad things. . . .

And she disappeared.

No matter how much Jane squinted her eyes, no matter how hard Jane tried to look for her, Jemima was gone.

Jane listened. It was all she could do, listen, because her body seemed frozen in place. Her heart was beating out of control; she felt sweat creeping down the insides of her thighs. The Rapunzel dress was too hot, too scratchy. The hair extensions were weighing down her scalp. Her eyes were stinging.

She heard a thump. From above her.

"What was that?" Jeff asked.

It made Jane smile, just a little, to hear the fear in his voice.

"These old houses make all kinds of noises," Melanie replied.

It was the same thing Jane used to tell herself.

Jane smiled wider.

The fear she felt was slowly being replaced with anger. Good, strong, pure anger. It unstuck her limbs and calmed her heart and filled her with a gentle kind of peace.

Another bump, and something else . . . A low, long moan.

"What was that?" Jeff asked.

"It's the wind. Are you scared of the *wind* now? Look, these are actually her journals. This is amazing; we need to take pictures of all of this."

"Are you hearing this? Mel, are you listening to this?" Jeff's voice was rising in pitch and so was the moaning. It was absolutely unmistakable: the moaning of an eight-year-old girl. How could Melanie possibly mistake that for *wind*?

Unless she was hearing something different altogether, Jane realized.

Unless Jemima was trying to get Jeff out of the house, but leave Melanie unafraid.

"Here, take this," Melanie said.

"What do you want me to do with this?"

"Just take it," Melanie said.

What had she given him?

The moaning was even louder.

"You're not hearing anything? Seriously?"

"Jesus, Jeff, get your shit together."

"I'm out of here," he said. "Come on, we're leaving."

"We're not going anywhere until we find it."

"This house is huge, Melanie, there's no way we're going to find something as small as—"

"We have to find it!" Melanie said, her voice rising to a sharp yell.

Jane cocked her head, listening. Find what?

"It's been, like, twenty years. I know you want to find it, but what are the chances it's even still here anymore?"

"I don't know what the fucking chances are, Jeff, but we have to try. Okay?"

"And I don't understand why we never looked for it before? Like, before they moved back?"

"Because I didn't know the truth before, okay? Look, maybe you *should* leave. If you're just going to ask questions and get in the way."

"I'm just trying to be a voice of reason, here, babe, I

mean—we're trespassing in someone's home. And the chances of us finding this fucking teddy bear that—"

A heavy, deep thump from above.

Like the sound of a body hitting the floor.

And Jeff finally had enough.

"Right. I'm out. Call me if you need someone to bail you out of jail."

And Jane heard him leave the bedroom, stomping down the stairs so quickly it was a wonder he didn't trip. Melanie followed him halfway down the hall, then stopped.

"Jeff, are you kidding me?" she called, but the front door had already opened and closed, and Jeff was long gone and probably hadn't even heard her. "Fine, I don't need you anyway!" Melanie called after him, and she turned and headed back to Jane's room, and Jane absolutely *adored* the way Melanie screamed when she saw her, standing in the middle of the hallway, blocking the way.

"Jane, what the *fuck*?!" Melanie shrieked, recovering quickly.

"You seem surprised to see me," Jane said calmly. "But this is my house. So that's a little strange."

"I didn't know you were home," Melanie replied. Her voice was hesitant, just the teensiest bit shaky. She had the tail end of a black eye, the bruising faded to a sickly yellowish green. It made Jane happy.

"What are you doing in my house?" Jane asked, her voice quiet.

"I was just leaving." Melanie took a step backward, to the stairs, but faltered.

"You didn't answer my question. What are you doing here?"

"I'm just...It doesn't matter, okay? I'll go."

"You shouldn't come into other peoples' houses without their permission," Jane said, her voice even, calm. The lights in the hallway flickered, on and off, on and off.

Melanie looked around. "Why's it doing that?"

Jane laid a hand on the wall. "Don't you think there's something...creepy? About this house?"

Melanie rolled her eyes but she looked unsure. "It's just a nickname."

"That's what I thought. At first."

"What are you talking about?"

"This house doesn't like visitors. She doesn't want you here."

"Look, I'm sorry, okay? I know I shouldn't be here. I'll leave. You won't..."

"Call the cops?" Jane guessed. "No, I think we can settle this just the three of us."

"The three of us?" Melanie repeated uncertainly. "Is somebody else here?"

"You know it happened on Halloween, right?"

"Everybody knows that."

"But you don't believe in stuff like that, do you?"

"Stuff like what? Like *ghosts*?" The lights flickered again. And there was a creaking from somewhere. Like someone opening a door, like a house settling. Sometimes it was impossible to tell those two things apart. Melanie looked around sharply. "What's wrong with the lights?"

"Tell me why you're here, Melanie. Why are you *really* here? You told Jeff you were trying to find something. What are you looking for?"

"It's none of your business," she replied through gritted teeth.

"How can it not be my business? Whatever it is, you're looking for it in *my* house."

"Why did you even come back here? Your family was supposed to be gone for good," Melanie said softly, spitting out the words one by one. "Everybody was happy when your grandmother died. The last of the Norths were gone from Bells Hollow. Nobody wanted you to come back. But you *did*."

"Sorry to disappoint you," Jane said. "But I didn't want to move here any more than you wanted me to."

"Just let me look for it," Melanie said, shaking her head back and forth. "Let me look for it and I'll leave, and I won't come back. I'm done. I promise."

"You still haven't told me what you're looking for."

Something seemed to snap inside Melanie; she drew her hands to her face and wrapped them around the back of her neck, squeezing. Then she took a slow breath and said, "I'm looking for something that belongs to my sister." And a pained expression passed over her face, she flinched as if she'd been slapped. She corrected herself: "*Belonged*. I'm looking for something that belonged to my sister."

"Your sister?" Jane repeated.

A flash of memory, a conversation she'd had with Alana:

Melanie's older sister is very...ill. Because of something that happened when she was younger.

"Your sister is Annie," Jane whispered.

Cansler. She knew where she'd heard that name before. On her first day of school, Rosemary had introduced Alana as Alana Cansler.

Alana and Melanie were cousins.

Melanie Cansler. Annie Cansler.

"You don't know, do you?" Melanie asked, her voice flat and dull.

"Your sister was with my sister when she died," Jane replied.

"But you don't know anything. Do you?"

"What else is there to know?" Jane asked. "My sister died. Your sister died. We should be *friends*, if anything. We should be helping each other. Instead you're breaking into my house in the middle of the night looking for—what did Jeff say? A teddy bear?"

"Helping each other," Melanie repeated, suddenly wild, suddenly angry and crazed. "Helping each other! Your sister ruined Annie's life! And then she fucking killed her!"

"What are you talking about? They were kids, Melanie. They were *friends*."

"Is that what your mother told you?" Melanie said, suddenly unstuck from the floor, pacing back and forth in a tight circle, her hands pulling at her hair, giving her a dangerous look. Jane was alarmed to see that she had started crying. She didn't move to wipe the tears that rolled slowly down her cheeks. She just let them fall, blinking quickly. "Is that what you believe? You're just as bad as all of them. Just as bad as your mother, just as bad as your dead sister."

Your dead sister.

The words cut right into Jane's chest, ripping their way through her rib cage to settle in her heart.

"My sister was eight when she died, Melanie. And that was over twenty years ago. You never even knew her. *I* never even knew her."

"I know what she did," Melanie said. "And you act all innocent but then you go full psycho on me. You're just like her."

"I didn't even know I *had* a sister until an hour ago. How could I possibly be like her?"

"Maybe it just runs in your blood. Your mom, your grandmother. All of you are evil. Fuck, I *hate* this town," Melanie said, still pacing. "I hate this selective history bullshit. I hate how the real story doesn't even matter anymore, and the only thing people remember is the poor little girl who died!"

"Okay," Jane said. "You're here now. It's just you and me. So tell me the real story, Melanie. Tell me what happened to Jemima and Annie." She had that warning bell in the back of her head again, the same warning bell she'd heard in the bathroom with Susie and Alana. The same feeling that she was about to find out something she didn't want to know.

"Do you really want to hear it, Jane? Because it's not the neat little story you think it is." Melanie had stopped pacing;

she was facing Jane again, and her eyes were wild, wide in her face, her irises surrounded by too much white.

"I want to know what happened," Jane said. "I want to know the truth."

"My mother was a housekeeper here," Melanie started. "She'd leave Annie with my grandmother when she went to work. But my grandmother got sick one day. There was no one else who could watch Annie, so my mother had to bring her here. She tried to hide her, to keep her in the kitchen, but Jemima found her. My mom thought she was going to be fired, but Jemima was so sweet. She pretended to be sweet. She told Emilia she wanted Annie to stay, to play with her. So my mother started bringing Annie to work with her more often. Jemima was always sweet in front of the grown-ups, but Annie started telling my mom about the things she'd do when it was just the two of them."

Jane hardly breathed. Melanie was red-faced now; her hands were balled into two tight fists.

"What things?" Jane asked.

"Little things, at first," Melanie replied. "If Annie didn't do something Jemima wanted, she'd push her. Pull her hair. She'd tell her Emilia would fire my mom. Things like that. But my mom needed this job. It paid well, the hours were good. My grandmother was getting older, sicker. She couldn't watch Annie anymore. My mom was backed into a corner. So she told Annie to deal with it. And when they were six, Jemima cut off all her hair."

Jane's stomach turned. A quick flash of Claudia Summers's face appeared in the back of her mind. Her hands felt heavy with the weight of the dull scissors; she could feel the memory of their resistance as she'd hacked her way through Claudia's thick ponytail.

"What else?" Jane whispered.

"When Annie was seven, Jemima brought her into the woods to show her where a cat had laid a litter of kittens. She had my sister pick one for her own. She said she could take it home and have it as a pet. But then she grabbed the kitten back from her and twisted its neck until it died. She killed *all* the kittens."

Jane felt sick. She crossed her arms over her stomach. "I don't believe you."

"She pushed her down the stairs. She broke her arm, but Annie was too scared to tell anybody what really happened. She said she tripped."

"None of those things are true."

"And do you want to know the worst thing about it? Your mom *knew*. Your grandmother *knew*."

"Even if any of this was true, how would you even...How could you even know this?"

"Because Annie told me." Melanie paused, her voice breaking. She squeezed her eyes shut for a long moment, and when she opened them again, she looked twisted with grief. "She didn't talk that much. Sometimes it was nonsense, sometimes she would recite the plot of a TV show that aired fifteen years ago, get it confused with reality. But something changed a few weeks ago.

I went to visit her and she was lucid, clear. She said, 'You have to find my teddy. It's in that house. I dropped it in the backyard. You have to bring it to me. You have to get it away from her.'"

"Away from who?" Jane asked.

"Somehow, she knew you were back," Melanie continued, ignoring Jane, maybe not even hearing her. "She started telling me things. Things she'd never told me before. Things no one had ever told me before. All about what your sister did to her."

Jane kept her mouth shut. The lights in the hallway flickered again and Melanie looked around at them, but she seemed stronger now. Surer of herself.

"Your sister's birthday was on Halloween. Did you know that? Annie was going to go out trick-or-treating with friends, but Emilia made her come here instead. She made our mom bring her here."

Jane dug her nails into the skin of her arms. A sharp, stinging pain. Melanie continued.

"Jemima was being nice. She took Annie's hand and led her out to the backyard. To the rosebushes. She told her she wanted to show her something really cool. There were all these big holes. They were doing landscaping, digging trenches for something. Big piles of dirt everywhere. Jemima picked up a handful and threw it on my sister. She was dressed as a nurse. A white uniform. Jemima laughed and laughed. And then she tried to push her into one of the holes. She came up behind her and pushed her, but Annie jumped out of the way. Jemima fell in herself.

"She tried to kill her, Jane. She tried to kill my sister. She knew she wasn't supposed to go near the holes; they were too deep, too dangerous. She was going to cover Annie up with dirt and kill her. And now nobody cares about any of that. All anybody cares about is that she died. Nobody wants to listen to what Jemima really was because how could they believe such a nice, pretty little girl was really just the opposite: She was *horrid*."

Jane didn't move.

"And then she killed herself," Melanie whispered. "You came back to this town, and my sister killed herself. She kept saying... '*She's back, she's back, she's back.*' She was so scared. Every time I went to see her... she had this look in her eyes. She said, 'I can't do another Halloween. She always comes to see me on Halloween.'" Melanie was crying now; the tears were pouring down her cheeks and her shoulders shook. "I didn't know what she meant. I didn't know what she would do. That was the last time I ever saw her."

She pushed me in, Jemima whispered into Jane's ear. *She pushed me in and I tried to climb out and all the dirt fell on top of me. I drowned in dirt. I was just having a little fun. But she pushed me in and I died.*

Jane turned around but the hallway was empty. She faced Melanie again and said, "Annie killed Jemima."

"She tried to kill her first," Melanie spat.

So Jane knew it was the truth.

"And then she tried to save her life," Melanie continued.

"She tried to dig her out of the dirt, she tried to save her, but she wasn't strong enough. Years and years of different therapists and medications and treatments, but every single night she had the same dream. Every single night she tried to save Jemima's life, but she couldn't. That's what she told me. That Jemima still tormented her, all these years later. That she was never alone, never truly alone, because your sister was always with her."

Jemima's voice was so close it was almost inside Jane's head. *She tried to save my life after she pushed me in the hole and covered me up with dirt. She tried to save my life when it was already too late.*

Jane pressed her hands against her ears, but she knew it wouldn't do any good; Jemima's voice was inside her head and there was no way to block it out.

"Did you really do all those things to her?" Jane whispered to Jemima.

I'm your sister, Janie. I love you. I wouldn't ever do anything bad to anyone.

She should give Melanie the teddy bear. She knew where it was. She'd seen it the first time she'd opened Jemima's closet door. It was sitting on a shelf with rows of tiny shoes. She should just give her the teddy bear so that Melanie would leave her alone.

But that won't be any fun at all. We should have some fun with her first. She shouldn't have come inside without knocking. I bet she's done it before.

Before?

Of course. The night of the break-in.

Jane hadn't made it up.

"You were in my room," Jane said. "What were you doing in my room?"

"I *told* you. I was looking for the bear."

"No—before."

"Before? I've never been in this creep house before."

"You're lying."

She's lying, Janie, she's lying, lying, lying. I can see into her brain. I see past her skin and her bones. I can see the lie and it's bright, bright red.

"Why would I lie? Why would I come in here? This house is evil. You can literally feel it."

"Evil," Jane said. "You keep saying that word. You think my sister's evil, you think my family's evil, you think my grandmother's evil... But it sounds like all the things you don't like about us are actually things you don't like about yourself. It sounds like maybe you know your story has holes in it. Maybe you know Annie could have done more to save my sister... and didn't."

Melanie's eyes were flashing, dark, dangerous.

Jemima's singsong little-kid voice: *Oh, I think you made her mad, Janie! Poor mad girl, so mad, so sad.*

"You don't know anything," Melanie said. "You don't know *anything!*"

And Jane watched Melanie hear something. The creaking of the old house. The sounds of settling. Her eyes grew wider. She looked past Jane into the empty hallway. "Did you hear that?"

"Hear what?" Jane asked.

"I heard…"

"What did you hear?"

"Nothing. I'm leaving."

But she didn't move.

I don't like this girl, Janie. She's just as mean as her sister. Remember what she said to you? Remember how mean she was?

Jane whispered, "You told me my family was dropping like flies."

"I don't feel bad for you," Melanie said, shaking her head. "You came back to this house. You came back to this *town*. After what your family did. After what your sister did…"

"Well, she's dead and your sister is dead, and it feels like all of this is a little fucking pointless, doesn't it?"

Jemima giggled. *Well, I'm having fun. So it's not completely pointless.*

Melanie heard something again. She took a half-inch step backward. "Did you hear it that time?"

"Hear what?" Jane asked innocently.

What do you think, Jane? Do you want to have some more fun?

Melanie pressed her hands to her ears. She shook her head. "What *is* that?"

"It's these old houses, Melanie. They're always making noise," Jane said.

"Fuck this," Melanie said. "You're right: It *is* all pointless. I never should have come here."

She turned and walked down the hall, a quick walk that wasn't quite a run. Jane followed her to the top of the stairs.

She walked halfway down. She watched Melanie reach the front door, grip the doorknob, and twist.

The door didn't open.

Melanie twisted around and looked up at Jane. "Just stop," she pleaded. "I just want to go home."

"I'm not doing anything," Jane said honestly.

But Melanie tried the door again; it still wouldn't budge. She slid the dead bolt open and shut a few times, but nothing she did made the doorknob work.

Jane felt her own stomach twist painfully inside her, a sliver of fear that worked its way deep into her body.

"What's happening?" she asked Jemima, but Melanie heard her and answered instead.

"How am I supposed to know?" she said, her voice rising to a shriek. "The fucking door won't open! Why won't the fucking door open?"

"I...I don't know," Jane said. She took another step, then another, and then all the lights went off. They were plunged into complete darkness.

Melanie screamed.

And Jane felt something very much like a small, cold hand take hers. And squeeze.

And when the lights came back on, Melanie was gone. The foyer was empty.

Jane lowered herself to a seat, pressing her body against the railing, trying to make herself as small as possible.

"Jemima?" she whispered. "Melanie?"

There was no answer.

The silence of the house stretched out in every direction, it became an alive thing, an entity that wrapped itself around Jane's body and squeezed her too tight.

But then something else, a muffled vibrating—her phone buzzing in the pocket of her dress. She fished around in the fabric until she found it, then she pulled it out.

A FaceTime from Salinger. She pressed Ignore.

The home screen lit up with twenty-seven missed text messages. From Sal, from Will, from Susie and Alana.

She opened the one from Will. He'd finally responded to her last message, but he hadn't answered the question. It was from just a few minutes ago, and it said: *Are you home yet? I'm coming over I can't talk about this over text.*

As if on cue, the beam of headlights sliced through the foyer, passing over Jane like a lighthouse's reassuring glow. Will, turning into the driveway. Jane felt numb as she waited for the car to park, for the engine to die, for the headlights to go off. She waited until the doorbell rang. It cut through the silence of the house like an ax.

The silence of the house—where had Melanie gone? And where was Jemima? And why wasn't Ruth waking up?

Jane placed her hand carefully on the banister and pulled herself to standing again. She felt shaky and strange as she made her way down the sweeping staircase. She felt like she was just slightly out of her body. She wasn't exactly watching herself from above, but she was an inch or two off, like something had gone wrong, just a little off center.

Will rang the bell again; she was walking too slowly. She could see the outline of his body through the stained-glass cutout of the door. She had the sudden thought—*I don't want him to see me in my costume*—but it was too late, and her hand reached out and gripped the doorknob and turned and pulled it open and there he was, Will, and he tried to step into the house, but she blocked him.

"Can I come in?" he tried again, confused.

"It's not a great time."

"Jane, I just want to talk to you."

"I know. I'm sorry. I can't let you in right now."

"Is it because of my text? Was I right?"

"Did I not know?" she said. "No. I didn't."

"But you know now?"

"I know now."

"Jane, I'm so, so sorry. Will you let me come in?"

"I can't."

"I want to talk about this."

"It's been a long night," she said, and it was the truth, of course, but it was also the biggest understatement of the truth, and Jane almost laughed out loud when she heard herself say it.

"I can't even imagine," he said.

"Some other time."

"Are you sure you want to be alone?"

"I'm not alone," she said.

"Your mom is home?"

"Yeah."

"And you don't want to go somewhere? We could go to Sam's, we could get pancakes or milkshakes or...whatever you wanted."

"I'm okay, really. Thanks, Will." She tried to make herself smile. She thought she mostly failed. "Did you like the book?"

"Yeah," he said. "I did."

"How about that ending? The *secret de Polichinelle*? Maybe I sort of knew all along," she admitted. "Well—not what happened. But that *something* had happened."

Will took her hand. "I'm *so* sorry," he said.

And for a moment, a flash, she saw herself leaving with him, getting into his truck, letting him drive her away from this house. Maybe they *would* go to the diner, sit and eat fries and drink milkshakes and talk and laugh and have a normal evening. Maybe when he brought her back, Ruth would be awake, and Melanie and Jemima would be gone, and this house would be just a normal house, just a too-big, drafty house with no weird noises and no weird dead girls haunting the corners and hallways.

But that couldn't happen.

She pulled away her hand and cleared her throat, and she said, firmly but not unkindly, "Thanks for stopping by. I think I just need some sleep tonight. I'll see you later?"

He made a face. "You're sure, Jane? You're sure you're okay?"

"I'll be okay," she said. "Have a good night, Will."

"Okay. You too. If you need anything..."

"I'll call you."

He walked back to his truck and she shut the front door.

And locked it.

The click of the lock sounded like the loudest echoing crash.

She turned around to face the foyer.

The house was both quiet—

And not quiet. She cocked her head a tiny bit, listening.

A buzzing sound.

Her phone again.

She was still holding it in her hand but she hadn't even felt it vibrate. She looked at it and saw she'd gotten another message from Salinger.

It was hard to imagine that just a month ago, she had told Salinger everything. Just a month ago, she would be calling Sal at this very moment, crying or screaming into the phone. Sal would be cool and collected. Sal would have an explanation for everything. Jane would hang up feeling better.

But there had been an almost palpable *snap* as Jane and her mother had driven out of California, past a great big sign that said WELCOME TO NEVADA. And with each state line they'd crossed—Arizona, Utah, Colorado—the snap had gotten louder and louder, until they'd pulled off the highway right in front of a large blue sign that said, in three-foot-high letters, WELCOME TO MAINE. At the time, she'd thought she felt nothing, but looking back, how had she missed it? The great, final *snap* that fully severed her from the life she used to have. From Greer. From California. From Sal.

She had lost Greer, but she had also lost Sal.

She had lost Greer, but she had also lost *everything*.

There was nothing she could say to Sal now, nothing Sal could say to *her* that would repair what had happened between them. The distance, the snap, the *ending*, so abrupt and unexpected that Jane hadn't even noticed it at the time.

She scrolled down in her phone until she reached the last message she'd gotten from Greer.

Outside!

In the real world, in this world, Will was backing slowly out of the driveway. The headlights landed on Jane's face for a moment and anyone watching would have seen how the glow made her skin look sickly and strange, too bright and waxy. There were bags under her eyes. How long had those been there? When was the last time she had really slept, an entire night's worth of rest, a night uninterrupted by strange dreams and strange noises?

But if she pretended, the headlights were made by her father's truck, and if she closed her eyes, she was back in California, before he died. If she closed her eyes, she was a child again, five or six or seven years old, and Greer was sitting on the edge of her bed, reading her a story. He always said the same thing, no matter what book they were reading. He always opened it and brought it to his nose and inhaled deeply and said, "Ugh. I *love* this book."

"You say that about every book," Jane would say, giggling.

"Because I love every book! Don't you just love books, Janie? I love books so much I could eat them."

"You can't eat books," Jane would reply, still giggling, not knowing then that there would be a day when Greer was gone, when all she would want in the entire world was one last story from him, because when Greer was reading her a story, she felt truly safe, truly brave, truly okay. Like the words were sinking into her very body, becoming a part of her, making her better than she actually was.

And Greer would pretend to bite the book, and Jane would pretend to shriek in fear, and Ruth would poke her head into the room and jokingly scold them both to keep it down.

Jane opened her eyes. And Greer was gone and she was alone and Ruth had lied to her. For Jane's entire life, her mother had lied to her. She'd had a sister. And Ruth had had long, curly hair just like Jane's. And she had eaten it. Just like Jane ate her books, just like Jemima had eaten the roses.

Three little girls all eating things they weren't supposed to eat.

Three little girls all eating things in order to fill their bodies with something other than the anger, the rage, that would otherwise consume them.

Jane hugged her arms around her stomach.

But Ruth had *changed*. Ruth had kept her hair short and moved across the country. Ruth was even-tempered and calm, rarely ever angry. She had designed a new life. She had left when Jemima died and gotten away from her father, her controlling mother.

Had Emilia been like the rest of the North women?

Like her daughter and her granddaughters?

Had she managed to get it under control, transforming herself, instead, into the buttoned-up version of herself Jane had always been a little frightened of?

Would Jemima have gotten it under control, had she lived a little longer?

Did Jane have it under control now?

Do you think you do?

And there she was—a little girl ghost. Sitting on the bottom step of the staircase, her hands folded neatly on top of her knees, looking like something out of the 1800s, not like a girl who had lived just twenty years ago. That really wasn't that long at all.

Grandma Emilia dressed me like this, Jemima explained, although Jane hadn't spoken aloud. *She used to call me her little doll.*

"Is it true, what Melanie said?" Jane asked.

That I was mean to Annie? Jemima considered. *Yes, I was.*

"How mean?"

She started it. She made fun of me for my dresses. She made fun of me for my hair. I don't like being made fun of. I get so angry when people make fun of me.

"Where's Melanie?" Jane whispered, and the ghost faded. Or it wasn't a ghost at all. Jane rubbed at her eyes. They felt tired, dry. And her hands ached suddenly. She looked down at them now. Was there dirt underneath her fingernails? Were there sores on her palms?

She wiped her hands on her dress. She closed her eyes again.

"Where's Melanie?" she repeated, even though it felt like she already knew.

She took a little walk.

"A walk where?"

In the backyard. I think she went to see the rosebushes. Our rosebushes are famous, you know. Have you ever tasted a rose petal, Jane?

Jane opened her eyes but nobody was there. She was alone in the entranceway, and her hands hurt, and her eyes hurt, and she was so tired, a deep, aching tired that she felt in every inch of her body.

She wanted to go upstairs. She wanted to go to sleep. She wanted to walk out of this house and never come back.

There was something wrong about this house; she knew that now. She'd known it the second she first stepped through the front door, but it had taken her this long to finally understand it.

Melanie went to see the rosebushes. Why had Melanie gone to see the rosebushes?

Jane started toward the back of the house. She reached the mudroom and opened the door, not bothering to close it behind her. The night was mild and pitch-black, and for once she didn't shiver as she stepped out into it. Maybe she was finally getting used to the cold.

She could see the rosebushes at the far end of the lawn; they almost glowed in the moonlight, bright spots of color against the blackness of the night.

There was a numbness that had spread across her chest, perhaps out of some sort of survival necessity, like if she stopped and thought about what was really happening, it would be too much for her, she would just break altogether.

But then she heard the first cry for help, and she was brought suddenly back to herself, and she took off at a run toward the rosebushes, toward the shouting.

She was running so fast that she tripped, landing with a jolt on the cold ground, hitting her head so hard she saw bright spots of light dance across her vision.

She waited a moment before she pushed herself up.

Her head swam. She felt a rush of nausea. She took a deep breath, then another.

Are you okay?

Jemima was sitting on a wooden swing that hung from a cherry tree just before the rose arbors started. Had that swing been there before? And had that tree? It was hard to focus. Had she hit her head hard enough to give herself a concussion?

You don't look so good.

"What did you do to her?"

We're just having a little fun.

Another wave of nausea. Jane folded her arms across her stomach. She was still on the ground, kneeling back on her calves. She took a breath and let it out slowly.

"You can't hurt her."

You're my sister, and sisters have to be there for each other.

"Jemima, please..."

Go back inside, Jane. You don't have to do anything else.

Jane tried to stand but her head spun too much to find the ground, to even tell which way was up or down. "Where is she?"

She isn't nice, Jane! She's mean, just like her sister was mean to me! She isn't nice and PEOPLE SHOULD JUST BE NICE*!*

Her last few words were a scream, so loud they felt like a knife in Jane's head. She was going to throw up. She was throwing up. No, she was dry heaving.

Go inside, Jane. You hit your head.

Jane dug her hands into the ground and breathed deeply, in and out, in and out, deep purposeful breaths that cleared her head enough so that she could finally bring herself to stand.

Another scream, this one choked and painful.

She made herself start walking, pushing herself forward, toward the rosebushes, past the not-real wooden swing and the not-real cherry tree and the not-real ghost.

She stopped when she reached the edge of the rosebushes. Her foot caught on something, and she almost fell again, but she managed to stop herself, grabbing on to a rose arbor for support.

She looked down for what she'd tripped on.

A shovel.

Ruth must have left it there.

Her hands ached again.

And then she saw, just past the first rose arbor, a circle of disturbed dirt. The top of someone's head, just barely above the surface.

And as she watched, Melanie was sucked underneath the ground.

And the soil buttoned itself back up, closing on top of her.

So you couldn't see anything of Melanie at all.

Just a hand reaching up through the dirt.

A hand that was even now sinking, sinking...

Jane took a step toward her.

She stole your journal!

Jane paused. "What?"

When she was in your room. She gave it to the boy. I saw her.

The nausea in Jane's stomach was replaced with cold. A heavy block of ice.

Here, take this, Melanie had said.

It was your last journal. The journal where your dad is alive. I told you. She isn't a nice girl.

The ice warmed, warmed, and Jane's stomach was on fire suddenly, the heat was coursing through her body, filling every inch of her with rage.

"I have to get it back," Jane said.

By your feet.

Jane looked down. Melanie's phone was on the grass; she bent down to pick it up.

If Melanie asks nicely, I'm sure he'll come back for her. He'll bring it back to you.

"I have to help her...," Jane said, but her voice was uncertain, wavering. "If I help her, she'll give me the journal back."

Or she won't, because she's not nice.

"I have to help her...," Jane repeated. She could still see Melanie's hand, opening and closing weakly, grabbing at nothing but air.

Or you could not. You could go and meet your friends. You could go and meet Will. You could go inside and go to sleep.

"Just because somebody isn't nice, doesn't mean they deserve *this*," Jane said.

Greer's voice: *You can't go around punching all the punks in the world.*

Jemima's voice: *But you* can. *That's the thing, Jane. You can.*

And why should she help Melanie, anyway?

Melanie *hadn't* been nice; she'd been mean to Jane since the beginning. Maybe Jemima was right; maybe this was what happened to people who weren't nice. Maybe this was what they deserved.

But still, Jane couldn't just *leave* her. . . .

She dropped Melanie's phone on the ground.

She took a step into the rose arbor.

And another.

She was close enough to reach out and touch one of the thorns.

She was close enough to pluck a tiny, perfect petal off its blossom.

She let it lie in her hand.

The scent of the rosebushes was overwhelming, and for the first time it brought a comfort with it. It felt like it was enfolding her, wrapping itself around her. Keeping her safe.

She closed her hand around the rose petal.

No, no—the scent of roses was too much. It was like a drug. It forced its way into her brain and made everything cloudy and fuzzy and hard to understand. Why did her hands hurt? Why was there dirt underneath her fingernails? Why had she come outside to the rosebushes in the first place? Where was her mother? She needed to wake her up. Ruth would know what to do. Ruth would help her.

She turned, and there was her sister, blocking her way, brighter now than she had ever been, as bright as a real live girl.

It's fair, Jemima said. *It's only fair.*

Jane closed her eyes. She was so tired. So, so tired. Jemima's voice was all around her, just like the smell of the roses.

"I can't let her die," Jane said, weakly now, so weakly that her words were barely a whisper, barely audible over the howl of the wind.

They let me die.

"That doesn't make it right...."

You're my sister. You're supposed to protect me. You're supposed to hurt the people who hurt me.

So tired. So cold.

This is where I died, Jane.

And Jane could feel it in the back of her throat, the dirt Jemima had drowned in. She was covered up in it, inhaling mouthfuls of it until her lungs had turned brown and gritty.

This was where Annie had let her die.

Melanie's sister.

Melanie's sister had let her die. She'd waited too long to try to save her, and wasn't that the same as letting her die?

Jane felt tears stinging down her cheeks.

And wasn't it too late for Melanie, too?

Jane turned around to look and Melanie's hand was limp and lifeless. A twitch in one of her fingers that might have been the wind. The wind that picked up even now, blowing through Jane's hair, sending it flying in every direction.

It's only fair, Jemima repeated.

And it *was* fair.

Jane could see that now.

So much of Jane's life had been *unfair*—Greer's death, the upheaval of their lives, their move across the country. But this.

This was fair.

She uncurled her hand. The rose petal glowed in the moonlight.

Jemima smiled.

And Jane put the petal into her mouth.

And swallowed.

Acknowledgments

These books I write keep taking longer and longer and are harder and harder to finish, and I become more indebted each time to the people who make the journey easier—and in some cases, possible at all. This story particularly threatened sometimes to pull me down into darkness, just as Jane is pulled into darkness, and I have had the express good fortune of knowing people who routinely pulled me back into the light. And the light is good, friends. Three cheers for the light.

First and foremost, always, always thank you to my agent, Wendy Schmalz, for knowing exactly when something is ready—and when it is not.

Thank you to the two incredible editors who worked on *Horrid*. I feel infinitely lucky to have both started and ended this journey with women who cared so deeply for me and Jane. Pam Gruber and Rachel Poloski—you made this book so much better.

I still feel so happy to have found such a welcoming and

nurturing home with Little, Brown. It takes a small army to bring a book to life, and I have so many people who have ushered this one into existence, including Karina Granda and Tran Nguyen (don't tell my other covers, but this one is my favorite!!!), Regan Winter, Stefanie Hoffman, Natali Cavanagh, Savannah Kennelly, Valerie Wong (and everyone on the NOVL team!), Siena Koncsol, Victoria Stapleton, Lindsay Walter-Greaney, and Olivia Davis. My heart is filled with gratitude for all of you.

To my family, who, as far as I can tell in all my extensive digging in the rose garden, are not hiding any dead bodies or twenty-year-old secrets. Maybe because you are so good, I am able to write stories about families who are so not good.

To my friends-who've-become-family, you know who you are, and I truly cherish you.

And to S, of course. Without you, none of this is possible.

About the Author

Katrina Leno was born on the East Coast and currently lives in Los Angeles. She is the author of five critically acclaimed novels: *The Half Life of Molly Pierce, The Lost & Found, Everything All at Once, Summer of Salt,* and *You Must Not Miss.* While she has never eaten an entire book, she admits to tasting a page or two. You can visit her online at katrinaleno.com.

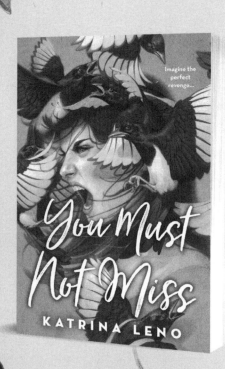